Felipe Marlo, Bullfight Shamus

by

Hugh Hosch / "Hugo el Verdugo"

First published by AuthorHouse 04/08/04

ISBN: 1-4140-6103-X (e-book)
ISBN: 1-4184-2237-1 (Paperback)

Library of Congress Control Number: 2004090049

This book is printed on acid free paper.

Printed in the United States of America
Bloomington, IN

Certain taurine critics believe the conflict between symbolic and phenomenological viewpoints on the subject of aesthetical toreo is multidimensional and, in the end, unresolvable. If this proposition is accepted, must it not follow that an inner reality -- that is, the expectations and values which we would impose upon toreo -- is infinitely more substantive than the exterior act in the ring itself, which we can know only through the visual sense?

Michael Rugram, *8Toros8*

Say, I dig groovy babes and bulls, pal.

Felipe Marlo, Taurine P.I.

Table of Contents

Felipe Marlo
Bullfight Shamus

Chapter 1

La Rejoneadora

Madrid could be nice in the springtime, I thought to myself. The temporada of '58 was finally underway -- gracias a Díos -- but the torrid heat of the Castilian summer hadn't yet arrived and driven Generalísimo Franco and his government out of town and off to San Sebastián with its cooling sea breezes. When the government moved north, so did the fatcats, and that meant a lot of places in Madrid closed up, not just some of the fancier shops but also a fair share of the better restaurants like Horcher's and the Jockey Club. And with places like that -- especially Horcher's -- shut down, where were all those "Dutchmen" who'd lived here for the past decade or more supposed to eat? ¡Carajo! Their problem, not mine. Horcher's was out of my class, anyway.

Well, if the weather was so great, why, I asked myself, was I wearing my trenchcoat and fedora in the office? I couldn't answer that. But while the weather might be fine, business wasn't. It wasn't because of the competition, I knew, because I was the only taurine P.I. in Madrid. Hell, maybe in the world.

I lit a Camel and tried to blow a couple of smoke rings. Finally I gave up and reached down and pulled open a bottom desk drawer, extracting a half liter bottle of Magno. I drew the cork with my teeth and took a big slug of the coñac, then sat the bottle on my desk. Might as well relax. Can't dance. Ha, ha.

I leaned back in my squeaky swivel chair and put my feet up on the desk, first snatching off its suface a flyer I must have found on the bar while I was having a quick one a little earlier in a taurine joint a couple of blocks away in the Plaza Santa Ana, folding the sheet into a paper airplane shaped like a long triangle with a lower fin. When I finished, I noticed that the black and white photograph of a torero was visible on the right fin. At least his head and shoulders, the latter clad in the chaquetilla of a traje de luces, were. Seeing as how I was a taurine P.I., I understandably unfolded the piece of paper and looked at it. It was one of those standard promotional handouts touting "Spain's next great figura" with a picture of a novillero and a pitch for his upcoming appearance in -- hmmm -- Las Ventas. Curro Azafrán, an andaluz from some hick town just outside Sevilla. Frankie Saffron. Never heard of him. I refolded my airplane and sailed it across the office. Señor Curro flew well, banking to the left in front of the empty file cabinets and going out the open window, headed for the Calle Victoria three floors down.

At that moment I heard the door to my outer office open, the one with the frosted glass panel and the imitation gold leaf lettering which read:

FELIPE MARLO SHAMUS
INVESTIGADOR PRIVADO
PARA EL MUNDILLO TAURINO

I removed my feet from my desk and got out of my squeaky chair, walking over to the connecting door and opening it. Holy Mother of God, I thought, sucking in my breath, for standing there all alone -- no dueña or nothin' -- was the most gorgeous female creature I'd ever laid eyes on, dressed in a black traje corto so tight-fitting she must have been poured into it. It bulged in all the right places.

* * *

Whew! Hey, let me back off for just a minute and explain some things, okay? Let's start with my name, Felipe Marlo Shamus. It's a Mexican name, I guess you could say. It ought to be, anyhow, because I was born in Mexico, a little chilango growing up in a shantytown which in the 'forties -- long after I'd left -- was finally torn down to provide a place to build what was now La Plaza Monumental de México. Or La Plaza Insurgentes Sur. Or La México. Hell, you know what I'm talking about -- the biggest frigging bullring in the world. Ironic, what with my old man being a torero. Well, okay, he was a torero cómico, dressed up like a clown and with vaquillas chasing him around the ring while the villamelones and their kids laughed their heads off. And all the while my mother, *née* Kathleen Shamus of County Cork, Ireland, wringing her hands like she did the washing she took in to earn us a few steady pesos, worried that my father would somehow end up on

3

the horns of some errant beast. Which of course he eventually did.

If she could have afforded it, my mother would've taken me with her back to Ireland -- but she couldn't swing that. Her late father had come to Mexico to create a new and mighty strain of irlandés-mexicano potatoes, but the noble experiment had been a colossal flop (the spuds had far too many eyes and they ogled the chicas nonstop, alarming the girls' mothers), after which he'd died of heartbreak hastened on by two bottles of tequila a day in the stead of Paddy's or Bushmill's. Her mother had disappeared with a traveling circus, leaving my old lady to be raised by some nuns in a convent out in the countryside -- until the revolution closed down the churches and the convents and she ended up working all hunched over in a tiny taco stand for toreros enanitos opposite the Plaza de Toros El Toreo, back in the capital.

Then in the mid 'thirties we did the usual thing and as a family of two headed up to the Colossus of the North, only for us it wasn't just for reasons of money. My mother longed to be back among people who spoke her own language, and the U.S. was a hell of a lot closer than Ireland.

So we ended up in L.A. I was fifteen and I went to school and grew up there. I didn't have many friends and I improved my English mainly by watching movies, especially Bogey flicks, which I'd figured out how to sneak into and avoid the twenty-five cents adult admission fee. I did my time in the U.S. Army, serving in the Pacific and shooting my quota of Japs, then I came back to the City of the Angels to find my ma dead and me with nothing to do and no training in anything.

The years went by. I tried all sorts of stuff -- I picked lettuce, I sold shoes, I even washed car windshields at stop lights, for God's sake. And because people thought I resembled Humphrey Bogart, I was able occasionally to hire myself out as a Bogey lookalike at Hollywood functions; I made more money doing that than anything else I tried, but the demand wasn't there for a full-time job at it. Then in the mid 1950s I finally sat myself down and said, look, you're past thirty-five. It's time you found a career. What do you want to do? Well, I answered, one does what one knows. Okay, great, I said to myself, but what do I know?

This question I really pondered. Finally, I answered: I know toreo -- and Spanish -- from my father and my upbringing in Mexico and I know private detective work from the movies. Especially Bogey movies. Actually, I also knew washerwoman work from my mother, but *that* I was not going to admit to *anybody*. Then I remembered: I knew how to shoot Japs. But I checked around and found out nobody needed a guy with that particular talent any more. So I decided to go into business as a taurine P.I.

When I floated my idea to people I knew in L.A., they all agreed that the city was perfect for a private investigator -- but a *normal* private investigator, certainly not a *taurine* one. There were no bullfights and no bullfighters in L.A., they said.

Maybe in Tijuana . . .

No, I told myself, I wasn't going to be a taurine P.I. in Tijuana. If I was going to really follow this thing through, I was going to do it where the most important corridas in the world took place. I would open an office in Madrid!

And I did. I scrimped and saved enough dough to get to Spain and open a dump of an office in a crummy building in the seedy Calle Victoria. But this street was the taurine center of Madrid, and I was in business. I had to admit to myself that if Spain hadn't been the cheapest country in Europe I probably couldn't have swung it. But I did. On the street level of my office building, at number nine, under the dingy orange and blue awning, was the central ticket sales outlet for taurine events. And on the second floor, just below my own world headquarters, was the office of Don Livinio Stuyck, empresario of Las Ventas and other bullrings, so I was well situated. Okay, so I wasn't in the city's newest office building, El Torre de Madrid on la Plaza de España, the only skyscraper in town unless you counted the ten-year-old Plaza Hotel building on the same square and the old Telefónica on Avenida José Antonio, la Gran Via, built just before the civil war -- but I was happy. And now my first client had come into my office, this stunning creature whose name I didn't know.

"My name is Maria Caliente," she said, dark eyes flashing and framed by flowing ebony locks, "and I am a rejoneadora."

"I'm impressed," I said. "Say, want a slug of Magno?" I held out the bottle to her.

She tossed her raven mane and sniffed. "No, gracias," she said, sitting down in my client chair and pulling a cigarette from a jacket pocket. She was, as I mentioned, wearing a black traje corto and she sported a pair of fine, tooled leather riding boots. She had a flat cordoban hat in one hand, which she laid on my desk while she got her cigarette out.

I quickly pulled a wooden match from a coat pocket; being a lefty, I naturally keep most stuff in my left pocket, just like I wear my rod in a shoulder holster under my right armpit. I onehandedly flicked the match alight with my left thumbnail, a trick I've always thought was classy, but then I dropped it fast as a small piece of burning phosphorus trapped under my nail caused me to cry out in pain. I grabbed the open bottle of Magno -- the nearest liquid at hand -- with my right hand and poured some on the end of my burning thumbnail, but the booze ignited and turned the entire digit into a blazing torch. I yelled out, louder this time, and ran over to the water cooler, holding the flaming finger under the spigot and with my right hand pressing the button which released a gush of water and extinguished the fire. I then popped my sore thumb into my mouth and sucked on it. Maria Caliente sneered and pulled out a lighter, setting her weed alight instead of her thumb.

"If you are finished," she said, blowing smoke in my face, "perhaps I can tell you why I'm here." Thumb still in mouth, I went back around my desk and sat

5

down.

"Shoot," I said, although the word sounded more like "Mmmmf." I removed my thumb and said it again.

"Have you ever heard the name Carlos Rojo?" she asked.

The name sounded vaguely familiar but I couldn't place it. I screwed up my face in thought but the girl spoke again before I could say anything. "He was a novillero when the civil war broke out in 'thirty-six," she said, blowing out another plume of smoke, this time toward the ceiling. "He was in Valencia, his home town, when the army revolted, thus he found himself in the republican part of Spain, and he stayed there with his father and mother and his newborn baby sister. He was twenty-one at the time."

I found my own cigarette and took a drag. "Plenty of toreros found themselves on the republican side at the start of the war, cariña," I said, shrugging, "but most of them made it over to Franco territory one way or the other, sooner or later. And why not? After a while, corridas in the nationalist zone resumed and even grew in number, while in the other zone the Fiesta Nacional all but dried up. A guy wanting to continue making a living at his trade didn't have a whole lot of choice."

"Yes, that's true," conceded the babe, "but Carlitos was a liberal dreamer and disposed to the republican line of thought, anyway. The progressive ideas of the Left appealed to him. He even used the name Carlitos el Rojo professionally, once the war began. And besides, with a name like Rojo he was bound to be suspect among the franquistas, anyway."

Yeah, I thought to myself, there was certainly truth in that. Just imagine a guy crossing the lines from the republican to the nationalist side during the war and him telling Franco's boys his name was Charlie the Red. Hah! Please step this way to the wall, señor.

"So he stayed in the republican zone," the girl went on. "At first he tried to continue his career as a torero but as the herds of toros bravos were slaughtered for their meat and taurine events came to an end there, he began working with the republican Minister of Agriculture Ruíz Funes to help collectivize farms. Agriculture, animal husbandry -- anything and everything. That is until finally, in a manpower sweep conducted by the unions the CNT and the UGT, he was put into a uniform of sorts -- a mono, really -- and sent into the front lines for the remainder of the war. Which he somehow survived intact."

"Bravo!" I said, clapping my hands. "I'm impressed again. Now please inform me as to why you're telling me all this."

"Because Carlos Rojo managed to come through all that, succeeded in avoiding being shot or going into one of Franco's internment camps after the war, and escaping to Cuba along with many of his comrades. Recently he returned, illegally, crossing into Spain via the Pyrenees. But as you know, the hunt for 'Reds' by Franco's police has never let up, and Carlos has had to use assumed names and move his place of living very frequently. But now he has vanished and I need someone to look for him. The police cannot be called in because they would put him in prison -- or worse. Señor Marlo Shamus, Carlos is my older brother." She looked at me defiantly, those magnificent black eyes flashing like . . . like. . . well, like my thumb only minutes before.

"I see," I said, stubbing out my cigarette in a cenicero. "And your name, Caliente, is, I suppose, a phony one."

"Yes," she replied, also putting out her own weed. "My original name is Maria Rojo, but my family -- except Carlitos and me -- was wiped out in the war. Carlitos fled Spain when the war ended, and I wandered about for years on my own. Eight years ago, when I was fourteen -- a very well developed, orphaned fourteen-year-old girl -- I was taken in by the Duque de Nuque and given a new name, Maria Caliente."

The Duque de Nuque! Holy Mother of God, I said to myself. The most notorious playboy in Francoland! A slick, goodlooking guy with billions of pesetas, virtual palaces in Madrid, San Sebastián and elsewhere, country haciendas, stables of polo ponies and sports cars -- and on top of that, a reputed amateur rejóneador of great skill and the owner of one of the country's top ganaderías, Gato Gordo. Oh yeah, and España's most eligible bachelor, with beautiful Hollywood movie stars at his beck and call. He must be in his early forties by now. Word was that as an ardent falangista and a dashing young captain in the Nationalist Army, he'd served with General Muñoz Grandes's Blue Division in World War II, fighting the Russians on their snowy steppes in 1941-42 as part of Franco's gesture of friendship to his old supporters, the Germans. I'd even heard he'd been awarded the Iron Cross First Class by Hitler himself -- although der Führer had reportedly been rather shaken when the young duke returned the kraut leader's handshake with a passionate Spanish abrazo. Hmmm. . . and now Muñoz Grandes was Franco's righthand man and designated successor to the caudilloship of España. The Duque de Nuque was well connected, no doubt about that.

"As I told you," the girl continued, "Carlitos returned to this country not long ago and somehow located, then contacted me. We met secretly on a weekly basis after that -- until he vanished. I don't know what happened, and he would never tell me where he was living. He thought it might be dangerous for me to know."

"You just want me to find your brother, that's all?" I asked. I didn't relish getting mixed up in a lot of political tomfoolery promoted by un rojo named Rojo.

"That is all," Maria Caliente replied. "Will this be enough to get you started?" She pulled a wad of pesetas big enough to choke a caballo from her chaqueta pocket and dropped it on my desk. I could see enough brown-and-white one hundred peseta notes with the Generalísimo's face peeking out from each to know this was a meaningful stash. At almost two dollars U.S. per bill, that was a handsome retainer in the Spain of 1958, when a dime American could buy a liter of tinto. I snatched up the pile of geetus before she could change her mind.

"Uh, yeah, that ought to just about do it," I said, stuffing the wad into my left trenchcoat pocket. My mouth twitched. "Look, ah, when's the last time you saw him or heard from him?" I asked.

"Two weeks ago," she answered. "We would always meet secretly at our usual place, an underground bar for ex-republican toreros, tucked away behind a basement shop selling only the cheapest wine, in a small side street off the Calle Mayor. He was excited over a plan he had devised to unite a number of small farmers and raisers of livestock, including some with a few toros bravos, into a large, ostensibly private enterprise which would secretly be a collective. It would be a continuation of his work from the old days in the republic. He -- he and his comrades, that is -- would develop their own ganadería of fighting bulls and then compete with 'the big boys,' as he called them. You know: Miura, Pablo Romero, el Conde de la Corte, and so on. And then Carlitos would resume his career as a torero and become a great figura, even at this somewhat late date. His enterprise would also raise cash crops, including saffron, rosemary and other herbs. He says herbs fascinate him. It would be -- it *will* be -- a very daring and successful scheme."

"*Daring* is the right word, sweetheart," I said. "Screwing around trying to compete with the people you're talking about, and him with his background -- sorry, but the way I see it, you might as well call in the priest for your brother's last rights, right now."

"No!" she cried. "You are wrong! He will succeed! And I will help him! But that is not your concern in any case." She reached into another pocket and pulled out a small box of wooden matches and laid it on my desk. "Here. Here is your . . . your clue, I believe you call it. It is all I can give you. Carlitos left it on the table when we last met. It may tell you something which will enable you to locate him."

I picked up the tiny pasteboard box and looked at it. *El Casino del Toro,* the flowery writing said. And, beneath that in smaller print: *30 km norte de Madrid (a la derecha), Carretera de Segovia -- pida Pepe. Mantenga discreción.* Hmmm -- a speakeasy taurine casino off the Segovia highway, ask for Joe. And mum's the word. Yeah, I guess so, I snorted mentally, seeing as how Papa Franco didn't approve of casinos in España Católica. Not officially, anyway. Of course, with a little dough slipped into the right government minister's pocket once in a while. . .

I knew the Casino del Toro. It was run by Paquito Duro "El Toro" and was a sort of rambling old hacienda with very high ceilings set back in the hills about forty-five minutes out of town and guarded by enough big ex-picadors to crack all the skulls in Castilla. I looked at the girl and held up the matchbox.

8

"From what you tell me about your brother, this doesn't sound like his kind of place. Señor Duro, the jefe, may be a former picador and a big aficionado, but he sure isn't interested in the welfare of the masses."

She shrugged. "I don't know that he actually went there. Oh, and here is a very old photograph of him," she said, pulling a dogeared snapshot of a young novillero in his traje de luces from yet another pocket. He looked strikingly like Tyrone Power in *Blood and Sand*. I studied the photo, then pocketed it.

"That picture was taken in 1936," Maria said. Carlos is proud of it. He gave it to me as a keepsake during one of our secret meetings."

"Okay," I grunted. "Say, before I forget it, what's this rejoneadora bit? You'll have to excuse me, but I've never heard of you."

She tilted her pretty head back and looked down her pretty nose at me. "That's because my career has not yet been officially launched. Rodolfo -- the Duque de Nuque, that is -- is going to see to that very soon. The day after tomorrow, as a matter of fact, I will have my debut in a gran festival at the tienta ring of the duque's estancia, Gato Gordo. Many important people are invited to come and see me. I will soon be the most famous torera since Conchita Cintrón."

"Ah, yes, good old duque. A guy with a heart of gold. I guess his, er, schedule leaves him plenty of time to play with his herd, maybe cut a pretty little vaquilla out from the rest and personally brand her with his hierro, eh, chica?"

She jumped to her feet. "You are insolent! Why, if there were another taurine private investigator in Madrid --"

"But there's not, baby," I said. "Hey, take it easy. I understand -- it sure beats scrubbing floors at the Telefónica, huh? Don't worry -- I'll find your brother for you. Just let me know how I can reach you."

She gave me a card, said a cool goodbye and left, slamming my outer door pretty hard. I stared at the door sucking on my thumb, which still hurt like hell.

Chapter 2

The Bull and the Mickey

I nosed my '39 Ford coupé through the last gate manned by overfed picadors at about midnight and parked in the big, unpaved area out front of el Casino del Toro. It was well hidden from the highway a couple of kilometers away on the other side of some hills, but once there the place was lit up like a cathedral's votive candle rack on Christmas Eve. I removed my rod from my shoulder holster and put it in the car's glove box, next to my New Testament with the slug. Maybe I better explain.

In my business I deal with all kinds of people, including some who are very religious or very superstitious; my Good Book can sometimes come in handy with people like that. See, I took this small, pocket-size version of el Nuevo Testamento and fired a .38 bullet with a very light charge of powder into the center of it. The slug embedded itself in the pages about nine-tenths of the way through. So, depending on who I'm dealing with, I'll sometimes slip the book into my left inside coat pocket, the one over my heart, ahead of time and later show it around as proof that I am a *very* lucky guy -- or maybe a very special one -- you know, like I got cartel with the Man Upstairs. Or even better, if I'm in a gunfight and I haven't shown it to anybody yet, I can pull it out afterwards, rubbing my chest like it's a bit sore, and then show the bullet-studded New Testament around. Nobody ever thinks to look for the hole in my coat -- if they're the type I'm going to show it to, they're already so overwhelmed they're virtually hyperventilating. I've had 'em go down on their knees, crossing themselves. Hey, with gypsies this thing is a gold mine. But for my visit to el Casino del Toro I decided to leave it in the glove box. I got out of my car and walked to the entrance.

The big front door was guarded by two very unsavory former picadors -- a couple of real gorillas -- who wore their traditional bullring garb for theatrical effect and were armed with heavy hardwood picas up to 2.7 meters long, plus pistolas under their armpits, partially hidden by their chaquetillas. They frisked me, then nodded me on in when I asked for Pepe, another ex-picador who was the casino's major domo. Just inside, standing under the stuffed head of a toro bravo, who should I happen to bump into -- literally -- but the boss man himself, Paquito Duro "El Toro." The short, thickset and bull-like Duro was decked out in a "smoking," as the local gente hermosa called a dinner jacket, plus frilly shirt and a muleta-red cummerbund. His black hair was so shiny I could see my face in it when I looked down at the top of his head. Using it as a mirror, I paused to pluck an unruly hair from an eyebrow.

"So, the bullfight shamus," El Toro said, holding a puro in one ring-festooned hand as he sneered at me. "Business so good you can afford to come to my place and drop a bundle -- or, por supuesto, win one?"

"Not tonight, Paquito," I said as I pulled out a Camel and a wooden match. I decided against striking the match one-handedly this time, using a stone wall instead. "I'm here on business." Over his head I could see well-heeled people playing roulette at a table. A picador-guard with his vara held straight up in the high-ceilinged room watched the patrons at play from his position against the far wall. For just a second there I got a glimpse of Domingo Ortega through the crowd.

"Yeah?" sneered the casino boss. "What kinda business, shamus?"

"Uh, it's not Shamus. At least, not *just* Shamus, that's my matronymic. It's Marlo Shamus. Felipe Marlo Shamus. P.I. for the figuras."

"Yeah, but you're still a shamus, ain't you?"

"Well, yeah, I guess so, but -- "

"So whattaya you want, shamus?" He was frowning.

"Look, Duro," I said, "I know a lot of matadors come here -- the top ones with plenty o' moolah to spare, right?"

"So what if they do? Sure -- Luís Miguel Dominguín and his brother-in-law Tony Ordóñez, Jaime Ostos, Marcial Lalanda. Some win, some lose. Some lose big time, like the one who's here tonight." He chuckled to himself. "What of it?"

"But do you ever get any, er, lesser toreros in here? Like maybe ex-novilleros?"

Duro's sneer increased until I thought his right upper lip was going to go up his right nostril. "Novilleros! Hah! This ain't a portátil, amigo. This is Las Ventas!" Then his sneer faded as The Bull seemed to ruminate on something. "O' course, there *was* that kid the duke brought in here. Seems to me *he* was a novillero. But then he was with el duque. If the Duque de Nuque brought a one-legged sereno from the Calle del Nuncio in here, the guy'd get credit -- as long as el duque vouched for him." Duro seemed to be thinking out loud, rather than talking to me.

"Do you remember the kid's name?" I asked.

El Toro looked at me. "Huh? Nah, I don't recall. Some young hotshot from down South. Near Sevilla, I think. I dunno."

"But no older, ex-novilleros?" I asked. "Like maybe one called Carlos Rojo?"

Duro's thick and shiny-topped head snapped up and he stared at me. Finally he said, "Let's go into my office." He led the way.

Ensconced in a stuffed chair in El Toro's spacious inner sanctum, like the rest of the place with a high ceiling, I accepted a snifter of brandy poured by my host. "Napoleon," he said. "None o' that cheap crap. This is Dominguín's favorite." I took a sip, then another. Tasted expensive -- but with a bit of an aftertaste.

"So who did you say you were looking for?" Duro asked, his voice sounding a bit odd, as though it were far away.

"I . . . I said . . . Carlos . . .Carlos . . ." And then the lights went out. I dreamed I was falling into a darkened pen full of Miuras. Then nothing.

Chapter 3

Marlo's Meat Wagon

I swam up out of a bottomless pit in a sea of blackness, occasionally aware of brilliant light which grew stronger, then suddenly disappeared with a whooshing sound. My head was splitting as I slowly opened my eyes and saw -- nothing. Pitch darkness. Then in the distance a pair of lights coming toward me. A car. As it got closer and I turned my head away to avoid being temporarily blinded, the car's headlights illuminated my surroundings and I realized I was in a car, myself. My own '39 Ford. And just before the approaching vehicle came even with me and flashed past, bringing back the darkness, I saw that I was not alone. There was somebody in the passenger seat, and he looked very dead.

I agonizingly fumbled for a match, struck it and held it in front of my passenger's face. I sucked in my breath. There was no doubt about it. He was considerably older than he'd been in the snapshot I'd seen of him in his suit of lights, but it was him. The ex-novillero with the big plans. The Tyrone Power guy. I'd found Maria Caliente's brother, Carlos Rojo.

I waved out the first match and struck another, studying the corpse. What the -- ? Rojo was dressed in, of all things, a traje de luces. But on his head was not a montera but a gorra, a cloth cap of the type worn by workers. On it and on his hands was some funny yellowish dust. What the hell was that all about? I looked for some sign of what had killed him and I finally saw it, on his right side, the side opposite from me. He'd been shot or stabbed in the ribs and was all bloody down his flank, but there was no hole or knife slit in his clothing. Somebody had done him in and then dressed the body in a suit of lights and stuck a gorra on his head. And then they'd put him -- and me, after I'd drunk that Mickey Finn in Duro's office, like a sap -- in my car. And next somebody had driven the Ford away from el Casino del Toro and back to the highway, then on a few kilometers to a point where it had been left parked on the shoulder of the road, facing toward Madrid. In the light from a car passing from behind me I could see up ahead one of those big silhouetted bull signs with the large white letters reading *Osborne* and, below that in smaller, yellow lettering, *Veterano*. Just to the right of the sign was a huge boulder, and the combination told me I was parked about five kilometers southeast of the turnoff to Duro's casino. Why here? Where anybody who cared to look could see the car and me and the former Rojo in it?

Wait a minute, I said to myself. Of course! *Anybody who cared to look.* And who would care to look at a car parked on the side of the carretera in the middle of the night? Answer: Those omnipresent patrolmen of the highways of Spain, that's who. The Guardia Civil. Holy Mother of God! If those guys found me in my car with a dead Red, I might as well volunteer to take on Sunday's miurada at Las Ventas as única espada, all six of 'em at once -- and without a cape. It was time to clear the scene, and fast.

Chapter 4

Saints and Sinners

I leaned against the bar in the Cervecería Alemaña in the Plaza Santa Ana and ordered another Magno. Some punks drinking cañas who didn't know my face were eyeing my trenchcoat and hat outfit warily, probably figuring I was one of Franco's plainclothes boys, or maybe even Seguridad. The place was starting to pick up business now, or at least it had been until I'd come in; it was almost eight o'clock on a warm spring evening. The nice thing about Spanish bars, I told myself, was that you didn't have to listen to rock-n-roll from a jukebox all the time, like you did in the U.S. You could enjoy a little peace and quiet -- unless a couple of old pensioners with voices like they gargled three times a day with kerosene were arguing about the bulls or fútbol or something. Back in the states you'd have Gene Vincent wailing *Be-Bop-a-Lula* or Jerry Lee Lewis hammering out *Great Balls o'Fire* at forty thousand decibels.

I was looking in the mirror behind the bar, grimacing Bogey style and trying to decide if it was too early to head on out to my next appointment. I'd finally gotten a few hours of sleep after I got back to the Calle Victoria at dawn and crashed on the ratty sofa in my outer office -- like I did every night; I didn't have a flat or even a rented room, just the office. Home sweet home.

I'd managed to avoid the Guardia Civil on the highway, but only just. As soon as I cranked up the Ford and gunned it toward Madrid, my headlights picked out two guardia walking along the carretera in the direction of where I'd been parked, not 500 meters away. My car lights reflected off their shiny, patent-leather hats and their belt buckles. Their carbines were slung over their shoulders. They didn't try to flag me down as they sometimes did, purely out of curiosity or boredom, but they tried to get a look at me as I roared past. I made it as hard as I could for them, mashing down on the high-beam button on the Ford's floor with my left foot, hopefully blinding them. I'd already pulled my hat and that of the dead Red down, to obscure our faces. Hombre, I sighed, that was too damned close!

Fortunately for me, Madrid was a late-night town, and even at 3:30 de la madrugada there were quite a few cars on the streets and people walking around, so I didn't draw any undue attention. I pulled in and parked alongside the old Convento de la Encarnación, only a block or two from the former Royal Palace. If the palace had been where Franco actually had his pad, as opposed to just using it for formal state ceremonies, I'd have been wary, as uniforms of all types -- and trenchcoats, too -- would've been swarming all over the place. But with el Caudillo way outside of town at his real snoozery, the Pardo Palace, I figured it was safe enough. The dark and quiet little Calle de la Encarnación which ran beside the convent was in deep shadow as I dragged Rojo's body from my car to some trash bins at one of the big rear doors of the convent, stuffing the stiff into the last one, then brushing off as best I could that yellow dust which had gotten onto my hands and coat. The nuns'd have a surprise the next morning when the novice hauled out their bucketful of half-eaten gruel or leftover holy wafers or whatever it was that composed their garbage, for the city's basura boys to collect. I hated to do that to what was left of Maria Caliente's brother, but I couldn't risk letting the cops tie me into his murder. They'd find his body soon enough.

And they did. By the time I woke up in the late morning, the word was already out in the bars and ticket reventa kiosks in the Calle Victoria. Félix, the old bartender at the joint near the corner with the Calle de la Cruz, a place with lots of carteles on the walls featuring the previous year's Número Uno in the escalafón, Gregorio Sánchez, first told me when I came in for a carajillo.

"No official announcement yet," Félix said *sotto voce*, looking furtively over his shoulder as he spoke," but a cuate o' mine, another oldtimer who cleans up down at the city morgue, told me he heard 'em talkin'. Says they identified a dead guy they found this morning behind the Convento de la Encarnación, all dressed up in a traje de luces, as a novillero from back during the civil war, guy they called Carlos Rojo, or Carlitos el Rojo. Stayed in the republican zone till the war ended, workin' to start collecta -- collectivo -- uh, you know, them farms owned by the people. Between you and me, Señor Marlo, he don't sound like a bad fella. But don't tell nobody I told you so, está bién?"

"Sure, Félix," I said, sipping my coffee and coñac. "Say, did your friend learn how Rojo was killed?"

"Sí," growled the barkeep, again looking around for eavesdroppers, "that he did. He said the guy was stabbed through his ribs on his right side, not too far below his armpit. Pierced his heart. Now, who'd stab a man that way, Señor Marlo? It ain't natural. It's lucky for the killer it even did the job. And get this: whatever it was did it, it wasn't a knife. Hole was too big and the distance from the guy's side to his heart was too long, even for most daggers. Said some of 'em are talkin' about maybe an army bayonet."

"A bayonet?" I looked up from my drink.

"Sí. But not a standard issue bayonet of el ejército español -- hole's not big *enough* for that. Maybe a bayonet from some other country's army."

"Hmmm. Interesting," I said. "Thanks, Félix." I plopped some coins onto the zinc counter for the carajillo, plus a few more for the info. Félix deftly scooped them up.

"Oh, one other thing, Señor Marlo," the old barkeep called out as I was heading for the door. I turned and went back to the bar. "My pal at the morgue was in the war like the rest of us from 'thirty-six to 'thirty-nine -- that's why he's got only one arm -- and the side he was on, well, keep this under your hat, Señor Marlo, it wasn't Franco's, if you know what I mean." He looked around again, then went on, "Well, he said his outfit had a couple of, er, advisors, from Russia they was, and he says they wore their own bayonets on their belts, and them bayonets was long and smaller-bladed than the Spanish ones. With blades just about the right size to make that hole in Comrade -- er, lo siento -- in Señor Rojo's side. And he also told me that these Russkis had a funny way o' killin', at least they did if they had any sayso in the matter: they'd shove their bayonets through a guy's ribs, from the side, all the way to his heart. But, you know, Señor Marlo, all that don't mean nothin'. It don't matter a damn who killed this Rojo fellow. You know why? The police, they have already decided to blame the murder on the Reds, anyway -- you know, a falling out among traitors, something like that -- and this latest stuff about a Russian bayonet may even make such a charge believable to some."

"Ah, *very* interesting, Félix," I said, smiling. I tossed another coin onto the bar, one of the old, big, twenty-five peseta pieces with Franco's profile and the wording running around the circumference which read, *Francisco Franco Caudillo de España por la Gr. [Gracia] de Dios,* and then the year it was minted: 1957, last year. I'd known it wasn't brand new because this year they'd come out with smaller sized coins. But Franco and all the wording were still there, of course. I started out of the bar but Félix called me back yet again. "Uh, Señor Marlo," he said, somewhat sheepishly, "can I ask you something?"

"Fire away, Félix, " I said.

"Uh, you know this Convento de la Encarnación where the cops found that Rojo fellow's body?"

"Yeah?" I said. "What about it?"

"Well, uh, maybe you know that they say they've got a bottle or a jug or something in that place with some dried up stuff in it, and that every year on July 27, el Día de San Pantaleón, that stuff, uh, turns into real blood. The blood of San Pantaleón."

"Yeah?" I said. "So?"

"Uh, do you believe that really happens, Señor Marlo?" Félix's eyes were open wide and his forehead was wrinkled questioningly.

"Yeah, sure," I said. "Why not? Only a Red wouldn't think so, right?"

"Oh, sí, sí, for sure, Señor Marlo," he said hurriedly, starting to wipe off the bar. "I was just asking."

I walked on out of the bar and back down the Calle Victoria, noting just how sooty black all the buildings were, from the soft coal burned in the wintertime. But what the hell, wasn't every building in every street in Madrid -- with the exception of the few relatively new constructions -- like that? And wasn't every other major city in Europe in the same, soot-black state? Well, maybe not Sevilla and a couple of other places way down south where little or no coal was ever burned, but just about everywhere else. So what could you do about it, I asked myself, then mentally replying: nothing. Once all the buildings turn sooty black, then they'll be that way forever; I couldn't see any way all those facades could be cleaned up, like you could your neck. Your shirt collar'd be pitch black inside from the soot, but at least you could wash the old cuello, right? You could also get a pain in it.

I went back to my office, where I telephoned Maria Caliente, using the number on her card. She might be at the Duque de Nuque's place but she obviously had her own telephone line because she and not some domestic hired help answered. I broke the news to her about her brother, and she took it pretty hard. I didn't tell her about my necrophilic pre-dawn ride with him or my social call at the nuns' place or my chat with Félix the bartender. As gently as I could, however, I did ask her if she knew anyone who might possess an old bayonet of Russian manufacture, or if Carlos had owned one. As to Carlos, she told me between sobs that she didn't know, but she *did* know someone who owned not one, but several Russian bayonets of World War II vintage, someone who had, in fact, brought them home as souvenirs after two years in the early 1940s on the Eastern Front with the falangist Blue Division: the Duque de Nuque. My, my. Of course, she had no idea why I was asking, and I didn't volunteer the info.

I'd figured my job with the rejoneadora was finished, but not so. She told me that my quest now was to learn who had murdered her brother. She had access to funds these days, she said; she could afford to pay. I said okay and hung up.

Chapter 5

A P.I. with Nobleza

And now I was ready for a little further peeper work. I sat my glass on the bar, lit a fag and left the cervecería, heading up the Calle del Prado to the Hotel Reina Victoria. I nodded to the one-legged vet with the single crutch who "kept an eye on" cars parked around the plaza for a small propina -- as if anybody's car needed watching in Franco's Spain. The vigilante smiled and tipped his motheaten peaked cap to me. Hell, I could drop a wallet full of pesetas on the sidewalk and I'd probably find it still lying untouched in the same spot the next morning -- unless someone had rushed it to a cop, who in turn would've returned it to me fully intact, if he'd been able to determine where I lived or worked. And if he couldn't, they'd keep the thing at the station until I reported it missing. Yeah, petty street crime was hard to find in el estado de España. Rubbing out Red ex-toreros -- well, that was different.

At the Reina Victoria I went through the revolving door and walked past the square columns sporting colorful taurine carteles promoting corridas and novilladas at rings in and around Madrid, for this week and future dates, too. The carteles for San Isidro were up, I noticed. I stopped and checked them out.

Hmmm -- there would be eleven corridas in this, the twelfth year of the feria. Holy moley, I thought, at this rate in a couple of years San Isidro will be up to fifteen corridas. Could Madrid really sustain that great a number of actuaciones, one day after another?

Who would be featured on the carteles this year? Well, I read and found out. I saw lots of names, including those of some of the guys I particularly liked: three appearances each for Antonio Ordóñez, Gregorio Sánchez, Manolo Vázquez and Julio Aparicio; two each for Antonio Bienvenida, Jaime Ostos, Rafael Ortega, Luís Segura, César Girón, Chicuelo hijo, Chamaco and the rejóneador Angel Peralta; and single appearances for Antoñete, Solanito, Joaquín Bernadó, Cayetano Ordóñez (there only because brother Antonio insisted, folks were saying) and a second rejóneador, Josechu Pérez de Mendoza. Toros from some of the top ganaderías were scheduled, too: Bohórquez, Cobaleda, Carlos Nuñez, Atanasio Fernández, Pablo Romero, Tabernero. Nothing from Gato Gordo.

I also saw other carteles with the names of a couple of current top novilleros, Diego Puerta and Miguelín, but I didn't see anything that could recall to my mind the name of the kid the Duque de Nuque was supposed to be shepherding around these days, the one from just outside Sevilla. Curro something or other.

I stuffed my cigarette butt into one of those fancy stand-up ashtrays the better hotels have, the ones with white sand in the top and the hotel's crest impressed into it like the seal of the pope's ring mashed into hot wax. I screwed up the pretty design with my butt. Too bad.

Off to the left and up a couple of steps was the lobby bar, which had a taurine theme. Pictures of Manolete were on the walls and a mounted bull's head was opposite the bar itself. A lot of the taurine crowd liked to come here and, according to the scuttlebutt in the Calle Victoria, I just might find who I was looking for here at about this time. I eyeballed the crowd, which was about as big as could comfortably squeeze into the small bar. Sitting around a tiny table in a corner were three people, one of whom was a great bear of a man with his back to me. While I couldn't see his face, I could see those of his companions, a man and a woman. The dame with the auburn hair and the green eyes and the high cheekbones would have been familiar to most Americans from the movies and to many Spaniards from the bullring -- always in a barrera sombra seat sobre los capotes. It was Ava Gardner. The debonnaire caballero to her right, with his left hand on La Gardner's knee under the little table, would also be recognized at the plaza de toros -- by *all* Spaniards: Luís Miguel Dominguín. Then someone called out "Harry!" and the big man with his back to me twisted around in his chair, revealing the smiling moonface of Orson Welles. I could've sworn I heard zither music.

I had decided to approach the threesome on some pretext, just to rub shoulders with the glitterati, when out of the corner of my eye I became aware of the man I'd come hoping to find. I turned and looked at the entranceway to the bar and saw him. He'd stopped to shake hands with an enthusiastic aficionado but was obviously trying to extricate himself. Good, because now *I* wanted to latch on.

Señor Domingo López Ortega, better known simply as Domingo Ortega to the world's taurinos and villamelones alike, was a trim man of fifty years or so and still making the rare appearance in the ring from time to time.   A couple of years earlier I'd seen him in a newsreel shot at a bullring in Mexico, I think it was. He'd apparently come as a spectator, dressed in a business suit and leather shoes, but somebody had spotted him and he somehow ended up out on the sand with a muleta and a toro bravo, passing the animal as beautifully and confidently as if he'd been in a suit of lights and in his prime. In his inimitable style -- which, as every taurino knows, was one of continuous walking, guiding the bull, passing it and walking on, crossing its path, pulling it through and around, walking, walking, walking -- he put on a show which had everyone in the plaza on his feet, applauding, yelling and screaming. And all the while wearing business attire and wingtips. Quite a guy.

And apparently a generous type, too: during the four years since his most recent (and presumably last) despedida, he had helped out in various festivales benéficos. He had even been awarded the prestigious Orden Civil de Beneficendia. It was said that he would appear again soon this temporada, in one of the taurine benefit performances. He'd draw a good crowd, that was for certain.

Ortega finally shook the fan after signing his autograph, and I chose that moment to pounce. Thanks to some dope I'd gotten from a reventa tout in the Calle Victoria, I thought I knew something that'd get his attention. I eased up to him and took his arm gently. "Holá, matador," I said quietly. "I think we've got a mutual friend. Paquito Duro."

Ortega whipped his graying head toward me and stared through black-rimmed spectacles with an expression which reflected both anger and fear. His eyes took in my trenchcoat and hat. "Who are you and what do you want?" he snapped. But he said it in a low voice so others couldn't hear.

"What would be your guess, matador?" I asked, smiling slightly and pushing the brim of my hat back a little with my thumb.

The old figura looked around quickly, then said in a low and controlled but irritated voice, "Look, I *told* Duro I'd get his money to him soon. Why is he sending his muscle to me already?" Sweat was breaking out on his forehead and upper lip. Oh, this was going even better than I'd hoped.

"Hey, you know how it is. El Toro suddenly realized he's running a little short and --"

"But he *knows* I'll get him the money!" Ortega interrupted. "I *have* the money. I'm a ganadero, a rich man. He knows that. It's just that I don't have, er, that *much* in ready cash. It will take a while for me to --"

Now it was my turn to interrupt. "Look, what if we gave you an extension, in return for some information?" I looked at him quizzically.

The torero studied my face suspiciously. "What information?" he finally asked. A muscle in his jaw twitched.

"Nothing that'll hurt you or anybody else. On a subject that really has nothing, or very little, to do with you. It's about an ex-novillero named Carlos Rojo. Does the name mean anything to you?"

Ortega looked away and frowned, apparently thinking. Then he started walking from the bar into the hotel lobby. I walked with him.

"Carlos Rojo," he muttered, still walking, not in a straight line but rather in a sort of ellipse. We proceeded in this fashion, circling first to the left, then to the right, through the lobby and out the front entrance of the hotel. Ortega would walk a bit ahead of me, yet looking back and watching me all the while. Then I would catch up with him and, as he motioned with his open hand held low and in front of him in a sort of "after you, Alphonse" gesture, I would find myself going past him and then, although I wasn't sure why, *around* him to the right or to the left, depending on which hand was doing the gesturing. It was weird.

"Why are we walking like this?" I finally gasped, beginning to tire. "What's going on?"

"I'm sorry, mi amigo," the veteran torero replied, looking somewhat surprised, "but it just comes natural to me. It is my estilo." As he finished speaking I realized I had once again gone past him and was circling around him, his flat, open hand held in front of me at all times. By now we were across the Calle Nuñez de Arce and walking elliptically into the grassless, packed-dirt Plaza Santa Ana, where quite a few people were strolling, relaxing on park benches or tending small children at this evening hour. Finally I understood what was happening. *I was being passed like a toro bravo by Domingo Ortega, in his ever-walking, never-stopping style!* He had worked me like a bull on rails -- curving rails -- in a faena from the hotel's bar all the way to the plaza!

"Stop it!" I yelled, freezing in my tracks. Several people in the plaza looked at me, including Ortega, who did finally stop. "You think I'm some crummy bovine?" I snarled. The old figura looked surprised.

"Crummy?" he asked, using the same Spanish word I had -- *ínfimo.* "Why, no, not at all. I thought you were quite noble, if perhaps a bit lacking in casta and trapío. No signs of your being sentido or even manso. No, certainly not crummy."

"Well, er, thanks -- I guess," I said, then, "Wait a minute! We're getting sidetracked here. Okay, Ortega: Carlos Rojo. Start singin'! And for God's sake, sit down on that bench!"

He reluctantly sat and told me what he knew, while I lit up again. If anyone would have had a chance to be made aware of an obscure young novillero in the mid 1930s, it was Domingo Ortega. He headed up the escalafón six out of seven years, from 1931 through 1937 (and once again in 1940), and by performing in more corridas than any other matador year after year he was obviously in more places and around more different toreros than any of the others, giving him more

22

opportunities to see or meet or hear about new talent.

Yes, he remembered a kid by the name of Carlos Rojo, although after the civil war started he began going by the apodo Carlitos el Rojo, remaining -- obviously -- in the republican zone. Although the kid had very few novilladas, his presence was made felt through his socio-political activities, something very rare for a torero in those days. He recalled Carlitos showing up at some lesser plaza de toros either before or just after the war started, dressed in his traje de luces but wearing a cloth gorra instead of a montera, and with his left arm raised in the clenched-fist salute of the Left during the paseillo.

"Yeah! That's the guy!" I blurted out. "Now, think carefully. Have you seen him? Or have you heard anything about him lately?"

The matador-ganadero sighed, then said, "I have not seen him in over twenty years, not since August of 1936, a month after the war began. I was still honoring some contracts in places which ended up being in the republican zone, and that's where I last saw him. In Valencia, to be precise. I hadn't had a decent meal in some days and, frankly, I was not comfortable going to the usual restaurants in the city at that time. The waiters were all euphoric over being 'just as good as' the rich, and if they perceived a patron to be un rico, they would often go out of their way to be sure he got poor service, or none at all. Maybe throw in some insults or spit in the soup for good measure. Well, I *was* rich; I was Número Uno in Spain, so I was suspect. I was lamenting this fact in a local taurine bar where I felt more or less secure, when a young man came up to me and introduced himself as Carlos Rojo 'Carlitos el Rojo.' I had seen him in a novillada or two -- toreros like to go to the bullfight, too, did you know that, señor? -- so I knew who he was. He told me he could not help overhearing me talking about the restaurants, and he invited me to come with him to a place where he could guarantee me a warm reception. The management and the customers were all his friends and of his own political persuasion, but they were taurinos first and foremost and would heartily welcome el Número Uno. I thanked him and accepted, as long as my cuadrilla could go, too. He agreed, and we proceeded in some automobiles, which had been confiscated from local landowners by his republican friends, out to the beach at El Grau. There, at a seafood restaurant which still served excellent fare but whose service was now atrocious -- though friendly, I must admit -- we finally had a most enjoyable dinner. Despite the fact that the waiters and the cooks had to vote on everything, including who got served first and how big his portions should be.

"The young Rojo had quite a magnetic personality and talked to me at great length of his dreams of turning Spain into a vast agricultural state with a benevolent republican government taking over all the ranches raising toros bravos and combining them into one gigantic ganadería, mixing the best breeds together to create a single super-breed which, in his daydreams, he would call Rancho Obrero. I didn't tell him his idea, if ever actually implemented, would spell disaster for the

Spanish fighting bull. But I was enjoying my dinner and I let him talk. He was also very interested, I remember, in agricultural schemes and vast collective farms. As to industrialization, however, this young idealist had no thoughts whatsoever, and this of course pointed up more clearly than anything else how incomplete his thinking was for one who saw himself as a future guiding light for a Red Spain. Not only that, but his vision of that same Red Spain as a monolithic ganadero was as off the mark as it could possibly have been. As he was outlining his dream to me, some of his fellow travelers were probably at that very moment slaughtering some ganadero's herd in the republican zone, not just killing enough cattle to feed themselves and any other needy persons in the area, but shooting the rest of the animals anyway, to be left to rot in the fields, simply because they belonged to a rich landowner."

After a moment of silence I said, "So that's the last you heard of Carlos Rojo?"

Ortega looked at me and replied, "No, that is the last time I *saw* him. That was your first question. Now, as to the last time I *heard* about him, that was last night."

"Last night!" I sat up straight on the bench and my jaw flopped open, allowing my cigarette to fall all the way down to my right shoe, where it neatly dropped down between the inside of the shoe and my sock, the glowing ash end resting against and burning a hole in the instep of my foot. I began yelling and cursing and hopping around on my left foot, trying to get my right shoe off. Everyone in the plaza looked my way; men with female companions hurriedly ushered them away, all the while looking back over their shoulders, while little children either laughed and pointed at me or else began crying and running to their mommies or their dueñas. Finally I had my shoe off and I shook out the damned butt. Ortega was just staring at me, mouth agape. I put my shoe back on and nonchalantly sat back down on the bench as though nothing untoward had occurred.

"Now," I rasped, "you were saying you heard something about Rojo last night?"

Ortega looked at me as though unsure how safe he was with me, but at last he spoke. "Yes, at Duro's casino."

"And what did you hear?" Damn! My right arch hurt! I tried not to show it.

"Not very much," he answered. "A distinguished-looking, elderly, white-haired man I would say looked like a university professor or a doctor or something along those lines was speaking to Paquito Duro, your boss, saying something like, 'Where is Carlos Rojo? I know he is here.' Something to that effect. And that's it. But why am I telling you this? Duro already knows it all."

"Uh, yeah, sure," I said. "Well, that's not your worry. Okay, you've got your extension. Now if you don't want to miss your rendezvous with that little chica, you'd better get back inside the hotel and head for the bar."

"Wha --? How did --?" Now it was Ortega's turn to look surprised. The sadist in me wished he'd had a fag in *his* mouth that he could've dropped into his shoe like I did.

"Never mind," I said. "Buenas noches, matador." I turned and walked off down Nuñez de Arce, toward the Calle de la Cruz. Ortega went back to the hotel.

Poor bastard -- what was he going to think when Duro's *real* goon eventually came along and pressed him for the dough he owed and told Ortega he didn't know anything about an "extension"?

Chapter 6

Adios to a Canine

I walked back the two or three blocks to my office, climbed the three floors and found the outer door cracked open but no lights on. Instantly alert, I pulled my Spanish-made snubnose .38 Moxley from my shoulder holster and kicked the door the rest of the way open, at the same time flicking on the light switch with my right hand. A couple of guys dressed like me were sitting on the ratty sofa -- my bed -- on the other side of the outer office. One of them, the younger and bigger one, jumped up quick; the older one took his time. Cops. Nobody but a cop -- of one type or another -- would dress in trenchcoats and snap-brim fedoras in warm Madrid weather, I thought. Except me, of course. The older cop spoke.

"Gimme the gun, shamus," he said, holding out his hand. His simian partner glowered at me, his right hand inside his trenchcoat, ready to draw. Tough guy.

"I've got a permit for that thing, you know," I said as I handed over the pistol. "Turned out the Generalísimo knows all about private eyes from Hollywood films, and he thought it might be a swell idea to have a taurine P.I. in old España, especially as he's an aficionado, himself, so I got a license. I'm sure you know he's a big fan of American movies, just like his old pal used to be, that other head of state. Uh . . . what was the other fellow's name? Oh, yeah -- Hitler."

With a nod from the older cop, the younger one stepped forward and punched

26

me in the mouth. Hard. And I went down hard.

After a minute, I propped myself up on one elbow and wiped a little blood from my lip with my other hand. "I guess that love tap was because Hitler lost, huh?" I said.

"Funny hombre," the older one said, sneering. "Keep that up and you'll find yourself in one of those basement rooms beneath the Dirección General de Seguridad on the Puerta del Sol, where lots of questions get asked in a not-so-gentle fashion." He was mustachioed and reminded me of the Mexican movie star Pedro Armendariz.

I got to my feet slowly, keeping an eye on the other guy, the trenchcoated escapee from the circus. He needs to wear thick gloves, I thought to myself, to keep from scraping his knuckles when he's walking over concrete or other rough surfaces. I worked my tongue around in my mouth and finally spat out a bloody tooth.

"That didn't hurt," I said to the young goon, smiling a red-stained smile at him, now with a gap where my left canine used to be.

That really got to the guy. His eyes bulged out as he drew back his fist to hit me again, but the other cop grabbed his arm. "Leave it," he said to the animal.

"But Capitán Gilipollas, El Toro said --" the younger one burst out.

"¡Cállate la boca!" barked the captain. After telling his man to shut up he turned to me and said, "We don't want any trouble, Marlo. This is purely a routine call, you might say, just checking to be sure your license is in order. You wouldn't want to lose it, now would you?"

"You haven't even asked to see my license," I said, dabbing at my mouth with my handkerchief.

"Yeah, well, I figure it's probably okay," the boss cop said airily. "Just keep your nose out of places it doesn't belong. You ain't been here from los Estados Unidos too long. It'd be too bad if we found out you were one of Eisenhower's CIA spies, wouldn't it? Or, even better -- we could always discover that you were a Red. And you know what happens to Reds. I could say you started shouting 'No pasarán' in the Avenida José Antonio. You'd be carne muerto, mi amigo."

"Yeah, sure," I said. "Can I have my rod back now?"

The older cop looked at me a moment, then handed me back my pistol, butt first. "Take my advice, Marlo," Gilipollas said, "make yourself invisible." He looked at his goon and said, "Come on, Bálthazar." He made for the door. I started to point at the young cop and amusedly cry, *"Bálthazar?"* then die laughing, slapping my thigh, but I thought better of it and just let the two of them leave. The outer door slammed shut.

I went into my inner office and sat at my desk, putting my feet up and pulling the Magno from the drawer for a couple of good slugs straight from the bottle. I probed the gap in my teeth with my tongue and mused that the cops apparently didn't know anything. Paquito Duro had put them onto me to try to scare me off the case, that's all. They probably wouldn't know anything about Duro's part in the murder of Maria's brother, or the part I'd played in getting rid of the body. But Duro, or somebody above Duro, had sufficient clout to have the police jumping when he said jump. Frankly, I couldn't see "The Bull" with that much pull, by himself; he was really no more than a succcessful thug. I'd just have to keep an eye out for danger from the ex-picador *and* the cops. I sighed; hell, I was a taurine P.I., wasn't I? Danger came with the job. Every assignment was a giant Miura. I took a hand mirror out of my top desk drawer and began practicing Bogey-type mouth twitches in it.

After a while I went out and had a couple of drinks at a taurine bar and ate some tapas, then I went back up to my office and crashed on the sofa. I needed to figure out a plan to find out who the distinguished old guy was who Ortega said was asking Duro about Carlos Rojo. I had no idea who this bird might be. What I did know, however, was that Duro was responsible for Carlos's murder. At least he had seen to it. But why? What was the connection between Carlitos el Rojo and a taurine casino hood like El Toro? Why had Rojo been killed? Why try to frame me for it? Yeah, I needed answers to all those questions. But right now I was beat and needed sleep. If I had to dream, I hoped it'd be something like me facing a sweet little novillo with blunted horns. It wasn't.

Chapter 7

Pic a Winner

At six a.m. the dawn was beginning to break in the east, to my back. El Casino del Toro was as quiet as it would ever be, its patrons all gone by now and the staff either vamoosed or in bed there on the property, at last. With the help of a ring of skeleton keys and a lock-picking tool, I'd gained entry to Paquito Duro's office seemingly without having been seen.

I'd waked up on my sofa at about five a.m. and gone to my car, driving out the Segovia carretera. This time, however, I turned off the main highway well before I came to the private road to the casino, circling around to the rear and parking on the other side of some rock hills behind the gambling joint. I scrambled over the rocks, up the hill and then down, keeping to the shadows. I spotted the two night watchmen and avoided them.

Now, inside Duro's private office, the biggest such place I'd ever seen, I made sure the drapes were pulled before I turned on my flashlight and began looking for -- what? Something which might tell me . . . something. Finally, in a filing cabinet I found an interesting item. It was a manila file folder marked *Azafumo*. What kind of name or word was that? I pulled out the file and opened it. There was a single sheet of paper inside, originally just a piece of white typewriter paper, but with a crude map of sorts drawn on it in blue fountain pen ink. There were several rough-drawn rectangular shapes and a smallish circle, plus a curving double line which I at first thought was perhaps meant to represent a river -- except that it ended in an open space between some of the rectangles. At the bottom end of the double line, where it ran off the page, two words were printed, along with a tiny arrow pointing downward: *to Madrid.* The curvy double line was a road of some type.

All of a sudden I sneezed. I got out my handkerchief and when I did I noticed, in the flashlight's glare, some yellowish dust on my hands. I looked at the map and saw that the paper was lightly coated with the stuff. I pulled out my handkerchief, balancing my flashlight on the top of a filing cabinet, and wiped it and my hands as free of it as I could, then put the pañuelo away.

I studied the rough map more closely. There were several notations in blue ink, all of them hard to read, as though they had been very hastily written. But one leaped from the page: *ruedo de tentaderos.* A tienta ring! So this was a map of some place with its own tienta ring. That meant some ganadero's place out in the countryside. But whose? El Toro probably knew most of the ganaderos in Spain. I deciphered more of the writing. The words *casa mayor* were connected by a line to the largest mass of rectangular block shapes. *Caballeriza* referred to a longish block. Stables. And with an inked line pointing to it, a square shape near the tienta ring was marked *cojones* -- and there was an arrow drawn pointing to it. Bingo! This had to be the place they were holding the old guy I was looking for, the professorish type Domingo Ortega had seen asking Duro about Carlos. Once I got to the ranch, I'd know where to look: in the building where they kept the, you know, after they cut them off the bulls. Wait a minute! Why would they cut the, you-knows, off the bulls? Toros bravos went into the ring with their, er -- they went into the ring *intact.* Then why did they need a building to store the bulls'. . . I looked at the map again. ¡Carajo! I slapped my forehead with the palm of my hand, hard. The writing on the homemade map said *cajones*, not *cojones*!

I started over. Okay, the place I needed to search was the building where they stored the cajones, the wooden crates into which toros bravos were lured, preparatory to shipping them from the ranch to the bullring. The only problem was that I didn't know *which* ranch. And there were ranches with toros bravos all over Spain.

I was folding the piece of paper and stuffing it into my inside coat pocket when the door to the casino was suddenly flung open and the lights flicked on, revealing Paquito Duro "El Toro" and a 600-kilo picador I recognized as Pepe, Duro's major domo. Pepe was gripping his long wooden garrocha tipped with pointed steel and wearing an expression like he'd been constipated for a month. I noticed that the cruceta, the restraining crosspiece at the base of the steel point meant to keep the shaft from penetrating a bull's neck and back muscles to any real depth, had been removed.

"You're a real fiero, shamus," Duro said with a snarl, "and one that's developing too much sentido. But now it's time for the first tercio to really get underway -- the act where the picador --" he pointed a thumb at the mountain of beef beside him -- "takes on the as yet unmarked toro bravo. And today the matador has given his picador orders to *destroy the bull!*" He pointed at me while looking at Pepe.

If the ceilings hadn't been so high, the guy never could've paraded around inside the casino with his long, steel-tipped vara, but they were, and he could. But now Pepe was lowering the thing and pointing it at me, across the room. He cradled it up under his armpit exactly as though he were on a horse, but then he broke the rules: he didn't wait for me to charge; instead, he charged me. I'd had a feeling this guy probably played dirty.

At the last moment I jumped aside, dropping my flashlight and pulling out my gat as the steel point of the pica rammed into the metal filing cabinets. I fired wildly, as I knew Duro would have his own gun out by now and I needed to make him flinch and think about getting out of my line of fire, rather than pausing to take a shot at me. Sure enough, he bolted through the open door, heading into the empty main room of the casino. Pepe had dropped his vara when I'd fired my Moxley, and now he was lumbering after El Toro into the big casino hall. He wasn't a total dummy -- he worked at the casino and he knew that one gun beat no varas.

I picked up the long hardwood pole and went through the door after them. Duro was running down the wide center aisle between the tables, heading for the main exit, and the lanceless Pepe was waddling after him. I put my rod back in my shoulder holster as I chased after the two of them with the staff in my right hand. Ah, Marlo, I thought to myself, thy rod and thy staff they comfort thee.

Once I was also in the wide main passageway of the casino I shifted the vara until I had it by the blunt end and then, still running, I jabbed the punta, the steel-pointed end, into the carpet and polevaulted myself high into the air in a perfect salto de la garrocha, barely clearing a chandelier hanging from the very high ceiling. I came down on the other side of Duro, between him and the exit; I quickly pulled the pica out of the carpet and held it under my armpit, just as Pepe had done, pointing it toward the two onrushing forms. El Toro ought to stop when he saw that. I wanted him alive.

But neither of the heavy men could brake that fast. Inertia simply carried them forward when they tried to stop. The long, hardwood pica almost nine feet long pierced Duro's heart first, then the gut of his major domo right behind him, as the hired muscle crashed into his boss from the rear. Olé! Just like two huge chunks of beef on a skewer.

The steel-tipped end of the pole now protruded from Pepe's back by at least three feet. The two men stood there jammed together, the big goon plastered to Duro's back and the long pole holding them together like the world's largest shishkebob.

Both had incredulous expressions on their fat faces. Then they crashed to the floor, falling over to the left. Duro was already dead and Pepe would be in a couple of minutes. Damn! I wouldn't get any answers out of El Toro now. I really blew that one, I thought to myself.

"So long, fellas," I said, touching the brim of my hat out of courtesy. I went out the way I'd come in. I didn't think anybody else had seen me.

Chapter 8

A Ducal Invitation

I sat in my "thinking position" at my desk: leaning back in my squeaky swivel chair with my feet up on the desk. I'd caught a couple more hours of shuteye after returning from el Casino del Toro and now I was studying the hand-drawn map I'd found there, trying to see if there were any clues as to just which ranch it was supposed to be. I was stymied.

Through my open window came the sounds of the Calle Victoria below. The city was just about at full steam now, as it was almost ten o'clock. The day's edition of *ABC* was on my desk, already perused. The lead story was typical of lead stories in the Spanish papers: Franco had dedicated a new dam someplace in Navarra. A photograph showed him in full dress uniform, cutting a long ribbon with a pair of scissors. Elsewhere, the bankers in the "real" Europe were telling Spain her money would always be worth crap until she cleaned up her act -- whatever that meant; of course, *ABC* didn't phrase it like that. Hey, here was something of interest in the *Fiesta Nacional* section: some Frenchie named Francois Bouyard, appearing on Curro Meloja's regular radio program *Tauromaquia*, proposed that moñas be awarded as premios during corridas instead of orejas -- and some people were apparently taking the damnfool suggestion seriously! Who the blazes cared about seeing a triumphant torero taking a vuelta holding aloft a frigging pretty-colored doololly sort of like a divisa, instead of an ear? What was the world coming to? And over here, I read, the old five peseta coins made of nickel would soon be biting the dust.

Buried in a back section I'd found what I'd been looking for, a piece on the Carlos Rojo business. Seems the cops had determined that the ex-novillero, a known Red, had come back to Spain for nefarious purposes but had had a falling out with his comrades, who had bumped him off with a pistol shot to the back of the head, checa style. I had sighed and laid the paper down; why couldn't these government people ever come up with something original?

I heard someone come into my outer office, so I moved my feet from the desktop, got up and walked over to the connecting door. An elderly chauffeur in a gray uniform and cap and highly polished riding boots was standing there, an envelope in his hand.

"Señor Marlo Shamus?" he asked.

"That's me, pal."

"I have a message for you, señor." He held out the envelope. I took it and he gave me a little bow and turned and strode out of the office.

I looked at the envelope. It was not of the usual business letter variety. It was squarish and cream-colored and it smelled faintly of perfume. I took it back into the other room, picked up a letter opener and slit it open. There was a sort of invitation inside; I pulled it out, unfolded it and read:

THE DUQUE DE NUQUE
REQUESTS YOUR PRESENCE
AT THE DEBUT OF
SRTA. MARIA CALIENTE
REJONEADORA
AT THE RANCH OF GATO GORDO

Underneath was today's date and the time, 5:00 p.m. On the back of the card stock was a simple map showing how to get there. I looked at it and saw that it was off the main road to Colmenar Viejo, to the north. So that's where Maria Caliente was shacked up with el duque. And I'd bet dollars to churros the layout of Gato Gordo corresponded to the map I'd gotten at El Toro's casino.

I turned the invitation over in my hand and thought, this has to be Maria's doing. The Duque de Nuque doesn't know me from the south end of a northbound jackass. Well! It certainly came at an opportune time, for with a little luck I could, just maybe, locate the old professor-like guy and grill him as to what was going on. Sure, Paquito Duro's picadors had undoubtedly done Rojo in, but they were just doing Duro's dirty work. And Duro was doing the same for somebody else, I just knew it. Too bad I had to skewer him before I could pump him for info, but that's the way the churro crumbles.

Wait a minute, I said to myself. Churros don't crumble, they're kind of greasy and they'll bend a little. Ah, never mind. I knew what I meant.

It took me over an hour to reach the turnoff to el duque's spread. A discreet bronze plaque set into a stone marker read simply, *Gato Gordo*, with no gate or guards or anything except a small sign which said *Entrada Privada.* But just over a rise I came to a checkpoint which even the Russkis would have envied, with iron gates and armed guards. A big turnaround space was in front, for the occasional motorist who might drive up the narrow but nicely paved road from the highway out of curiosity. One look at those carbine-packing neanderthals and the curiosity would quickly fade. I showed my invitation to a guard and, after he cased and sneered at my '39 Ford, he checked a clipboard on which he apparently found my name. Then he opened the gate and waved me on through. In my rearview mirror I saw him go into his little guardhouse, no doubt to phone ahead of me.

The macadam road wound its way through some scrubby and rocky hills for a couple of miles. Then at the crest of a ridge I braked and looked down into a fertile valley dominated by a sprawling white hacienda with a red tile roof and lots of outbuildings. Lots of cars, too -- this looked like a big shindig, all right.

A series of guards posted at intervals made sure I went where they wanted me to. I was finally directed to stop and park at the tienta ring, between a huge Hispano-Suizo and a brand new Rolls. No Seat 600s were in evidence. I looked up ahead and saw that a crowd of well-dressed people was already there. Patting my right armpit to reassure myself that my gat was still in place, I started walking toward the low, white stucco structure reflecting the brilliant late afternoon sunlight which was gaining that yellowish tint it gets toward the end of the day. I was aware that I was the only person present wearing a trenchcoat and fedora; most of the men wore expensive sport coats with an open collar or with a silk cravat, although some were in traje corto. The ladies for the most part wore colorful, chic dresses and high heels, but a few of them as well wore traje corto outfits. This was certainly a switch from what one usually saw in Spain, where probably ninety percent or more of all the women over forty -- and lots of younger ones, too -- wore mourning black for their late husbands. And in España, once the black dress went on, it was on forever. A sixteen-year-old widow at war's end in 1939 -- a not uncommon situation, expecially in the sticks -- would still only be thirty-five now, but the black dress remained. Unless she found another man, of course.

I was headed toward the stairs leading up to the guests' observation gallery overlooking the tienta ring when I stopped short. Holy Toledo, I thought, reminding myself that I was referring to Toledo, Spain, not Toledo, Ohio -- there with a small, stemmed glass of fino in his hand, chatting with some broad, was the Tyrone Power lookalike, Carlos Rojo!

I walked over toward him, my mind reeling. Whose body was that I had

35

dumped behind the convent? When I was about ten feet away from him a platinum blonde bombshell, drink in hand, cut directly in front of me, making for Rojo. Hey, I knew her, too! Holy Mother of -- Hollywood's Mamie Van Doren! Didn't she start out as a Shakespearean actress? Nah, on second thought, I guessed not.

"Tyrone!" she squealed, running up to the darkly handsome guy and proferring her cheeks to be kissed, one after the other. "Oh, Tyrone!" she gushed, "I want you in my *power!*" The guy smiled hugely, said something and dutifully bussed her cheeks. The woman he had been talking to previously glowered. So did I -- this wasn't Carlos Rojo the Tyrone Power lookalike. This was Tyrone Power. Nuts.

I followed others up some steps to the larger than usual viewing gallery which boasted ascending rows of padded chairs instead of hard benches. Up at the top, a small banda taurina made up of zit-heads -- probably the kids or other young relatives of the staff -- was warming up. Below, two white-jacketed waiters were serving drinks from large silver trays -- fino, Scotch whisky and something bright red, probably that Campari crap which the ladies liked but which I thought tasted like Lavoris mouthwash. A third waiter was passing out puros, and many of the men in the crowd were lighting up the stogies. Me, I grabbed a whisky, then walked back to the top of the short staircase and leaned against a wall. From there I could see everybody and I could also leave the area of the seats without sticking out like a sore thumb. The very thought reminded me that my left thumb was still sore as hell from my matchlighting trick with Maria Caliente a couple of days earlier.

And speaking -- or at least thinking -- of Maria Caliente, I wondered where she was. She wasn't in the ring yet, although several people were, including a matador and a kid in his early twenties, both dressed in traje corto. Looking down into the ruedo -- like most tienta rings, this one had very high walls -- I checked out the matador and recognized him easily by his big smile: Antonio Bienvenida. The kid I didn't know, although his face seemed vaguely familiar. Oh, yeah -- Curro whatsisname, the novillero pictured on my paper airplane, from near Sevilla.

Now a dapper gentleman dressed in a very expensive pearl gray traje corto and riding a magnificent white stallion came out into the ring to applause, dismounted and gave an abrazo to Bienvenida, then to the kid. The caballero was a tall, dark and handsome devil probably in his early forties, with the same dashing looks as Errol Flynn, pencil-line mustache and all. He was obviously very much at home here; this had to be the Duque de Nuque. He turned to the crowd sitting high above in the gallery -- it was too big to be called a palco -- clapping his hands and calling for attention. The chattering soon trailed off and el duque made a little speech, welcoming everyone and promising a good show. He then said that today's featured artists would follow the traditional order of seniority and that the first one on the bill would be none other than the great figura from that legendary dynasty of figuras, Antonio Bienvenida. The crowd applauded.

Bienvenida's smile got even bigger, if that were possible, and he called out to the spectators that he was delighted to be there. He also made a little joke, saying it was always nice when he could appear in a ring without the threat of danger being present. Everybody laughed and applauded him again.

When they let Bienvenida's foe, a feisty eral, into the little ring, I put down my drink, slipped down the stairs and looked around. Yep, the crate storage building marked on the map I got from Duro's files was right where it should be, about a football field's length off to the left, past a rocky hillock. From behind the hillock one of the male guests was coming my way, zipping up his fly as he walked. Perfect! Now I had a reason to be heading in that direction.

I went around the hillock from the right side, fumbling with the front of my pantalones as I walked, just in case anyone was watching. But once behind the little hill of rocks I kept going, circling around to the back side of the storage building which was my goal. Then I realized that all that business about playing around with my fly had made me really need to pee. I hurried back behind the hillock and did so. Then I resumed my trek.

As I walked, I thought. Yeah, I can do both at the same time. Ambidexterity nonpareil. I asked myself, who wanted Carlos Rojo dead? Who killed him? Who was the old professor guy? Who shanghaied him out of Duro's casino? Who left yellow dust all over everything? Who . . . Who . . .

Who put the bop in the bop-de-bop-she-bop?
Who put the ram in the ram-a-ram-a ding-dong?
Who was that man? I'd like to shake his hand,
He made my baby fall in love with me .

Damn! I thought, tossing my head in an effort to clear it. Get that new rock-n-roll ditty from the U.S. out of your mind, Marlo, and concentrate on the job at hand!

I walked around the rear of the storage building, keeping close to the wall and listening for the slightest sound. From the direction of the tienta ring I could hear scattered *olés* and applause.

The way I was sneaking around behind this building suddenly made me think of the popular U.S. TV show *The Lone Ranger*. More specifically, of "the Lone Ranger's faithful Indian companion, Tonto," because the masked man always sent Tonto to "go surround the house." Yeah, and Tonto always got knocked out by the bad guys, too, I mused, suddenly concerned. Well, what could he expect, with a name which meant "stupid" in Spanish? Think about something else, I told myself.

The main door to the structure I was surrounding faced away from the tienta ring, so I hadn't yet been able to see if it was guarded. When I finished sidling my way along the wall, my back and the palms of my hands to the whitewashed stucco, I peered around the corner very slowly. Two big picadors were on guard, and like those at el Casino del Toro they were armed with long hardwood varas and pistolas tucked under their left armpits. No wonder the Mexicans always booed those guys. They were smoking and joking. Then something prompted me to look at my hands; they were snow white from sidling along that whitewashed wall, and now I knew the back of my trenchcoat was, too. Damn!

I backtracked a way, then stepped back and looked up at the building, a one-story job about fifteen feet high. There were no windows back here, but there was an open space between the top of the wall and the tile roof; if I could just get up there . . .

Doing the human fly bit, climbing a sheer wall, is hard enough wearing a track suit and gym shoes, but when you're wearing a hat, trenchcoat and leather wingtips it's a bitch. But never-say-die Marlo did it, although I was sweating by the time I heaved myself up onto the top of the wall. The space between there and the roof overhang was only a couple of feet. I looked down into the interior of the barn-like structure, letting my eyes adjust. Making use of the faint daylight reflected from the gap at the top of the building's four walls, I could make out two rows of the cajones in which the bulls of Gato Gordo would be transported by truck to rings all over Spain.

I eased myself over the inside of the wall, just holding onto its top edge by my fingertips, then I let go, falling into a pile of straw. I remained motionless for a moment, listening. Nothing. Finally I got to my feet and began moving cautiously from one wooden shipping crate to the next. The crude, yellow-dust-covered map I'd filched from El Toro's files had an arrow drawn to what I had to assume was a shape representing this building. So if he was here, the old guy must be locked up in one of the cajones. I tentatively whispered, "Anybody here? Can you hear me? I'm a friend."

Silence.

I tried again, increasing my volume to that of a stage whisper: "Listen to me! I am a friend of Carlos Rojo! Can you hear me?" In the distance was the sound of cheering and *olés*, mixed with some pitos. By now they were probably for the novillero, Curro whatsisname. Too bad I had to miss the show. But I did find something very big. Only I didn't understand its importance until later.

Chapter 9

In Father's Footsteps

The shouting and applause continued from the tienta ring, along with pasodoble music by the zit-head band. El duque was evidently putting on quite a show for his guests. I wondered if Maria Caliente had made her appearance yet; I had really hoped to see that.

How much time had passed, I didn't know -- my watch didn't have a luminous dial and the light was too poor for me to read it without striking a match, and it wasn't that important. I didn't have my flashlight any more. I supposed it had been twenty minutes or so since I'd located what it was the map in Duro's office had been about. In the far back corner of the darkened crate storage building I found a mountain of sealed wooden boxes, each one maybe two feet square, stacked all the way to the ceiling. I struck a match and saw that everything was coated in a yellowish dust: boxes, floor, everything.

One of the boxes at the bottom of the pile had a busted corner and grainy yellow stuff had spilled out onto the floor in a little pile. I took a pinch of it between my thumb and forefinger and sniffed it. Then, like all good P.I.s do when checking out any unknown substance, I put some on the tip of my tongue. Hey, I know some people say that's a dumb thing to do, but that's the way we do it. Hell, it can be cocaine, heroine, arsenic, plutonium, you name it. That's the way we check stuff out. On reflection, I'm not sure why we always test things in this manner, but it has occurred to me that maybe some of us P.I.s don't get the tips of our tongues on some things we'd like to, so we make do with whatever comes our way. I don't know, it's just a theory.

Anyway, my tongue-lab test worked. It was azafrán. Saffron. Now why the hell would the Duque de Nuque be hiding a ton or more of that stuff? It didn't make sense. I sat on a box and tried to puzzle it out, but nothing ever came to me. I decided to test the stuff again. I sniffed it first, and this time I sneezed. Big. Then I heard shouts from just outside the cajonería, or whatever the hell they called this place. The big door at the end opened and daylight flooded in, silhouetting the two picadors. I heard another round of cheers in the distance.

"Check the stuff," one of the round shapes said to the other, "and watch out for that peeper."

Crap! Somebody knew I was on the loose and had alerted the two guards. I could now see that they were carrying their long picas and were advancing slowly into the building, headed toward the back where I was. I thought about that old song title, *Run into the Roundhouse Nelly, He Can't Corner You There.* Too bad I was in a square barn instead of a roundhouse, and already cornered, to boot.

Cornered! Like a rat in a trap! *Come on out, Marlo!* they'd probably yell any time now. Would I reply? If so, what would I say? How about, *Come and get me, copper!* Like Bogey in *High Sierra.* No, no -- these were bad guys, not coppers. Oh, well, I'd think of something. What I thought of, however, was not a snappy answer but a way out.

I sneaked along the side wall in a space maybe a yard wide between the loading boxes and the stucco wall itself. Fortunately this area was in deep shadow, and on top of that the two picador-guards' eyes hadn't yet had time to adjust to the dim confines of the interior of the building. I scurried on and made for the open door. Just as I ducked out, headed for the relative safety of the crowd of guests at the tienta ring, I heard one of the picadors yell, "There he goes! Out the door!"

I had to hold my hat onto my head with one hand to keep it from blowing off as I ran, while the skirts of my trenchcoat billowed behind me. My knees were "high-steppin' it." Up ahead, between me and the stairway entrance to the tienta ring's gallery full of guests, two more hefty picadors were running toward me, one of them with his pica, the other with a pistol at the ready.

I immediately changed directions ninety degrees to the right, now running toward the holding pens adjacent to the tienta ring. I leaped and got a handhold on the top of one of the eight-foot-high stone walls which separated the various pens and runways, and I pulled myself up, rolling over on the top of the wall. I quickly got to my feet and looked back in the direction of my pursuers just in time to see the business end of a picador's vara jabbing upward at my crotch. I retreated toward the tienta ring along the top of the divider wall, until I stepped back -- into space.

Falling backward, I twisted around and plunged face-down into the chiquero, landing square on the back of a big novillo. I found myself straddling the beast, exactly like a bull-riding rodeo cowboy preparatory to shooting out of the toril, the gate of which was in fact already in the process of being swung open. And shoot out of it we did, like a watermelon seed being expelled from the puffed-up cheeks of a good ol' boy. It seemed the three-year-old bull I had fallen onto was to be Maria Caliente's opponent in her informal debut as a rejoneadora, because she was in the ring, riding a -- well, a horse; that's about all I could make out, under the circumstances. My own mount, an azabache-black, 375-kilo novillo, thundered straight out into the center of the tienta ring with me on its back, leaning forward and holding onto its horns as though I were riding a Harley-Davidson with the California Highway Patrol on my tail. Where was the boxing-ring bell? *The Gillette Cavalcade of Sports* was on the air!

The guests in the gallery thought it was a planned gag, and they laughed and applauded the funny man riding a bucking novillo while wearing a fedora and trenchcoat. From my tenuous position astride the bull, the world looked like the projected image of a movie film which has jumped out of the projector's sprockets: everything was jerking up and down so fast it was all just a blur.

I don't want to disparage the Gato Gordo hierro unfairly, so perhaps I should say that the fact that I was riding the novillo probably kept it from reacting to the horse and rider as would normally have been the case. As it was, the bull ignored the mounted Maria Caliente and seemed to concentrate instead on getting me off its back, bucking and kicking in fine rodeo style, while continuing to run in circles. Several times I would have been thrown clear, had I not been gripping the beast's two horns with all my strength. My crotch and tailbone were taking a real beating, however, flying up and then banging down on the novillo's backbone every couple of seconds.

I later learned that the bizarre happening at first astonished, then infuriated Maria. This was, after all, supposed to be her big "coming out" party and here I was, screwing everything up. I could hear her screaming at me to get off her bull, as she chased us around the ring, all the while with the beautiful guests shrieking with laughter and applauding like crazy.

Finally my novillo stopped for a breather and I could at last see without everything appearing to jump around. Maria was off to my left, while on the far side of the ring I saw a gate open and el duque come riding out on his white caballo, a farpa in his right hand all gaily festooned with red and yellow colored paper frills.

"Rodolfo!" cried Maria. "What are you doing in the ring?" This is not colleras! This is my novillo!"

"Just helping, querida," the duke laughed, spurring his mount in my direction, the long stick with its barbed steel point raised in the air. The crowd was cheering their host's entrance and the band began playing *El Gato Montés*.

Still gripping my bull's horns handlebars-style, I kicked him in the ribs with my heels, spurring him into sudden movement. And just in time, too, for el duque had been swooping down on me, his farpa poised to plunge. But my novillo's unexpected charge caused the duke to swerve away and circle around for another go. Maria was still screaming for him to stop, but he came on anyway, the smile on his face replaced by a fierce, rictus-like grimace.

This time he had it timed right, and the novillo -- ignoring my presence at last -- was going for the horse, as he was supposed to do. At the last second, as el duque and his upraised farpa approached elliptically, I realized that the spot on the bull where the spike should enter was exactly where my crotch was! Without releasing my handhold on the horns, I slid back as far as I could, and just in time, too. The steel barb plunged between my outstretched arms and into the bull's shoulders a bare hair's breadth from the juncture of my legs. The crowd roared. The band played.

Maria continued to plead in vain for her benefactor to leave her animal alone, but the duke was paying no attention. Twice more he planted the colorful barbed sticks between my legs, each time just a little further back. I was stretched to the limit and I could feel my grip on the horns weakening. Yet now el duque was coming not with mere barbed farpas but with el rejón de muerte! He closed for the kill.

I knew that the death-lance was *supposed* to be placed forward of the farpas, but in the case of el duque, well, I couldn't be certain. And sure enough, when the moment came -- when he put the metal to the cattle, I guess you could say --his placement was muy atrevasada. So far back, in fact, that if I hadn't turned loose of the horns and allowed inertia to slide me backward, I would have instantly qualified for the job of eunuch in some sultan's harem. I could've sung the falsetto lines of the Diamonds' hit song *Little Darlin'* that goes Laaaaa. . . la-la-la-laaaaa . . . etc. -- in a glass-shattering pitch which would now have been my normal voice. Whew!

As it was, I found myself lying face down in the sand in the middle of the tienta ring, the bull sinking to its knees a little distance away. El Duque de Nuque was smiling and saluting the cheering crowd with one hand held aloft, although I noticed that he turned and glowered in my direction. I really believed he was angry because he had missed his mark: me. Maria had exited the ruedo at some point -- in anger and mortification, I felt sure. Yeah, I knew the feeling. I also knew the feeling of relief -- and it *wasn't* thanks to *Bromoseltzer-Bromoseltzer-Bromoseltzer* . . . although one probably wouldn't have hurt about now.

The happy guests were filing out of the gallery as I got to my feet and began trying to dust off my trenchcoat and hat. Fortunately, they were both sort of dust-colored, anyway. The Duque de Nuque cantered over to me and spoke to me from the saddle, a smirk on his handsome face. He removed his flat cordoban hat and executed a mock bow.

"Mil gracias para la diversión, Señor Marlo," he said, "I'm sure you realized that at no time were you in any real danger. I am grateful for your surprise demonstration of toreo cómico. I hope you enjoyed it as much as I did."

"Yeah, sure," I replied, still slapping my hat, "probably about as much as Maria did. I understood this was to be her debut as a rejoneadora."

The duke waved his hand, airily dismissing the notion. "Oh, Maria is just a girl, Señor Marlo. She will get over it. There will be many more opportunities for her. But today, ah, I found I could not restrain myself, ha, ha."

"Uh-huh, well bully for you," I said, "but I doubt Maria will look at it so glibly."

"Maria will do as she is told, Señor Marlo. You see, I am what I believe you americanos would call, ah, her billete de comidas."

"Yeah," I said, It was all I could think of. Her meal ticket. Damn!

"But wait. I am not being a good host. Please to come inside the hacienda and have a cooling drink after your, er, ride. Luís!" He waved to a white-jacketed waiter. "Take Señor Marlo into the house and see that he is refreshed." He touched the brim of his hat and guided his white horse away. I trudged after Luís into the house.

Inside it was cool and there were taurine decorations everywhere: two mounted bulls' heads, crossed banderillas, old carteles and trophies on shelves. Luís fetched me a Carlos Primera coñac, then left. A few guests were present, sipping drinks and chatting in groups. But I could see through a window that most of the gente hermosa was outside, around the pool, where a bar was set up and a rock-n-roll band made up of guys wearing ducktail haircuts was playing *Don't Be Cruel* while a Spanish kid tried to impersonate Elvis Presley. He was supposed to be singing in English, but I couldn't understand a word he crooned. Man, el duque was up to date. Most madrileños wouldn't know what to think about all this. I shook my head.

When those present in the room I was in saw me they smiled. Ah, the clown. Ha, ha. Amusing fellow. But the devil of a way to earn a living, eh? Then I was dismissed from their thoughts. I looked out the window again and saw a couple of babes in the pool. But I noticed that despite the air of internacionalismo here, they still took care to stay within Franco's law and wore full, one-piece bathing suits. Chickens. Bienvenida and Curro were off in a far corner of the pool area, surrounded by admirers.

Suddenly Maria was by my side. She spoke urgently and softly. "I -- am sorry I was angry with you in the ring. Now I know it was all Rodolfo's fault. He -- he can be so maddening! I . . . I *hate* him! But . . ."

Yeah, I thought to myself, but he's your billete de comidas. What a world. Prior to my actually replying, however, she grabbed my face with her two hands and kissed me. Then, before I could say anything, she slapped me, hard.

"Hey!" I said, rubbing my cheek. "What was that for?"

"For letting me kiss you, you fool!" she snapped. Then she went on: "But back to Rodolfo. I want to hurt him," she said breathlessly, "but without him knowing it was me who did it. He is hiding something, I do not know what, but I am sure it is something illegal. Come with me!" She walked out a far doorway and into a darkened hall, and I followed.

"Go down this corridor and take those steps down," she said, pointing to a shadowy staircase at the end. "You will find another hallway below. His secret, whatever it is, is in the room at the far end. You will have to find some way to open the door, for it is locked. But perhaps you can unlock it. And discover his secret. And hurt him with it!" And suddenly she was gone.

I found the room. There was nobody around and so I listened at the door for a minute or so but could hear nothing. It was quiet as a tomb down here; the walls were very thick. I got out my batch of skeleton keys and picks and went to work. It took me less than a minute before I heard and felt the bolt move. I pushed the door open.

The tiny room was pretty dark, although a bit of light filtered in from a small, barred basement window at the top of a high wall. As I let my eyes adjust, I heard the unmistakable sound of a gasp. I peered into the far corner and gradually began to make out the shape of a man. An old, whitehaired man in a rumpled suit who looked at me fearfully. He looked like a professor or a doctor or something. I smiled broadly and pushed the brim of my hat up a little with a thumb.

"Holá, tío," I said. "Don't be afraid. I'm a friend of Carlos Rojo."

Chapter 10

Never-Get-Enough Marlo

It was about a half hour later when I went back upstairs. I told old Doc Probeta -- that was his name, I'd learned -- that I'd have to lock the door when I left, but I promised him he wouldn't have to languish in his makeshift prison too much longer. Not now that I thought I knew the whole story. Well, almost everything. I still didn't know who had actually killed Carlos or exactly how, but that was just a matter of time. I *did* think I knew *why* he had been killed.

As I walked back into the ground level taurine trophy room Maria saw me and came quickly to my side. She was obviously full of questions and she grabbed my arm, drawing in a breath. I held up a hand.

"Not now. Yes, I discovered el duque's little secret, and yes, it is illegal. I'm afraid it's going to mean -- er -- a big fine and -- er -- some loss of face for him." I didn't want to tell her it would also almost assuredly mean la penitentiaria and ruin for him, because I didn't want her to realize it could spell adiós to her sweet setup -- she just might back out and queer the deal if she heard that. But a fine and a reprimand, yeah, she could handle that -- as her twisted smile showed.

"Bueno!" she said. "Now come speak to Rodolfo, so he will not begin to wonder where you have been. He already knew you were a private investigator -- he has his ways of finding these things out, you know -- but I explained that as you were a *taurine* P.I., you were interested in his toros and that you had gone to look at them."

"Does he know you hired me?" I asked her.

She looked up at me, defiantly pretty. "Sí, I told him I wanted you to find my brother Carlos for me."

"I see," I said, "and now that he knows Carlos is dead, does he know I'm on the trail of his murderer?"

Now she lowered her eyes. "No, I did not tell him that," she replied. "I told him I had already invited you to my -- my debut." She curled her lip at the thought of her ruined coming-out. "But he doesn't know you are still working for me. Because officially Carlos was killed by lós comunistas, a ridiculous tale of some 'falling out' among traitorous friends, and Rodolfo believes that."

"Oh, he does, does he?" I said, cocking an eyebrow.

"Yes. Oh, here he comes now. Rodolfo! Señor Marlo was saying he enjoyed seeing your toros."

The Duque de Nuque had cleaned up and looked smarmier than ever, all dolled up in a white dinner jacket with a burgundy silk cravat in his open collar. Like Errol Flynn sheep-dipped in oil of owl shit and cologne. "Oh, how interesting," he said, all choppers. "Funny, I would have thought you'd have had enough of *bos taurus ibericus* for one day, ha, ha."

"Uh, yeah," I said, "well, that's me -- old never-get-enough Marlo."

"Really?" el duque replied with his dazzling smile. I wanted to bust him in the chops. "Well, if you're really that insatiable," he went on, "how about joining us for the novillada at Las Ventas on Thursday? I have the palco next to el Generalísimo's. He of course uses the one King Alfonso formerly occupied in the old days. El Caudillo won't be there, I'm afraid, not for a novillada, but my protegé Curro Azafrán will be on the cartel, as will my bulls. You missed him today, I understand. Why was that?"

"Uh, well, I, ah -- I had to take a . . ."   I glanced at Maria, who blushed. "That is, I had to see an hombre about a perro."

"Ah, well, too bad." The duke just brushed the subject away with no more concern or effort than I always flicked away the powdered sugar from my lap and tie after finishing one of those madrileño pasteles I liked so much. "Just ask for an entrada in your name at the taquilla de pases at Las Ventas before the commencement of the event. It will be at las cinco de la tarde. Important things happen in España at that hour, as I am sure you know, Señor Marlo. And afterward you may join us in the suite I have reserved for young Curro at the Hotel Reina Victoria and we can celebrate his triumph with several bottles of cava, eh?"

"Uh, yeah," I said, "sounds swell."

"Hasta jueves, entonces," beamed the duke, shaking my hand but foregoing the abrazo, "a las cinco de la tarde. A las cinco en punto de la tarde." Then he laughed.

I mumbled my goodbyes to Maria, shaking her hand quite formally and not kissing it, like the beautiful hombres were all doing to the beautiful damas's paws. Then I walked leadenly to my car as though carrying both a sábana blanca and an espuerta de cal and headed back to Madrid.

Chapter 11

Curro's Magic

Thursday, 4:40 p.m. The guy at the ticket window at Las Ventas had an envelope for one Señor Felipe Marlo Shamus, and inside it I found an entrada to what I supposed was a palco on the sombra side. I examined the ticket and determined that the number of the palco was 1900. Wait a minute! It wasn't in Sombra, it was in -- what? -- Solera. Solera? What the --? And was this the name of the palco: Terry Suprema Calidad? Oh. I was reading the advertising around the border of the entrada. Ha, ha, I knew that all along. There was no price on the thing, just the purple-stamped word *Invitación*. Well, I already knew that a good sombra tendido bajo 10, fila 1 seat cost 55 pesetas, so this baby admitting me to a palco in the Franco section had to cost a lot more than that. Even if you were so high up you couldn't see squat. It was the neighborhood you were paying for.

I made my way toward the plaza's big entrance doors, noticing old ladies passing out little purple and white flowers about an inch and a half long, plus stem, in return for some small coins. Many people were wearing these botanicals in their lapels or pinned to blouses. And I noticed yellowish dust everywhere. Then I remembered my conversation with Doc Probeta. Oh, yeah.

I went inside and climbed up to the grada level, then found the palco in question. Sure enough, it was right next to the box where Franco sat when he attended a corrida here. A goon in a tight black suit and with a fat armpit was standing outside the door. I showed him my ticket and he opened the door a crack. An eye peeped out and a voice said "Está bién," and the goon opened the door wide for me.

The duke and Maria were sitting in the front row of seats, el duque holding a puro and drinking cava from a flute, a chilled bottle in a bucket by his side. There were a few other assorted flunkies in the palco, all beefy men, but no beautiful people today. Except el duque, Maria and me. None of the others were introduced to me, and none of them were drinking anything, although they were all wearing those flower things in their lapels and smoking puros. But my own beautiful status was confirmed when the duke offered me a seat by him and some bubbly. Seeing as how there was nothing else, I accepted. And then he stuck a little flower thing in my jacket lapel.

"So how's it hangin', duke?" I asked, trying to seem friendly. Maria rolled her eyes and looked away.

El Duque de Nuque seemed a bit nonplussed, but only for a second. He then said, "Aha, Marlo!" and clinked glasses with me. "So today you will see Spain's next great figura for the first time! El Faraón de Colchones! And novillos de Gato Gordo!" He was grinning hugely. Maria seemed strangely quiet.

"Er -- *where?*" I asked. I didn't think I'd heard right. "What town did you say the kid is from?"

"Colchones," answered el duque. "It is a small town just outside Sevilla. Close enough for the sevillanos to adopt Curro as their own."

"Colchones," I mused. Mattresses. Funny name for a town. And this kid Curro was the Pharaoh of this burg? Jesus. Sure, and like they said, I was the King of Denial.

"Say, duke," I said, adopting what I hoped was a friendly tone, "what's all this vegetation you seem to be spreading around, like this stuff you stuck in my lapel and what so many of the spectators are wearing -- including your goo . . . er, your guests." With a thumb I indicated the silent hulking men behind us.

El duque waved a manicured hand. "Oh, the azafrán, you mean! Ah, that is some harmless talisman Curro likes to affect. As I am sure you know, saffron is one of the herbs indigenous to Spain and, in fact, to Curro's region. And it is of course his name. It's nothing more than a gimmick, really -- something to make the people remember Curro. If his family name happened to be the same as that of another herb, he would probably use that plant as his charm: romero, orégano, tomillo, curry -- whatever. Oh, perdone -- more cava?"

"Er, yeah, sure," I said, thinking: yeah . . . *if* the other herb could do what this one did. "Say, who are the other novilleros on the cartel today? I confess I didn't even look."

The duke's hand waved again. "Oh, just some local rifraff Don Livinio, the empresario, filled the bill with. Curro is enough. You know that for a novillada at Las Ventas a third of the plaza filled is normally considered excellent. Today, with Curro, we shall have close to half! I, Curro, say it!" Then he died laughing at his line from Blasco Ibáñez's *Blood and Sand*. Jesus, I thought, every plagiarizing bum around has used that quote.

"You, ah, didn't want to see your boy on a bill with some real talent?" I asked. "Chicos like, oh, say, Mondeño, or maybe Paco Camino?" I just had to get a dig in.

The duke shot me an icy glance that would've killed a lesser man. "No," he answered, finally, "that is not necessary. People come to see Curro, not others -- just as they will after he takes his alternativa next year." Then he dismissed me.

Curro was the most senior of the novilleros for today, so he went first. Why did the thought go through my mind: I'll bet he gets used to doing that. Huh? I didn't know. As the paseillo commenced, el duque leaned over and offered me a puro. Why not, I thought, and I lit up. I puffed away, enjoying the fine habano, one of Batista's export quality cheroots, breathing in the taurine atmosphere.

And now Curro was on. His novillo was pretty good sized, 420 kilos, and the kid was a magician with the capote. A good portion of the crowd, including me, was going nuts over what we were seeing below. The lances were timeless, ultra slow-motion works of art. I screamed *olé* till I was hoarse, just as did so many others. When the picadors came out I suddenly realized I was standing, and I sat down. That, it seemed, was all we were going to see of Curro until it was muleta time.

When the final tercio began, I found myself as excited as before, and rightly so: the genius was executing the most magical muletazos I had ever seen. Pure artistry. The best ever. Better than Arruza. Better than Manolete. Better than Dominguín and Ordóñez. He was incredible. I screamed, I applauded, and when the kill came and it wasn't exactly the greatest I'd ever seen, it still capped a wonderful, a marvelous, an *incredible* faena. I waved my white handkerchief like a madman, demanding two ears and the tail -- and I'm a pretty discriminating guy. When the presidente awarded only one ear, I was outraged. I whistled, I hurled epithets, I anguished. Finally I sat down and noticed that the duke was smiling broadly but Maria was looking at me with a strange expression. I suddenly realized that although I'd been "going ape," many if not most of the people in attendance had *not* been so enthusiastic and had not voted for multiple trophies. In fact, even the one ear had been a close call. What on earth --? Then I once again remembered my chat with old Doc Probeta and I sat back, somewhat subdued.

The other two novilleros, Luís Alfonso Garces and Victor Quesada, came and went, with me paying no attention whatever. I was thinking. Then it was time for the fourth bull and Curro. I noticed that ever since el Faraón de Colchones had finished with his novillo, the smoke from the puros had cleared out considerably. None of the other gentlemen in our palco -- those to the rear, the ones whose lips moved when they read -- had lit up a cigar since. Even the sprigs of saffron had been removed from lapels. But now that Curro was back, the puros were back out and so was the saffron.

"Er, 'scuse me, duke," I said, "but I gotta go to los aseos." I got out of my seat.

El Duque de Nuque did not take kindly to my idea. "But this is Curro!" he shouted. "You cannot go now!"

"Look, duke," I said patiently, "if you really want me to stay here and pee all over the floor, I'll do it, but . . ."

"Ahhh!" he gasped, waving a hand in exasperation at me to get out. Maria watched me as I worked my way out of the palco and touched the brim of my hat to all the scowling goons.

Once outside the palco I didn't go to the head; instead, I worked my way around the grada level until I came to an open doorway where I could see the ring, throwing my boutonniere of saffron down a stairwell. Curro was just going out with his capote, the bull having done a couple of initial laps around the arena after coming out of the toril. And lots of saffron-sporting curristas down below were puffing on their cigars.

This time I saw a different show, although based on their cheers and *olés*, the curristas didn't. To them, this one was even better than the first -- the one I'd loved so much. But what I saw was a kid who spent most of his time steering clear of his enemigo; a couple of the lances were pretty good, but not much better than those other two guys had done -- yet the Curro supporters in the audience went crazy. And then with the muleta it was downright disgusting, with lots of pico and enough space left open to drive a pair of two-wheeled burro carts, the kind you saw by the hundreds out on the road to Toledo, between man and bull. Yet Curro's fans were standing and screaming *olé* like Real Madrid was leading the Red Army fútbol team in the final seconds.

Finally it was time for the kill and Curro performed an outrageous end-run to the left, stabbing the bull in its right armpit. The worst bajonazo I'd ever seen. The beast took forever to die and the puntillero actually did his job before the animal was completely down. Horrible! And yet the curristas were jumping up and down and waving pañuelos -- just as I had done with the first bull, I ruefully reminded myself -- while a large number of others in the audience were emitting pitos and shouting derogatory things at el Faraón de Colchones. Well, old Doc Probeta had known what he was talking about.

I returned to el duque's palco to find everyone except Maria in a jubilant mood. She was very quiet. The duke saw me and waved his puro in the air.

"Marlo! Did you see it?" He was all grins.

"Yeah," I said, "yeah, I saw it, all right."

"Isn't he fantastic?"

"Well, he's certainly got something nobody else has," I replied.

"Exactly!" cried the Duque de Nuque. "Something nobody else has!" Then he almost died laughing. Maria looked at me, fearfully, I thought. I stayed cool.

"Está bién, amigos!" cried the duke, addressing everyone in the palco. "Now let us go to the hotel and celebrate with Curro!"

"But Rodolfo," Maria said, grabbing his arm, "there are two more to go. Don't you want to see them?"

"Hah!" the noble one shouted. "Two nobodies who will do no honor to my novillos! No! Let us go now! We will have lots of cava while we await our Curro!" And he started for the door at the back of the palco. Everybody else followed, including me.

Chapter 12

A Suite Ending

We were all settled in, real comfy like, in the suite el Duque de Nuque had arranged for his protegé in the Reina Victoria, a nice set of digs overlooking the Plaza Santa Ana; it was, I was told, the same suite Manolete had used in the previous decade. I'd begged off for a minute to go downstairs, saying I needed to call, er, my office, but now I was back. The party was in full swing, and Maria was there. All it lacked was young Curro, but he'd be along shortly. In the meantime the cava was flowing. I held a glass of the bubbly in my hand as I noticed two of el duque's goons hauling into the suite a huge wicker basket -- the kind toreros filled up with capotes, muletas and all that stuff. But what was kind of funny was the fact that Curro and his cuadrilla and all their junk hadn't yet arrived from Las Ventas.

But that absence was soon remedied. Curro entered the suite, followed by his peón de confianza and his mozo de espadas with the sword case, pursued outside by a throng of admirers, all of them wearing sprigs of saffron in their lapels or on their blouses or coats. The hallway echoed with shouts of "Curro! Curro! Curro!" All we lacked was *The March of the Toreadors* from *Carmen*.

Finally the duke's goons pushed the door shut and Curro, resplendent in his unbloodied suit of lights, walked over to el duque and gave him an abrazo. All in the room -- well, almost all -- applauded. El duque then made a long, dramatic speech about Curro and his future, el Faraón preening immodestly all the while. Then Curro said a few words of thanks to el duque, speaking in his native andalú. During all this I sidled over to the door, discreetly cracked it, and peeked out into the hall. I saw what I wanted to see. The crowd of fans was gone, but . . .

I turned back to the little gathering in the center of the suite's parlor just as the duke was saying that it was now time for Curro to repair to his sala de cama so that he could get out of his traje de luces, bathe and slip into some more comfortable attire.

"Un momento, duque, por favor," I called out, holding up a hand. Everybody turned and looked at me like I was Nat King Cole walking in cold at a Klan rally.

"Before you go, señor," I said to Curro, "perhaps you'd like to hear what I have to say to el duque."

Well, you could have heard a pluma drop. Ummm, on second thought, *pluma* meant pen, not pin. It also meant feather, and I reluctantly had to admit you probably *couldn't* have heard a feather drop. But, hell, it was quiet, okay? I spoke, raising my voice a bit more than necessary, it might have seemed.

"Duque," I began, "you might be interested to know that I found Dr. José María Probeta in the basement at your estancia and had a nice chat with him." The duke stiffened and a couple of his goons took a step in my direction, but he halted them with a mere hand gesture. I continued: "He told me the whole story. About how the novillero Carlos Rojo fled to Cuba at war's end and purely by chance got a job as an assistant to the good doctor, who for years had been experimenting with the hallucinogenic effects of certain herbal fragrances when mixed with some airborne gases. In particular, saffron and the smoke of puros, fine cigars. The breakthrough came one day when the doc was puffing on a stogie while messing around with various herbs -- rosemary, thyme, oregano . . . and saffron. He was at one particular moment sniffing the saffron as he smoked, looking out the window and watching some of the local Cuban boys shooting baskets with an old, patched-up basketball and an iron barrel hoop nailed to a palm tree. He found himself going ape, observing what he thought at the moment was the most profound display of athletic prowess he'd ever witnessed. He was so excited he was screaming and yellling; tears were running down his face. Carlos Rojo, his assistant, rushed in to see what all the hoopla was about, and when the doc pointed out the window and showed him, Carlos just saw a bunch of ragged kids shooting baskets, like kids anywhere. Then, after much retelling of the experience by the doc and an analytical consideration of it all, the secret of Azafumo was understood. Azafumo, that's what Doc Probeta named his discovery, the mixture of the fragrance of azafrán, *crocus sativus*, saffron, a purple and/or white flower producing a yellow coloring, with the fumo, or smoke of puros. Azafumo -- an unstable element, like ozone, yet potent enough during its short life cycle to create an hallucinary effect on human beings which makes them think they are seeing something of incredible beauty or artistry, when in reality they're seeing the mundane.

"But the only problem was that, as with marijuana or alcohol or certain other substances, not everybody was affected in the same way, even if they were breathing in the same fumes. Oh, sure, it helped if a guy had a bit of saffron in his lapel while he sucked in the cigar smoke -- but it still was no guarantee. For people who wouldn't voluntarily wear the flowers on their person and thus breathe the fragrance, the dust of powdered saffron in the air could achieve the same effect -- on those same susceptible types. Those old saffron ladies had only to unobtrusively flick a little of the stuff onto the clothing of certain people going toward the entrances to a plaza de toros -- those who appeared to be of weaker self will. You know the kind; they are easy to recognize. Because the dust, like the fragrance, did not affect everybody in the same way -- it worked best on those people with a procliivity to submission to certain influences. The shrinks would probably call them people with an urgent *need* to idolize something or someone, people with an underdeveloped sense of personal self, people who tend toward desperately grasping for fairytale heroes who don't really exist. For these people, Curro has been the answer to their prayers. But not everyone is included in this grouping and Dr. Probeta eventually realized this. At the same time, he understood that the temporary hallucinogenic could affect *enough* people in a crowd to, well, give a definite advantage to an individual in a competition situation -- *if* the supporters of the other toreros were not exposed to the same presence of fragrance of saffron, even though the cigar smoke would of course be in the air.

"Carlos Rojo," I went on, "was a dedicated socialist -- okay, a Red -- with one major failing: he wanted to be a matador de toros. Worse, he ached to be a figura. By this year, 1958, he was pretty old to still be thinking along such lines, but I suppose there are unrealistic dreamers everywhere." At this I cleared my throat, then went on. "So he and the doc decided to put the theory to the test, Carlos to become a figura and Doc Probeta to prove his Azafumo theory on a grand scale. Carlos slipped back into Spain, while the doc followed through legal means. But Carlos found that despite his virtually guaranteed method of success, he could not get onto any carteles without publicity and an apoderado and all that -- and those things cost money. So he went to Paquito Duro, who he saw as a taurino with money and a willingness to gamble on a sure thing, and he told him his tale, asking for backing and promising to give El Toro a big chunk of the profits, once he'd made it. But what he didn't know was that Duro was in el duque's employ -- I fugured out that you're the real owner of the casino, duke -- and El Toro spilled the frijoles to his boss without knowing that, purely by coincidence, el duque and his protegé Curro were onto the same exact thing, the saffron and smoke bit. Duro knew the duke had lots of azafrán stored at the casino, but he probably just thought his employer was trying to corner the market on herbs, or something like that. Maybe he thought romero and albahaca -- rosemary and basil -- would be next.

In any case, el duque couldn't have some long-in-the-tooth nobody called Charlie the Red coming onto the scene with the same scam, could he? It could screw up everything. So he had Carlos bumped off, probably by Duro, coincidentally on the same night I came around asking about him." I heard Maria gasp at this.

"He saw me for a patsy, so he drugged me and had Carlos's body stuffed into my car with me, leaving us in the Guardia Civil's path. Now Curro had carte blanche to continue wowing el público -- or at least a significant portion of it -- with Azafumo, as he had been doing, in fact, for the past year. Yeah, duke, you had Carlos's body dressed in a traje de luces after you had him killed, as a sort of warning to any other toreros who may have heard what Carlos had been up to and might decide to try the same thing. The worker's gorra on his head was just your little joke.

"That same night old Doc Probeta, who had gone to el Casino del Toro with Carlos but who wouldn't have been a part of any financial discussions -- or the murder -- became concerned after a while and started asking around about his erstwhile assistant. He was overheard making such inquiries by Domingo Ortega, who later told me. You heard about the doc's questions and decided to kidnap him and stash him out at your estancia; you'd figure how best to get rid of him later. You also moved the cache of saffron, tons of the stuff, from the casino to your ranch, just in case somebody like me came sniffing around and put two and two together. Too bad for you that hand-drawn map of your place wasn't removed from Duro's file cabinet."

I was winding down. "All you have to do now, duke, is kill off kindly old Doc Probeta -- and me, of course -- and Curro's future will be set. I now realize you aren't going to all this trouble for mere money. You're trying to relive your life through your creature, Curro, since you never made it bigtime as a torero, yourself. Oh, and by the way, I found the stash of azafrán at your estancia, just before I found the doc." I'd said my piece. Now I wanted to hear what el duque would say. Maria was looking at him in horror, a hand to her mouth.

The duke had recovered and was his old self, smiling and debonnaire. "I congratulate you, Señor Marlo," he said. "I never realized you could be so, ah, resourceful. But, regrettably, your investigation must now come to an end. Your death will avenge the poor, stupid Paquito Duro. You may have wondered about the presence of that big, empty wicker basket over there. That is to be used to take your body out of the hotel. The police will determine that, like Carlos Rojo, you were killed by the Reds." at this, Maria gasped yet again.

"And how do you propose to kill me, if I may ask?" I asked. I still had the Moxley under my right armpit.

"Ah," said the duke, "I do not propose to do it at all. I will leave that to the next great figura de España." At this he snapped his fingers and Curro stepped forward, holding his right hand out to his side and slightly behind him. His mozo de espadas rushed forth and placed the handle of a killing sword in it.

My left hand went for my gun, but a goon stunned my wrist with a sudden whip of a blackjack from my left side.

"The same as with the one named Rojo!" the duke commanded the novillero. "This one is the evil empresario I told you about. He will see that you never become a figura. Kill, Curro! Through the heart!"

Maria cried out, "No!" and covered her face with her hands.

¡Carajo! I thought, my dead left hand dangling at my side. I sure wished I'd put that New Testament in my breast pocket after all. I backed up until the wall stopped me.

Curro advanced, raising the gleaming estoque until he was sighting down the blade as though it were a rifle barrel. His left knee was bent, his right leg straight as he rocked back on it, but both were trembling.

Where the hell was Capitán Gilipollas? I thought, panic growing. I knew he and his animal were on the other side of the door and would have heard everything. So what was keeping them?

Curro launched himself in a sort of volapié.

I say *a sort of volapié* because instead of coming straight at me with the sword, he veered off to his left -- my right -- and did the same circling-around end-run I'd seen him perform that afternoon at Las Ventas. There wasn't much I could do; my back was against the wall and to my left was a table, so I moved forward, trying to get past him, but from far off to my right his estoque plunged into my side, the point finding its home under my right arm and felling me like a pole-axed steer. So this was what had killed Carlos Rojo, I thought -- not a thrust by a Russian bayonet but a horrible bajonazo by a Spanish estoque. No wonder it had been long enough to reach his heart from a rib-side penetration.

I lay on the floor, gasping, wondering if this was what all those bulls felt like at the end of their stint in the ring. Curro, sword in hand, had backed off with a fearful look, as though he were afraid I might get up and gore him or something. The duke's eyes were shining, his toothpaste smile gleaming. Maria had moved her hands from her eyes to her mouth and was staring at me in horror.

Propped up a little on my left elbow, with my right hand I slowly pulled open the right side of my trenchcoat to assess the damage, while I could still do so. I looked down. Damn!

"You -- you stupid hick!" I cried out. "You busted my pistola!" Curro's swordpoint had hit the cylinder of the .38 in the shoulder holster under my right armpit and knocked it completely out of the gun's frame. Crap! This would cost me a pretty peseta to get fixed, I thought. Then I realized my situation and called out.

"Capitán Gilipollas!" I bellowed. The door burst open and the boss cop rushed in, gun drawn. Bálthazar was right behind him, and other cops were peering in the door from the hallway.

I got to my feet uncertainly and spoke. "Well, you heard it all, capitán. Now you know what really happened to Carlos Rojo. And you can send somebody to set free poor old Doc Probeta at the estancia. I'd say the case is closed."

Capitán Gilipollas looked at el duque for a moment, blinked, then looked at me, now pointing his rod, a Walther P-38, in my direction. At last he spoke.

"Sí, now I know what really happened, Señor Marlo," he said, deadpan. "You are a Red, an American spy trained in Moscow, sent to falsely incriminate el Duque de Nuque, one of España's most celebrated heroes, a true patriot and an invaluable advisor to el Caudillo. But your attempt has failed, señor. We have found you out. Come with us!" He motioned to Bálthazar, who grabbed me by one arm and relieved me of my wrecked pistol with the other. He then shoved me toward the doorway, but I braked and looked around.

El duque was giving me his smarmiest smile yet, but Maria was looking at the floor, almost as though she were drugged. Curro was hiding around a corner, peering out fearfully. A trail of yellow dust -- saffron -- wound its way from where he'd been when he stabbed my armpit to where he was now. The stuff must exude from his pores, I thought.

"Maria?" I said. "You aren't just going to let it end like this, are you? What about Carlos? What about justice? Can you really live with it?"

She raised sad eyes to me and murmured, "Like you said, Felipe, it sure beats scrubbing floors at the Telefónica." Then she dropped her eyes again and the cops hustled me out.

Author's Note

1958 was my first year in Madrid. In the previous story I have tried to picture things as they were then, as best I could. As for the characters, well, most are fictional. Among the exceptions are Filipe Marlo (QEPD) and one other, whose name and botanical association I partly changed for the obvious reason: I don't want a bajonazo in the ribs.

Felipe Marlo's Dangerous Summer

Edited by

Hugh Hosch

"Hugo el Verdugo"

Editor's Note

If you are a taurino you may very well know Muriel Feiner. Even if you do not know Muriel personally, you probably know who she is. Muriel is to modern taurine literature what Amelia Earhart was to aviation: a true pioneer on behalf of the female sex, in her chosen field. Muriel knows her stuff, and she writes about it as no one else -- man or woman -- can.

Muriel also knows that I have always been interested in the exploits of the late Felipe Marlo, the Mexican-born but U.S.-raised taurine private investigator who was a presence in Madrid for a period of time beginning in 1958, which happened to be my own first year in Madrid. Indeed, prior to a recent encounter with Muriel I had written about Marlo's first case in a story called **Felipe Marlo, Bullfight Shamus**, and Muriel knew this. Thus it was that one day in March of 2002 when I happened to be in Madrid, where Muriel lives with her retired torero husband Pedro Alaéz and their kids, the noted taurine authoress telephoned me at my room in the Hotel Reina Victoria and told me she had come across something in which she thought I just might be interested. Intrigued, I met her for dinner at the restaurant Viña P in the Plaza Santa Ana and, over after-dinner glasses of ice cold licor de manzana, Muriel pulled from her purse and passed across the table to me a rather thick notebook bound in peeling imitation black leather and about the size of a paperback novel. I opened it and whistled softly: I quickly realized I was holding the private journal of the great taurine P.I. himself, Felipe Marlo, covering almost two months during the summer of 1959. A hasty flipping of the pages revealed an astonishing find, and I blubbered my profuse thanks to my friend Muriel, who indicated I was to keep it.

In answer to my question she said she had been visiting the building of the old taurine ticket office at number nine, Calle Victoria, just off the Puerta del Sol, and had gone up to the third floor -- where Marlo's office had been located in the late fifties -- looking for someone who, it turned out, had moved on. Renovations were in progress and a worker who had just ripped out a wall was marveling over a pistol he had found secreted behind a camouflaged compartment, a .38 calibre Spanish Moxley. He had tossed into the hallway other items from the cache which were of no interest to him, one of them a ratty, scribble-filled notebook which Muriel, with her eagle eye, had immediately retrieved. She instantly recognized the handwritten treasure for what it was and held onto it, although she soon decided that, professionally speaking, it was "not her bag." And that is where I got lucky -- when she offered the journal to me.

"How can I repay you?" I beseeched her, clutching my new treasure as though it were the Holy Grail.

"Just put more women in that trash you write," she answered, giving me a good natured pixie smirk. I said I would try to do that.

And so, with a minimum of editing, I am able to present to you here and now, in Felipe Marlo's own words, the actual, behind-the-scenes story of one of the most notable epochs of twentieth century taurine history -- the period from June to August of 1959 which the noted shamus called **Felipe Marlo's Dangerous Summer.**

—Hugh Chowl

Chapter 1

Marlo's Journal of 1959

If you've never spent a year in one of Generalísimo Franco's jails, you ought to try it sometime. It can be educational, especially if you're not in a regular jail for ordinary thieves and murderers, but a jail of the Policía Taurina. I did, so I speak from authority.

What's a taurine jail, you probably ask. Well, it's a place where they put guys -- and a few chicas now and then, as well, in a separate section -- from the mundillo taurino whose suerte ran out. Everything from espontáneos to horn shavers who didn't pay the proper mordida to toreros who kill men instead of bulls. Me, I got sent away for exposing a taurine scam run by a duke who had too much clout with Franco.

Funny thing is that I think the Caudillo liked me. I know he liked American movies about private eyes, especially Bogey movies. And here I was, Felipe Marlo Shamus, a naturalized U.S. citizen raised in L.A. but born in Mexico of a torero cómico father and an Irish mother née Kathleen Shamus, a guy who just happened to not only be an estadounidense taurine P.I. who habla-ed the old español fluently, but a dead ringer for Bogey, as well, with a Bogey-tinged American accent when speaking English. That's the reason the old boy approved the idea of me becoming the first and only taurine private investigator in Spain -- probably in the whole

64

world -- last year, in 1958. Putting it all in the proper perspective, I guess only a year in one of his jails was the Generalísimo's way of saying he loved me.

But, as I say, I got an education of sorts in la cárcel. Like, I learned to blow halo-shaped smoke rings -- that is, flat circles of smoke like halos, not upright circles like the letter "O." This little trick I learned from a fellow taurine inmate, a gypsy kid from Jerez -- a novillero who called himself Rafael de something. Polo? Palha? I forget. He was in for a short stint for stabbing some banderillero -- not fatally, fortunately for both of them -- who he said had given him the evil eye. Anyway, he would blow these smoke rings that lay flat in the air like little hula hoops. He liked to puff them out and make them hover above people's heads, because he claimed the halo effect took away evil ideas the people might have, or something like that. Weird guy, but a neat trick. I finally got it down pat, myself. I called it "blowing Rafael halos."

But enough of that. What I'm getting to is the reason why I got sprung from my ward-of-the-state situation. I was sitting in my cell one afternoon in June of this year, 1959, puffing on a weed and blowing a few Rafael halos. My trenchcoat and fedora were making me sweat a little, but I still had my pride. A taurine P.I.'s gotta dress the part, even if it hurts. Then my cell door opened and my jailer, old Gordito the ex-picador, muttered that I was to come with him. What now? I asked myself. I found out soon enough.

In the warden's office was a slick looking, fortyish guy in an expensive suit and a pencil-line mustache who I pegged right off as some kind of government bigshot with a soft job and probably a rich daddy. The warden wasn't there. The guy motioned for me to have a seat on a wooden chair and introduced himself as Colonel Medidas. He got right to the point.

"Señor Marlo, you are an americano and style yourself as a private detective. Would you say that your talents might include being a bodyguard for a rich countryman of yours? If," he added with eyebrows arched, "it might mean your release from this pleasure hotel?"

I looked at him for a moment, then spoke. I was no dummy. "Sure," I said. "Tell me more."

He plopped a photograph in my lap. It was a straight-on, black and white glossy of Ernest Hemingway in a rolltop turtleneck sweater, looking kinda sad. "You know who this is, I presume?" he said.

"Yeah. Sure."

"Señor Hemingway, as I am sure you are aware, is a notorious Red. His writings and other efforts during our civil war against the Bolsheviks were most harmful. He is an enemy of España. But politics require strange actions. Señor Hemingway is a powerful force in the United States and elsewhere and he professes interest in our country. Therefore, against our better judgment, we have permitted him to come here in recent times, purportedly to attend corridas. He is here in Holy Spain once again, claiming as before to be interested only in los toros. But we think otherwise. We do not know what is his true agenda, but we wish to stay informed." He paused and lit a cigarette.

"That's swell," I said, "but where do I come into the picture?"

Mister Slick blew smoke in my face and said, "Your countryman Señor Hemingway is apparently not as macho as he would have people believe. He fears for his life, it seems, and he is looking for a guardaespaldas -- a bodyguard. But despite his mouthings about his love of everything Spanish, he in truth wants a yanqui protector." At this Colonel Medidas spat dramatically at the floor, then continued: "In fact, he has apparently heard of you and has asked about hiring you."

"Why me?" I asked. "There are plenty of bodyguards in the U.S., and surely some of them would qualify to enter Spain."

"Yes," said the dandy man, blowing more smoke in my face, "but he has been told of the world's only taurine private investigator, one Felipe Marlo, and as a self-styled taurine expert himself, it seems he wants *you* as his shield against -- what? Us? It is infuriating!"

I smirked. "Everybody loves somebody sometime," I said.

He ignored me. "As you may have gathered, I am not with la Policía Taurina. I am with Seguridad del Estado. The Taurine Police have, in the interests of Spain, agreed to release you into our custody. We want you to take the job Hemingway is offering. Protect the famous 'Papa.' We are not going to harm him, anyway. At least not my department. And report to us exactly what it is he is up to. He says publicly he is here to observe a series of mano a manos between two matadores de toros, Luis Miguel Dominguín and Antonio Ordóñez, but that is patently too simple. He is up to something, but we do not know what. Contact his old friends, the Reds, in some plot against España Católica? You, as his bodyguard, will find out and you will tell us."

"Uh, yeah, sure," I said. This was screwy, but if it got me out of the hoosegow, that was fine with me. And not only that, it meant gainful employment by the writer -- for what? To watch for nonexistent assailants? It sounded like a really swell deal.

"Está bién," the colonel said, getting up and walking to the door of the office. "You will be released immediately. Go to Madrid and take up quarters in your old office in the Calle Victoria -- you will find we have kept it as it was for you. Expect to be contacted by the Red Hemingway or one of his sycophants very soon. And accept the job. Our people will keep in touch with you." He paused at the door and gave me a hard stare. "And remember: mess up and you will be back here before you can say 'John Robinson.'"

"Jack," I said, absentmindedly.

"¿Qué?"

"*Jack* Robinson, not John," I replied. "Oh, nothing. Look, I agree to everything, okay?"

The colonel paused with his hand on the doorknob. "Oh, one more thing, Marlo," he said. "El Caudillo likes to divide up his security groups. You may find that another department -- one not under my control -- will very likely make its presence known to you. It is Colonel Herculo Descolorado's Sección Trece, a rather singleminded outfit, I might say, one which sees Bolshevist traitors behind every tree, so to speak. They wear black leather trenchcoats and hats and their motto and rallying cry is "¡Muerte a los Rojos!" The Sección Trece people are more precipitous than are we in my own, more reasoned department, I feel, but they are there nonetheless. I am afraid I cannot help you with the good colonel and his, um, boys." He looked at me, then walked out and shut the door.

And that was that. Pretty soon I found myself back in downtown Madrid and my old office at number nine, Calle Victoria, one floor above the offices of don Lavinio Stuyck, the big kahuna of Las Ventas. Everything was pretty dusty, but that's the way it always had been anyway. I let the belt to my trenchcoat out a notch and sat down in the squeaky swivel chair, propping my feet up on the desk. I was fumbling with the bottom drawer to the desk, hoping -- in vain, it turned out -- to find an old bottle of Magno, when the stand-up telephone rang. I lifted the earpiece off the hook and put it to my ear, grabbing the pole of the speaker part with my right hand.

"Marlo," I snarled.

"Uh, Mister Marlo," a tinny voice said in American English, "my name is Davis. Bill Davis. I am a friend of Ernest Hemingway . . ." And so began Felipe Marlo's Dangerous Summer.

Chapter 2

Marlo Meets Hemingway

Hemingway looked just like his photographs. We sat over plates of trout and glasses of rioja blanco and ate while I and not the fish got grilled. We were in a joint in Alicante near the bullring not too long before corrida time; I was supposed to have been there earlier in the day but my '39 Ford had broken down en route from Madrid just outside Ocampo and I just made the meeting. The writer ("call me Papa") was very friendly and seemed to make much of the fact that my old man had appeared in the ring with bulls, if only in a clown costume and a barrel. Other than that, he was full of shit but I could live with that. Then he let me have a hint as to what it was all about.

"Marlo, I'll level with you," he said, spearing a forkful of trout into his mouth and glancing over his shoulder. "I'm here in Spain but that doesn't mean the Feds aren't still out to get me. I want you to watch my back. Understood?"

I paused in my own eating and said, "Feds? Like U.S. Feds?"

"Damned right I mean U.S. Feds! The bastards are after me everywhere I go! I want you to watch my back, you understand me? If you can't handle the job, you tell me now!"

I leaned back from the table. "I can handle it, Mr. Hemingway, but --"

"Call me Papa. Call me Papa," he said, fussing with his napkin.

68

"Okay, uh, Papa," I said, "I'll watch your back. Where all does this apply? Everywhere?"

"Everywhere!" the writer shot back. "Yes, everywhere! From the moment I get up in the morning until I go to bed at night -- and while I'm asleep! Marlo, you don't understand: they're out to get me!"

"They are?" I asked. "Uh, do you know exactly who they are? What they want?"

"Of course I know!" he exploded. "They are . . . they are . . . the Feds! And they're out to get me because . . . because . . . they're Feds!" He glowered at me.

This was screwy but I reminded myself it was keeping me out of jail. "Oh, yeah, sure," I said, "the Feds. Of course."

"They're everywhere, Marlo," Hemingway said, leaning over the table conspiratorially, "you just don't know."

"Uh, yeah, I see what you mean," I said, squirming a little.

Hemingway drained his wine glass and then signaled the waiter for more. "This is a good, clean rioja. Its flavor is true. It is a good wine and we will have another bottle and we will drink it because it is good and clean and true."

"Sure," I said. "Nothing beats true wine."

"Papa" leaned across the table and spoke, lowering his voice. "Marlo, your part in all this has to remain confidential. I don't want the Feds to know I've retained you -- it might make them even sneakier."

"Well, how are we going to swing that?" I asked, forking down another mouthful of trout. "I mean, I can't be the invisible man. They're gonna see me."

"Correction," said Hem. "They will see *someone*. I will introduce you as A. E. Hotchner, a writer from the U.S. who was originally planning to join me for a few weeks here in Spain, no doubt to provide himself with more background on the inevitable book he will write about me. Hotch had to change his plans at the last moment, but nobody else knows that. And, more importantly, nobody else here knows him or even what he looks like. So you will be Hotch!"

"Uh, yeah," I said. "That's me. Good old Hotch."

"Fine!" he said. Then he gave me a sort of fisheye squint. "Uh, Marlo, do you really have to wear that hat and trenchcoat all the time? For God's sake, man, it's summertime!"

"Sorry, pops," I said, lighting a cigarette, "but the hat and coat are part of my persona. You'll just have to get used to it." I blew a flat smoke ring and it hovered over the writer's head like a halo, but he didn't know it was up there.

Hemingway sat there for a moment, just looking at me. Then he seemed to make up his mind about something.

"Right!" he said, slapping the table and thus pronouncing the session finished. "We'll just pass you off as an eccentric writer. There are plenty of those about, I hear." He paused for a moment, frowning and looking absentmindedly off into space, then he spoke again. "Speaking of eccentric writers, I guess you heard Raymond Chandler died. You know, the author of those Philip Marlowe detective stories."

My mouth dropped open and my fag fell out. I just stared at Hem, like I was in shock or something.

"What's the matter with you, Marlo?" he asked, looking concerned. "Are you okay?"

I recovered, wiping my face with a hand. "Uh, yeah, yeah, I'm fine. I dunno -- I just had a funny feeling there for a moment, like somebody had just walked over my grave or something."

Papa looked at me for a few more seconds, then with a mock-jovial air said, "Well! Let's go to the corrida!"

"Ah, what about the other good and clean and true bottle of wine you just ordered?" I asked, belting my trenchcoat and putting on my hat. "Do you want to have it?"

Hem looked at me and said, seemingly more to himself than to me, "To have and have not." He then waved to the waiter. "We will take it with us," he said as he got up. "Just like in Ronda."

"Ah . . . what's like in Ronda?" I asked.

"Never mind," he said. "Let us go. It is good to be going."

We got going and it was good.

Chapter 3

Dinner With Ordóñez

At the Alicante bullring Hem introduced me to his pal Bill Davis, a sixtyish fellow who it turned out served as the writer's personal chauffeur and general aide-de-camp. Someone had described Davis as having a "Pickwickian" face and, on looking at it, I decided it did look sort of Pickwickish. He was friendly enough and he, in turn, introduced me to Dr. Manolo Tapapas, the famous taurine surgeon who was big buds with both Dominguín and Ordónez. Then Hem, Davis and I went in and stood behind a burladero against the back wall of the callejón and watched the corrida from there. I could see that hanging out with this Papa character could have its benefits.

Of the two matadors I'd been told to watch out for, only Ordóñez was on the day's cartel, with bulls of Juan Pedro Domecq. The kid from Ronda cut a tail on his first and an ear on his second. Not too bad. Throughout the event I kept glancing at Hemingway, watching for any telltale signs of him secretly schmoozing with any characters who might be Reds, but I couldn't detect anything out of the ordinary. He just seemed intent on watching his boy Ordóñez and calling out advice and warnings which I'm sure were superfluous. As I recalled reading, old Hem had never actually faced a bull, himself -- not even a becerro. How could a guy like that become such an authority on toreo? Beats me.

After the corrida the three of us went to Ordóñez's hotel room, so Hem could introduce me to the matador. For a second there I forgot who I was supposed to be, and I sort of froze. What was my name? Hutch? Hosch? Oh, yeah -- Hotch.

"Hiya, Tony," I said, sticking out my paw, "I'm Hotch."

"Holá, 'Otch," said Ordóñez, smiling, as he shook my hand. He was getting out of his traje de luces with the help of Míguelillo, his mozo de estoques. "You know, you look sort of like a banderillero I used to know. Ever do any bullfighting, 'Otch?"

"Why, er, not really," I answered, which was true. In the course of my taurine investigations I'd had an encounter or two with the bulls, but nothing you could really call bullfighting.

"Perhaps we can remedy that," Antonio said jocularly, punching me lightly on the arm. "Luis Miguel and I have several mano a manos coming up and we will need a sobresaliente each time. This could be your big chance, 'Otch."

"Uh, yeah, sure, peachy keen," I muttered uneasily, trying to smile. Surely he was joking.

We left Ordóñez amid promises to meet later that night at the beach restaurant outside Valencia which Hem called "Pepica's" -- actually La Pepica -- and headed north in Papa's car, Davis at the wheel, bound eventually for Barcelona and Ordóñez's next fight, this time on a cartel with Dominguín and Antonio Bienvenida. In the car, an English Ford painted a godawful flamingo pink, Hem sat in the front with Davis, while I sat in the back with my bag and piles of other luggage and a wicker hamper full of cheese, bread sticks and other food. Papa kept an insulated canvas bag between his legs, holding bottles of vino rosado, which he polished off one by one as we drove, talking all the while about Gertrude Stein and F. Scott Fitzgerald and other folks I didn't know. By the time we reached La Pepica at about 11:00 p.m. and met up with Ordóñez and his cuadrilla, he'd worked up quite an appetite. Hem, Davis, Ordóñez and I sat at one table in the busy restaurant, the cuadrilla at another.

"I like it here," Papa said. "It is a clean, well lighted place. An honest place." What he then ordered for the four of us would've been enough for the merienda for the entire plaza of Almería, the biggest intermission chow-down in Spain: sangría, salchichas, fresh tuna and prawns, fried octopus, steaks, chicken and rice, bread and salad, and postres. And more wine. I wanted to puke just looking at it all.

Hem saw my expression and said, "You will eat this good Spanish food, Hotch. You will eat it, and it will be a fine thing that you eat it."

In fact, I decided I had to get some air -- especially with my hat and trenchcoat adding to heat of the sultry June night -- so I excused myself and headed out through one of the big double doors opening onto the terrace overlooking the beach, fumbling for a cigarette as I did so. As luck would have it, another guy was coming in at the same time, and we bumped into each other. The fellow was big by Spanish standards, wearing a black leather trenchcoat and a fedora shaped like mine. As our chests brushed I felt the unmistakeable bulk of a gat in a shoulder holster.

"Perdone," he mumbled, pushing past me and into the restaurant. I noticed his right hand was sliding under the front of his coat.

At that moment some kids set off a string of firecrackers nearby on the beach, something fairly common for Valencia, Spain's fireworks manufacturing center. But this seemed too coincidental to me. I bolted back into the noisy, bustling restaurant just in time to see the big guy in the black leather trenchcoat over there behind a potted palm against the wall, taking aim with a long-barreled, small caliber target pistol -- the kind professional hit men sometimes used -- at the table where Hemingway, Ordóñez and Davis were eating. The fireworks outside were creating a hell of a din.

I drew my own rod, my trusty Spanish Moxley .38, from its holster under my right armpit -- I'm a lefty, see -- and I snapped off a shot which hit the other guy's gun just as he pulled the trigger. This deflected the big man's own aim just enough to alter the path of his bullet slightly to the left while knocking the pistol from his hand and into the base of the potted palm. The other guy's slug clipped a drumstick Hemingway was holding up to take a bite out of and sent it spinning away to land in a pitcher of sangría across the table. The cacophany of the still-exploding firecrackers and the forty thousand decibel level of routine noise in the tile-floored restaurant combined to cover up the sounds of the two shots. Papa, a bit fuddled by this time from all the wine he'd downed, looked at his now-empty hand, which was still positioned in front of his mouth, and blinked.

"Did you feel the earth move, Old Bill?" he said to Davis. "Or at least the chicken leg?" On the other side of the table Bill Davis was mopping at his sangría-soaked shirt with a napkin, grumbling to himself.

"I felt the sangría move," he answered, still mopping. "Onto me."

My disarmed man bounded for the restaurant's front entrance at the far end of the big room and I pursued him, but as I started out the door after him I collided with a beautiful woman who was on her way in. Sucking in my breath, I stared at her. Holy Toledo! It was Ava Gardner!

"Say, sorry about that, toots," I said, touching the brim of my hat.

"Why, you big oaf!" she cried, pushing me away from her. "Why don't you watch where you're going?" Her words were slurred a little, like maybe she'd been doing some partying of her own.

"What is it, Ava, dear?" squeaked a little gopher type of a guy who came bustling in behind the movie star.

"Oh, shut up, Melvin," she snarled. "Look, I see Tony back there with Ernest Hemingway, so Luis Miguel may be here after all. Go see if he's with them."

I removed my hat now and spoke to the feisty, auburn-haired beauty with the great cheekbones. Great other stuff, too. "Er, excuse me, Miss Gardner," I said, "but if it's Luis Miguel Dominguín you're looking for, he's not here. Just Ordóñez and Papa. And me."

"Who're you?" she sneered, Ah, but a lovely sneer. Nicest sneer I'd ever received, I told myself. I didn't mind being the sneeree at all.

"The name's, uh, Hotch," I said. "I'm a friend of Papa's."

"Really!" she said, tottering just a wee bit. "Hell, I thought for a moment there you were Humphrey Bogart! But that'd be kinda difficult, wouldn't it? Poor old Bogey went to the big studio in the sky a couple o' years back, dinee? Besides, you're younger'n him." Before I could answer, she grabbed the weasely gopher by the arm and headed back out the door. By now, of course, the guy I'd been chasing was long gone.

I retrieved the long-barreled gun from the potted palm and stuck it into the waistband of my pants, under my jacket. When I got back to the table, Papa was proposing a toast, so I hurridly grabbed a glass of vino and held it aloft with the others, in time for the graybeard's pronouncement:

"To the goddam prawns and the truly honest octopus and the chicken legs that fly into the sangría!" We drank.

Chapter 4

Dominguin's Revelation

I looked out the window of my hotel room in Barcelona. The sky was gray and the wind was blowing rain and the writhing palm trees could've been dancing in time to the pop song:

> *Goodness, gracious, whassa wrong with me?*
> *I'm itchin' like a man on a fuzzy tree . . .*

I thought, well, I'd be all shook up, too, if I was expected to appear before the bulls on a day like this. But the word was that the corrida was still on, weather or not. We'd gotten into town at about noon, checked into the hotel and hit the sack for awhile. Now it was late and almost time to head down the Avenida José Antonio to La Monumental.

I shaved, and as I looked at my mug in the mirror I recalled bits and pieces of the drive up from Valencia. Hemingway had grown philosophical and had stated somewhere along the way that the daylight between a matador's groin and the horns increases as his wealth increases. "Antonio will impale Luis Miguel on the horns of his own pride and destroy him," he proclaimed. "It is tragic, but like all tragedy, it is preordained."

Yeah, I thought, as preordained as Papa eating that chicken leg. I remembered a story I heard as a teenager in East L. A. about Presbyterians who believed everything was predestined. Their preacher was arguing with the spokesman for a dissident element in the church that didn't believe it was already all written down, so to speak. They were having a big Sunday-go-to-meetin' dinner on the grounds and all, when the old line preacher stood and held up a drumstick and cried, "It was preordained that I should eat this here chicken leg!" And at that, the other guy rushed up and grabbed the piece of chicken out of his hand and threw it into a gulch and a dog ran off with it. The schism occurred then and there. Moral: nothing's for sure, pal.

A bit later we were again in the callejón, waiting for the paseíllo to begin. The weather was still terrible.

"A three-day blow," Papa said, looking at the sky.

But old Balañá the empresa was determined to make the thing come off, and it did. The clarines sounded and the event was under way.

"Look at Bienvenida, Marlo," Hemingway said *sotto voce* to me, for the moment dropping the "Hotch" farce. "When he smiles it's in two movements. First, gritting teeth, then pulling back the lips to expose dental structure." I looked. Sure, enough, old Pops had it right. A grimace more than a smile.

"Have you seen them?" he asked me.

"Bienvenida's teeth?" I replied.

"No, you obscenity," he growled at me, "I mean the Feds! Have you spotted them yet? Did you see them at Pepica's? You were acting awfully strange. Hell, that's what you're here for, you know -- to protect me from the Feds!"

"Ah, yeah," I said, "I mean, no. No, I haven't seen any Feds." I was positive the guy who'd taken a potshot at the table with him, Ordóñez and Davis the previous evening hadn't been an FBI man. The guy was too tall to have been hired by the runt Hoover, and FBI men didn't wear black leather trenchcoats. Besides, this guy had obviously been Spanish. I didn't think anybody else had realized that any shots had even been fired, thanks to all the fireworks racket and the noise and hubub of the restaurant itself. But who then had the man been? One of Colonel Herculo Descolorado's Muerte a los Rojos squad trying to bump off the Red Hemingway? Or a Red assassin bent on rubbing out a former sympathizer apparently gone soft and playing footsie with the Franco regime in order to follow his torero friends around Spain? Or could it be somebody hired by Dominguín to knock off his uppity brother-in-law who was now claiming Número Uno status for himself? My mind reeled.

In any case, I enjoyed the corrida. Dominguín came out on top, cutting a tail, but Ordónez did well, too, earning an ear after a terrific faena. Bienvenida got zero.

After the corrida I got the chance to meet Luis Miguel for the first time. The tall, slim, arrogantly handsome matador was polite but cool, not down-to-earth like Ordóñez. As we were leaving his hotel room after congratulating him on his triumph, he pulled me aside for a moment and said something out of earshot of the others.

"Señor Hotchner," he said, "you may have heard my, ah, rather famous comment that although one cannot love all the women of the world, one must try. But I would add something for you: Even if one *has* loved at least all the *beautiful* women of the world, there is still a price to pay."

"You mean you really have loved all the beautiful women of the world?" I asked, goggle-eyed.

"Yes," he replied, "but it has not brought me happiness."

"Well, it would me, pal," I said.

And with that the door was shut. I left the hotel and went out in the street with the oblivious Hemingway and Davis, who were discussing how the weather was clearing now.

"After the storm," said Papa. "The end of something."

Jesus, I said to myself. This business gets curiouser and curiouser.

Chapter 5

The Sanfermines Begin

The caravan continued on, pausing in Burgos for a good corrida with Ordóñez and a bunch of Cobaledas, all of them difficult and dangerous and with Antonio cutting two ears off the second. Then we headed south to Madrid and, after that, on to Malaga and Bill Davis's ritzy place on the coast.

Davis's joint was called La Consula and it was the cat's pajamas. Ordóñez came, and all was cozy. On the second day there, Hemingway's wife Mary showed up with Davis's spouse Annie. Papa introduced me around and everything was fine. Yeah, fine -- but the dames would maybe mess up the works. I didn't know for sure -- it was just a feeling.

The next big deal was to be in Pamplona, the annual Fiesta de San Fermín. Neither Ordóñez nor Dominguín were on the carteles there this year, but Papa felt duty bound to attend, so off we went. The ladies would follow in a separate car. I was starting to get a little complacent by now; nothing had happened since the night at La Pepica and I was beginning to really enjoy my assignment: bulls, good food, vino, the company of famous matadors -- what more could a guy want? I could answer that: Hell, I'd been in the clink for a year, I told myself -- a guy could most definitely want something else! Ah, well . . .

Ordóñez would be in Pamplona as a festival-goer, he'd promised Papa that, and we'd all see the bulls, party all night and go on picnics in the wild Irati River valley up in the Pyrenees. But no nailbiting in the callejón. Not this time.

We were sitting at a table of the Bar Choko on the Plaza del Castillo just before noon on July sixth. "Miss Mary," Hemingway's wife, wasn't present at the moment, nor was Annie Davis, as they were still back at the place where we were staying, but Bill Davis, Hem and I were there overseeing the plaza.

"Pamplona is no place to bring your wife, Hotch," Papa said, taking a slug from a glass of rioja. "The odds are all in favor of her getting ill, hurt or wounded or at least jostled and wine squirted over her, or of losing her; maybe all three."

"Then why'd you have Mary come here, Papa?" I asked the writer.

He looked at me and said, "Pamplona is good and clean and the women are extra and superfluous. Here the congeniality is true and I obscenity on it."

"Uh, yeah," I said, "but I'm not sure what that means."

"Men without women. Well, you better not think about it," Papa said. Then he straightened up and declared, "We have to be forted-up and the joints all scouted before the eruption." He looked around. American college kids wearing teeshirts and chinos mixed with other young people from Spain and all over Europe. The dominant color for clothing was white with red neckerchiefs and sashes, but among the Spaniards the color royal blue was definitely second; this shade of blue was the official color of the Falangist Party and many of the various peña members wore blue shirts or pants or canvas shoes. "It's hell, isn't it?" Hem went on. "Forty thousand tourists added since I first came here almost forty years ago, when there weren't twenty tourists in town. In the old days it was good to be in Pamplona but it was bad to be too drunk to like it. To be too drunk was bad but that was good, really. But if being too drunk was bad, it was all bad."

"Hmm. I suppose you're right," I said.

Those forty thousand extra tourists had not only jammed the streets and bars of Pamplona, they had taken up all the hotel space, as well. Papa's friend from the old days, Juanito Quintana -- the former hotel proprietor on whom Hem had modeled the character of Montoya in *The Sun Also Rises* -- was supposed to have lined up hotel rooms and corrida tickets for us but something had misfired and we'd ended up buying our entradas from scalpers and crowding into a gloomy dump of a private apartment on a back street. Hem seemed to take it all very philosophically, saying that we wouldn't be getting but three hours or so of sleep a night, anyway, so what difference did it make?

Within a day I had an answer to that question, although I didn't voice it: the difference it made to me as opposed to sleeping in my own room in a hotel was that as of the following day, when Ordóñez and his party showed up, I'd be sharing a double bed with the mozo de estoques, Miguelillo -- and I was to find out that Miguelillo slept with all his swords in the bed with him. By the first day after we began sharing the cama I'd already run out of BandAids; they now covered my back and ass.

At exactly twelve noon the sanfermines officially kicked off, with exploding rockets and Raggedy Andy peña bands marching and playing riau-riau music through the streets to the Plaza del Castillo, where we sat. In the middle of the plaza some workmen were stringing up firecrackers and sparklers in the trees and bushes for young lovers to snake-dance under later that night, burning holes in their clothes and setting their hair on fire. *A hunk a hunk o' burnin' love,* I hummed to myself, thinking about it.

For most people in town, getting a table in a sidewalk cafe in the plaza was a near impossibility at peak times, but Papa's fame ensured him -- and us -- a permanently reserved table outside the Bar Choko, the site where, Hem told me, Quintana's hotel used to be. He also said he'd been in touch with a lot of friends and most of them would be arriving the next day, since that was the first day of the corridas. Among the lot would be Ordóñez and his cuadrilla -- including Miguelillo and his swords. Papa had gotten Antonio to promise to come to the sanfermines and party with him, as the matador had a few rare open days in his schedule at this time. Up to now, keeping one eye on Papa and the other on people in the immediate area, on guard for suspicious types, hadn't been too hard. But I could see that trying to keep up the task throughout the chaos of San Fermín was going to be a bitch.

Sure enough, the next day was when everybody showed up, friends as well as some new faces, friends of friends: a doctor and his wife from Ketchum, Idaho, where Hem and Mary had a house; a guy who was a calypso singer and guitarist named Hugh somebody, who had a real babe of a French wife; a movie starlet I'd never heard of and was pretty much a bubblehead; a sultry, dark-haired woman who said she was a reporter from Scotland but who spoke Spanish with a Cuban accent; some U.S. college kid type down from Paris who as best I could figure it was mooching off Papa; and arriving just before the afternoon's fight, Ordóñez and crew.

The first corrida of the feria "stunk up the joint," according to Papa. "Bad bulls, bad toreros," he said, despite the fact that one ear per matador was cut off the toros of don Angel y don Rafael Peralta by Curro Girón and Miguelín. Girón performed forty-eight muletazos on the bull off which he cut his ear. Chamaco did nada. Without Ordóñez in the ring, Hem paid scant attention to it all, and he and Antonio talked about all sorts of things as we sat in good barrera de preferencia sombra seats. At 425 pesetas per seat for the best in the house, they *ought* to be good, I said to myself. If I'd been footing the cost on my own, I probably would've been in a sol asiento general at 50 pesetas, or 85 cents U.S.

Papa spent a lot of time glancing around. Looking for friends, he said, but I tried to spot any contact being made. I couldn't.

Back at our table at the Choko, even though Ordóñez and his group had been delayed en route back from the ring, Papa was in his element, surrounded by admirers, and he expounded on all manner of topics, leaving no one in doubt that he was master of all. Until, that is, the American kid down from Paris started needling him.

"A question, Papa," he said, leaning back in his chair, cerveza in hand and smirk on face. "You're always talking about what every matador except Ordóñez does wrong in the ring, as though you could do it better than all of them. But isn't it true that you've never faced a bull, yourself? Ever?" The kid, who was a little pudgy and a real smartass, continued to smirk and he raised his eyebrows, waiting for Hemingway's response. The table went silent, with all eyes flitting back and forth between the college boy and the white-bearded author. Hem's jaw muscles twitched and his face went red under the checked gorra he was wearing. Finally he leaned forward, his beefy, white-hair-covered forearms on the table and his glasses reflecting lights from around the Plaza del Castillo.

"You little shit," he finally said, looking the kid straight in the eye. "The Feds put you up to that, didn't they? You're trying to rile me, that's it, isn't it? Me, the battler. You want me to challenge you to a boxing match, which you'll agree to do in some dark alley where your friends the Feds are waiting, right? The killers. Well, listen to me, young shit. I obscenity in thy cerveza and in the homogenized milk of thy Feds. Now get the hell out of here and don't ever come back!" The last line was roared, and people at surrounding tables were looking our way.

The college boy turned pale and then tried to recover, nervously chuckling as though it had all been a fine joke, but as everybody at the table just stared at him, saying nothing, he finally got shakily to his feet and melted into the crowd, never to be seen again.

A black cloud hung over our table now, and before long, in ones and twos, the various friends and guests began making excuses and got up and left. Pretty soon only Hem, Davis and I remained. Nobody said anything until Papa finally spoke.

"I was tight," he said. "But what I said was good, clean and true. He was a smartass kid from a fancy college and like a fool I helped him in spite of all that had happened and there will not be time to forget. He was a traitor. A goddam traitor. It showed, and he knew it."

At that moment Antonio Ordóñez and his peones and his apoderado Pepe Dominguín, Luis Miguel's brother, appeared and there was much shouting and the exchanging of pounding abrazos, and the black spell was broken. Their last corrida had been two days ago in Toulouse and now, with a few days' furlough, they were ready to party. More than ever, Papa wanted to drink and celebrate, too. The revelry was to go on all night long, up to and including the running of the bulls the next morning.

Chapter 6

Marlo Runs with the Bulls

Ordóñez and his gang stuck around for five days, partying like there was no tomorrow. Antonio ran with the bulls in the mornings and one day he took the point of a horn in the back of his calf during the encierro, while he was rescuing a fallen runner. To keep the wound from stiffening, he explained, he danced all that night. Basically he just ignored it. Papa said his own legs were too unreliable to run with the bulls as he used to, and he contented himself each day with watching from a good vantage point. I couldn't help wondering if he really had ever run.

Antonio wouldn't let up razzing me to run with him, but I told him my khaki-colored trenchcoat and hat would be out of place in the sea of white and blue. So he accomplished the impossible: I don't know where he got them, but prior to the morning run on July eighth he showed up with a white trenchcoat and matching fedora. To complete my ensemble, he gave me a red neckerchief and a red sash to wear in lieu of the trenchcoat's fabric belt.

"Está bién, 'Otch," he said. "Now you have no excuses left."

What could I say? I was stuck with it. If you've seen any of the newspaper photographs of the Pamplona encierro of July 8, 1959, you may have seen a guy running in the middle of the pack who's wearing a white fedora and white trenchcoat and carrying a rolled-up newspaper in his right hand. What you might not have noticed, however, is that the guy's left hand is tucked into the front of his coat, Napoleon style. That was because my hand was on the rod in my shoulder holster; if I got cornered by a 1400-pound juampedro, I was damned if I was going to try to defend myself with that little rolled-up paper. Hell, no -- old Ferdinand would get six .38 dumdum slugs between the eyes. Right in the anticone, so he'd never see them coming.

But fortunately I didn't have to resort to that; I made it to the bullring unscathed, and Antonio didn't insist on my running on the other mornings. At least I now had an outfit which allowed me to blend in with the crowds a little better than had been the case previously. I'm going to hang onto those duds in the event I ever land another case which takes me to Pamplona during the sanfermines.

After the encierro Papa said he wanted to catch a few Zs at our dump before we left around midday for a pre-corrida picnic excursion into the countryside. I stuck my head into the darkened room where Miguelillo and I shared the swaybacked bed; the little mozo de estoques was asleep in the sack -- with his swords. I muttered something to myself, absentmindedly rubbing my punctured and BandAided rear end with one hand, then headed down the almost pitch dark stairwell to the front entrance, fumbling for a cigarette as I did so.

Outside, I walked along the narrow sidewalk of the alleylike cobblestone street, aiming for a little bar about a block away for a pick-me-up. In the distance I could hear riau-riau band music and a few fireworks going off, even at this relatively early morning hour. As I made my way down the street, everything completely in shadow although the sky above was a cloudless blue, I heard a car rattling over the cobblestones. When it pulled even with me it halted and doors opened. I stopped and looked at two guys getting out of a black Seat, the Spanish-built Fiat. They were dressed like me, except that their trenchcoats and hats were khaki and not white.

"Un momentito, Señor Marlo," one of them said. They came up to me. I didn't go for my gun because I had a hunch these two were Franco's boys. I was right: they showed me Seguridad I.D. cards, then repocketed them. Both had pencil-line mustaches and looked like they could handle themselves.

"So, how's Colonel Medidas doing?" I asked in my friendliest manner.

"Never mind the coronel," the slightly smaller of the two said. "What we want to know is what you have to report concerning the purposes of your fellow countryman spy, the Red Hemingway."

"I've got nothing to report," I said, pushing my hat brim back a notch with a thumb. I took a drag on my fag and blew a Rafael halo, which settled over the talking guy's head. "I've been with him at all times but nobody suspicious has tried to contact him, nor he them. He's just having a good time." The weed in my puss wiggled up and down as I talked.

The smaller Seguridad man slapped the cigarette out of my mouth and said,

"All that means is that either you are not being observant enough, or else you are lying!" I said nothing, so he went on: "Remember, Marlo, you are out of jail on Colonel Medidas's tolerance. Wear our patience too thin and you'll be right back in there. ¿Entiendes?"

"Yeah, I understand," I said. "I'll try to come up with something. Just give me a little more time." I didn't say anything about Señor Blackleather -- I figured he was one of Colonel Herculo Descolorado's frothing-at-the-mouth, anti-Red goons of Sección Trece, and these guys in front of me were only interested in Reds, not rival Spanish agents. Maybe I ought to tell them to check out that so-called reporter lady from Scotland, the luscious brunette who spoke Spanish with an accent that sounded like it came via Havana. And who claimed such a weird name -- Urqfart or something like that -- that we all just called her Lorna Doone. She supposedly worked for a Scottish newspaper called *The Daily Haggis*, or something similar. Nah, I decided, I didn't know that much about Scottish accents and I could be wrong -- in which case I'd be putting young Lorna through a lot of hell for no reason. And then of course there was always the possibility that she was Hem's Red contact, the one Medidas was looking for. If she was really Cuban. After all, Fidel Castro had taken over Cuba back in January, and folks were already saying he was headed for the commie camp. I'd just have to keep an eye on this strange, good looking chick, wouldn't I?

"That time you talk about is running out, Señor Marlo," the Seguridad man said. "Our simpatía is not limitless. Remember that." And with that they turned and climbed back into the Seat and roared off down the bumpy, narrow street. I fished another cigarette from my pocket and continued on to the bar. People who had seen the Seat and the two men talking to me had all ducked back into doorways or around corners until the car had gone; then they came out again and watched me as I walked down the sidewalk.

Chapter 7

Papa's Prisoners

That afternoon a good-sized contingent from the Bar Choko went on the first of four afternoon picnics up the valley of the Irati River, which comes out of the Pyrenees. Ordóñez and Pepe Dominguín came, along with Bill and Annie Davis, the doctor from Ketchum and his wife, Calypso Hugh and the French babe, the starlet (whose name was Beverly), and the Scottish reporterette everybody called Lorna Doone. And Miss Mary, of course.

This was Papa's old stomping grounds from the twenties, where he used to come fishing, and he loved to remove his shoes and socks and wade in the edge of the ice cold river up to his ankles, and he bullied the rest of us into doing the same thing. I was glad for the opportunity to set down the huge wicker basket which contained the bottles of wine for our picnic. The thing was so big and so heavy that it required four of us to lug it the mile or two we walked up the pine-scented valley, Papa in the lead. Other people carried the baskets with the food and blankets, but they weren't nearly as heavy.

Our wading-in-the-river event, with Hem holding Miss Mary's hand and carefully picking out the way for us, me right behind, took us past a big rock overhang with small pines growing on its top. It was hard to talk, as the rushing Irati was pretty noisy here. It was hard to walk, too; the splashing water soaked the bottom of my white trenchcoat and made it heavy as hell.

"Where are we headed, Papa?" Miss Mary shouted over the roar.

"Across the river and into the trees," Hem shouted back.

I was glancing up at the overhang, one of nature's lovely creations, when I saw the silhouette of someone crouching down up there, near the end of the rock formation. Before I could say anything -- I probably wouldn't have been heard anyway -- a small boulder about the size of a breadbox plummeted down from the overhang, straight toward Papa. I lunged forward and pushed him to the left with all my might and he fell into the icy water, pulling Miss Mary with him. The huge rock landed right where the two of them had been wading a moment earlier, sending a geyser of water upward and outward. Miss Mary screamed, but though it was a close call, I didn't think she'd been hit.

Ordóñez, Bill Davis and some of the others helped me assist Papa and Miss Mary to the riverbank, where we sat them down on some grass in the sun. Miss Mary had jammed a big toe against a river rock while falling, and the digit was already blue and swelling fast. Broken. And there's nothing that can be done for a broken toe; you just hobble and suffer until it heals on its own. Pisser.

We found some brandy in the wine basket and had the missus guzzle as much of it as she could stand. Then somebody got some blankets and bundled the wet Mary and Hem in them. I figured we'd head back to Pamplona right away, but Papa, after mumbling thanks to me for saving his and Miss Mary's lives, declared that to go back now would be unmacho. I was the only one who'd seen the crouching figure on the rock overhang; everybody else thought the falling rock had simply been a freak accident.

"Miss Mary's tough, Hotch. Tough like me. Falling rocks and the big two-hearted river don't scare her! She'll want to have the picnic first. Then we'll go back. Isn't that right, Miss Mary?"

Miss Mary was in pain and clearly the last thing she wanted to do was to stay there in her wet clothes with her broken toe and have to sit through a lavish picnic prolonged by much wine and Papa's stories. But she had long ago chosen her path in life and she answered her husband by saying in a sing-song, mocking manner, "We'll have a good picnic, won't we? Oh, let's have a good picnic!" It was all I could do to keep a straight face, although Papa seemed to accept her words at face value, and he spoke to her again.

"You will have some more brandy, Miss Mary. You will have some more brandy and it will be a fine thing that you have more brandy."

"Isn't it pretty to think so?" Miss Mary answered, almost in a whisper.

Bill Davis tried to lighten things up. "So this is where you used to come fishing, eh, Papa?" he said, looking around. "By God, I'll bet it was great. I love to fish, too, but it's been a long time. Remember when we went deepsea fishing? You know who I like to go trolling for, don't you? Mr. Marlin, that's who."

"For whom the Bill trolls," Papa said.

I got my mind back on serious things fast. While the others busied themselves with setting out the picnic and opening bottles of wine, I mumbled that I needed to go see an hombre about a perro and went off into some nearby bushes. Once I was out of sight I climbed a rise and walked out onto the rock promontory from which the boulder had fallen. And then I froze. Somebody was there, crouching down behind a shrub.

I went for my gun and ducked behind a small, bushy spruce tree. Pulling back a branch, I watched the figure, maybe twenty feet away. Then it straightened up and I saw it was the Lorna Doone reporter lady with the Cuban accent who said she was from Scotland. I put my rod back in my shoulder holster and came out from behind the spruce. I spoke.

"Hiya, Lorna. Whatcha Doone?"

The lovely, dark-haired woman wheeled suddenly in my direction and her right hand went for the purse she was holding in her left. Then she slowly moved her right hand up to her hair and began patting it in a very ladylike manner.

"Oh, er, Hotch," she said, smiling I thought a bit nervously, "you scared me. I, ah, I was just finishing a trip to the loo."

So she'd come all the way up here to take a pee? Maybe, maybe not. "Sorry to have startled you," I said, touching the brim of my white hat. I didn't offer anything else; I just stood there. Lorna Doone started past me, then suddenly stopped and grabbed the sides of my face with her two hands and planted one on my kisser -- a long, passionate kiss of the French variety. Finally she stepped back and looked up at me. What a broad, I thought.

"Come with me back to where the others are," she breathed heavily. "I don't want to walk alone."

"Sorry, toots," I said, tipping my hat brim back a touch with the tip of my thumb, "but I gotta see an hombre about a perro. Just like you did," I added.

Lorna didn't like this and she turned on a heel and stalked off without another word, heading back to the picnic area. I watched her until she was out of sight, then I went out toward the edge of the promontory looming over the river.

A cursory look-see told me somebody had been there, all right, somebody other than Lorna Doone -- who, by the way, left no trace anyplace up there of having whizzed. Two or three fresh cigarette butts of a Spanish brand were lying about, and under a bush I saw something small and yellow. It was a box of matches with some advertising imprinted on it: *La Pepica, El Grao* it read, *Playa de Valencia*. Big Señor Blackleather. I wondered if he'd replaced the pistol I'd shot out of his hand and later confiscated. Well, he was gone now, so I returned to the picnic.

After much food and vino and stories by Papa we finally got a miserable Miss Mary back to the cars and returned to Pamplona. So far, I mused as we drove back, my investigation was producing more answers than questions.

The day's corrida was nothing special. Manolo Vázquez, Antonio Borrero "Chamaco" and Miguelín faced bulls of Juan Pedro Domecq. The only one cutting an ear was Borrero, who everybody hinted was queer. Maybe, maybe not -- but he can fight bulls, I said to myself. Afterward, we were all once again sitting at our table in front of the Bar Choko when Ordóñez, in a playful mood, asked for my white trenchcoat. I took it off and gave it to him; my gat in its shoulder holster didn't show because I was still wearing my suit jacket. Antonio walked out into the square where cars would occasionally drive by, and he began "passing" them as though they were bulls. People sitting at the tables of the many sidewalk cafes began "olé-ing" and applauding. Everybody was having a swell time. Even Miss Mary, who was limping about now with the aid of a cane, was putting on a brave face, smiling and clapping her hands. But despite the display, I didn't think she was having a very good time in Pamplona. I wondered if she ever did anywhere.

After a while Antonio apparently decided he'd had enough of the toreo de calle and began to fold my white trenchcoat under his arm exactly as though it were a capote, at the same time starting to walk back to our table while acknowledging applause. At that moment a small white Renault entered the plaza at fairly high speed. I think Ordóñez would have ignored it now that his act had pretty much wound down, except for the fact that the car's horn began blaring and the vehicle seemed to be veering toward him. Now the driver began riding the clutch, causing the little car to buck like a bronco -- or maybe even a bull -- as it approached. It was too much for Antonio, he had to "pass" this one last adversary. He performed a smooth verónica to which the cafe crowd roared *olé!* But the driver of the Renault, instead of continuing on across the plaza as the other cars had done, turned in a tight circle and came back for more. I could see a man and two women inside. Ordóñez was both surprised and delighted with this turn of events and this time he gave the car with French plates a beautiful chicuelina andante. More *olés!* and applause. Two more tight circles by the car and two more perfectly executed capotazos by Ordóñez -- the last one a graceful rebolera -- and the Renault turned, then seemed to stall. Antonio went down on one knee in front of the car, my trenchcoat folded under one arm, in a classic desplante. The crowd roared.

The Renault's doors opened and its occupants quickly got out. The two women were stunners, I could see now, a blonde and a brunette, and they rushed up to Antonio and began going goo-goo over him and hugging him and exclaiming things in American English. Antonio's face was one gigantic smile. He brought the girls over to our table with their male companion, the driver, trailing along behind. Introductions were made all around; the young ladies were named Mary Jo and Mary Ann, and Papa, standing at the table and beaming, announced that there was already one Mary present, so in order to keep things simple we would call the blonde Mary Dos and the brunette Mary Tres. Miss Mary would be Mary Uno. Their friend, the man, was then advised by Papa that these two women were his "prisoners of war" and that he should "bugger off." Which he did, taking the Renault with him.

Two more chairs were found and squeezed up to the table and the new additions to the group were invited to sit on either side of Papa, who draped a big arm around each babe's shoulders. Both lasses sported, uh, abundant charms, but the blonde, Mary Dos, was especially blessed, with blue eyes, ruby red lips, and creamy white skin. She was wearing a very low-cut dress and old Hem was getting an eyeful.

"Hills like white elephants," he said, grinning.

Miss Mary's improved mood, I noticed, had suddenly disappeared, replaced by a glowering, sulking one. I hate to say it, but it was the mood I had become accustomed to seeing her in ever since I'd first met her back in Malaga.

Papa was enjoying himself immensely, hugging the two dolls as he told them how he and a jeepful of "his men" had liberated Paris from the Nazis in '44, beginning with the bar of the Hotel Ritz. He saw me looking at him and he gave me a big, white-beard-framed smile.

"Just like in Ronda," he said, beaming.

Chapter 8

A Picnic with Fireworks

Mary Dos and Mary Tres quickly became a part of "the cuadrilla," as Papa called our gang, and they joined us each day at the Bar Choko, the corrida and afterward. They also went with us on more wine picnics up the valley of the Irati, although Mary Uno stayed in Pamplona, nursing her toe.

Beginning with the third corrida our luck changed. Oh, man, did it change! On hand were five astados of Alvaro Domecq, all of them applauded at the end and one given a vuelta. The only dog was the lone entry from Nuñez, which received a bronca. Gregorio Sánchez won two ears, Curro Girón two ears and a tail. Pepe Luis Vázquez came away emptyhanded.

The following day saw Gregorio Sánchez, Luis Segura and Miguelín on the cartel, facing a string of Pablo Romeros. As a surprise late addition, the rejóneador Angel Peralta appeared, taking on a single bull -- and that became the story of the day. Everybody's heard about Rodolfo Gaona's famous "par de Pamplona" of July 8, 1915, with the Saltillo bull Roderillo; well, on this day the caballero placed what everyone was later calling "the *other* pair of Pamplona," this set, of course, placed from horseback. Unfortunately, however, the kill was not what the crowd was hoping for.

And then we had a day billed as a miurada, although one bull was from

Escudero Calva, for Solanito, Curro Girón and Diego Puerta, the last two on the cartel cutting two ears apiece. This was not exactly a banner day for don Eduardo: one of his animals showed up dead -- I could've suggested a couple of matadors who probably could have handled that Miura -- and another broke a horn off on the tablas. Girón dedicated the fifth bull to Papa, but while Hem acknowledged the honor, it didn't seem to mean much to him.

On the second and third picnic trips with the full contingent -- including our two new "prisoners of war" -- nothing out of the ordinary occurred and everyone had a pleasant time. "It's better than *The Sun Also Rises*," Hem proclaimed.

On the fourth outing, however, it was a different story. This day's event at the plaza de toros, the final one of the feria, was a novillada and Hemingway declared that we would this time enjoy a longer excursion and simply skip the bulls -- it would be good not to be rushed getting back to Pamplona for a change. The novilleros we would miss were Parrita, Francisco Rodrigo and Pepe Ortíz, with novillos of Tulio and Isaias Vázquez.

Once the decision to skip the novillada was made, Papa extended the usual picnic trip to one going all the way up to the Pass of Roncesvalles, steeped in the legend (and history) of Charlemagne and Roland, and he spoke grandly of the adventure to friends and strangers alike from his breakfast bully pulpit in front of the Bar Choko before we left town in our caravan of cars. Ordóñez would not be with us; he and his cuadrilla had left for a corrida in El Puerto de Santa María with Dominguín and a string of Benítez Cuberos. Papa had decided not to go, citing concerns over Miss Mary's foot.

As usual, I rode in the English Ford with Hem and Bill Davis, and all the way up into the mountains Papa regaled us with the romantic tale of Carlos el Grande -- Charlemagne -- and the retreat of his Christian armies from Spain in the year 778, pursued by the victorious Saracens. Charlemagne entrusted the rearguard defense of the pass at Roncesvalles to his faithful lieutenant, Roland. Famed for his pride and valor, Roland possessed a fabulous horn which was said to be so powerful it could be heard miles away; he was to blow this horn if his situation were to become untenable, whereupon Charlemagne and his main force would return to the pass to help him out. But while Roland's valor was never in doubt, his undoing was his pride. When eventually overwhelmed by the arab hordes, the old boy just couldn't bring himself to sound the call for help; Roland and his men were destroyed to the last man, and the fabled horn which was not used disappeared forever.

Our little train of cars wound its way higher and higher into the Pyrenees -- lush and green at this time of the year, at least in this area -- as we drew ever closer to the French border. Banks of mist obscured sections of the road from time to time, and often the surrounding mountaintops were hidden by low clouds. The temperature grew cooler and it was hard to believe it was July in Spain.

Hem had picked out a place for the picnic and supervised the spreading of the blankets in the sun on the riverbank and the placing of the wine bottles in the river, to cool. He then told a story about how he'd received a wire from the Hollywood movie producer David O. Selznick, offering to pay him $50,000 for the rights to film *A Farewell to Arms* ("even though I'm not required to do so," Hem quoted Selznick as saying). Papa claimed he wired the producer back, saying, "Change your $50,000 into nickels and cram them up your ass until they come out your ears!"

Everybody got a good laugh out of that, then we broke out the food and Bill Davis opened the wine and everybody started chowing down. I selected a small, raw cucumber from a basket and held it up in front of my face.

"I dub thee Sir Francis," I intoned mock-gravely to the vegetable, then I ate it. "The short happy life of Francis Cucumber," I said. Most people laughed. Hemingway frowned. I decided to forego any more attempts at humor.

After a while, most of the group lay down in the sun with their jackets and coats on and were soon asleep -- everyone was seriously sleep-deprived by now. I was lounging in the grass, propped up on one elbow, when I saw sunlight glint off something in the undergrowth along the top of a ridge maybe two hundred yards to the north. Casually, I got to my feet and sauntered to the south until I came to a shallow ravine, through which I hurried east for a while, then doubled back to the north, staying in some rather heavy forest growth as I traveled. Pretty soon I was peering through a break in the growth, looking at the picnic site down and to my left. I could see Papa's white head lying on a red blanket, although a big wicker food basket hampered the view of him somewhat, and I could see most of the others, as well. I couldn't pick out Marys Dos and Tres, however, nor Lorna Doone.

I crept through the forest more carefully now, bearing north-northwest. The French border couldn't be more than a half mile away. I froze as the sun once again reflected off a shiny surface, probably glass. Whatever it was, it was situated between two huge granite rocks at the edge of a hundred-foot cliff, about fifty yards ahead. From those rocks anyone would have an excellent view of our picnic area below.

I carefully moved on, keeping to the shadows. All around me loomed giant, old fir trees, probably hundreds of years old. Could any of them have been here, I wondered, when Roland and his boys tried to stave off the advancing Muslim tidal wave from Africa twelve hundred years ago? How old did a fir tree live to be, anyway? Then: forget that, Marlo. Concentrate on what's ahead.

There were no pathways up here. Indeed, no sign human beings ever came this way. The only sounds were the wind in the trees and the faint gurgling of the river down below. Just to be ready, I eased my Moxley from its shoulder holster. I cursed myself for having worn my white trenchcoat and hat with red trim amid all this dark green foliage.

Suddenly I saw him. The same guy, black leather trenchcoat, hat and all. Only this time he had a scope-mounted rifle with him, and he was taking aim at our camp down and to the left. He was wedged between the two granite boulders at the cliff's edge. I glanced at the collection of aficionados, blankets, baskets and wine bottles far below and I saw Papa starting to stand up; the view of him was no longer partially blocked by the food hamper. I quickly looked back to the granite rocks dead ahead and just slightly below me. The guy was zeroing in on his target through the sniper scope; I could almost see his right index finger tightening on the trigger of the rifle, even from where I was.

I sure as hell didn't like the idea of plugging a Spanish agent, even if he was one of Descolorado's loony fringe boys who saw a Red behind every tree -- that'd still be sure to put me back behind bars. Or worse. But I couldn't just stand by and watch the thug take Papa out. I aimed the Moxley, bracing it against a tree trunk, and slowly squeezed the trigger.

Señor Blackleather jerked and the rifle flew out of his hands and pitched forward over the cliff -- followed by the body of the Sección Trece agent plummeting down toward the river below. Almost immediately, the sound of a pistol report reached my ears. And then I realized I hadn't yet squeezed off my own shot -- somebody else had plugged him!

The sound of the shot, I became aware belatedly, had come from over to my right. I moved my rod in that direction, trying to find something to shoot. Now two, three, four more shots came -- this time from ahead and to my left. Then two shots in reply back from the right. All pistol shots. And I still didn't see anybody. What the hell was going on?

I crept forward, doubled over and my gun at the ready, figuring to take cover behind the granite rocks where the sniper had been. Just as I'd almost reached the nearest boulder another man in a black leather outfit came charging out from behind it and headed in my direction, his eyes wide and swiveling to the left and rear, obviously concerned about whoever had been firing all those shots; he was emptyhanded. I held my own gat out front of me and barked at him to freeze. Instead, he collided with me and we both rolled down a steep incline, arms and legs flailing and our bodies bouncing over rocks and shrubs with branches like wooden spikes. Finally rolling to a stop at the bottom of the long slope next to the whitewater river, we each tried to overcome the other, but both of us were so dazed and beat up it was mostly futile. My adversary -- I could now see he had a Franco mustache and a bloody gash on his left cheekbone -- reached under his coat flap and whipped out a Walther P-38 automatic. My own gun had been lost on the hillside and I groped around frantically for anything I could find to use as a weapon. My hand closed around something round and metallic half buried in the riverbank soil; I yanked it free and threw it at Blackleather Dos, who fired as I did so. Whatever the thing was, his bullet hit it in midair, sending the metallic object spinning off to the side. Now the guy pulled the trigger to his P-38 again, but this time it emitted only a click. The automatic was either jammed or out of ammo. I lunged at the man, but he coshed me on the left temple with the pistol barrel and I went down. Lying in the grass, I was groggily aware of my assailant running off toward the treeline. Within seconds the only sounds I could hear once again were the river and the wind in the trees.

I got up slowly and tried to dust off my white trenchcoat, which was now a mess. I climbed back up the steep hillside, recovering my hat and my gun, but when I got to the two granite boulders at the top there was nothing to be found and no trace of anyone else having been in the area. Back down at the bottom again, I finally found what it was I'd thrown at the gunsel and spoiled his shot. It was a very old -- what? -- trumpet? Ancient, dented and dirty, apparently made of hammered bronze, the horn of some kind was covered with worn filigree work. It was -- or had been -- a beautiful work of craftsmanship, that was for sure. Blackleather Dos's slug had bent it all to hell, though. I turned it over, examining it in the sunlight. Down near the mouthpiece I could see some faint words engraved in the dark and discolored metal. They were written in some sort of flowery script and I strained my eyes to make out what it said. Finally I could read the last two of the three words: *ma corne*. And then the first word revealed itself to me: *Roland*. It was old French, but similar enough to Spanish for me to be able to figure out that it said *Roland -- my horn.*

Holy Toledo! The Horn of Roland! One blast on this baby twelve hundred years ago and -- who knows? Maybe Charlemagne would have come back and defeated the arabs and Spain would never have had to undergo all those centuries under the caliphs! Not the Caliphs of Córdoba, of course; I mean the real Muslim jobs. I whistled softly and tucked the horn into my trenchcoat pocket, then I returned to the picnic area.

The body of the sniper in black leather had fallen into the river behind some rocks, so his presence was not known by the Hemingway party -- or not by most of them, in any case. Everybody was up and watching me as I strode back into the little encampment. Mary Dos and Mary Tres were now in evidence, as was Lorna Doone, who didn't look at me. All three were smoking cigarettes and looking very blasé. Hemingway walked up to me, frowning.

"Where have you been, Mar -- er, Hotch?" he barked at me.

"Why, I was just taking a hike, admiring the scenery," I replied.

"What the hell was all that shooting?" Papa asked.

"Oh, that," I said, reaching for a cigarette, "ah, that was just some kids shooting off fireworks."

"Fireworks! At the Pass of Roncesvalles? In the middle of nowhere?"

"Uh, yeah," I improvised, "it seemed a little odd to me, too. But kids will be kids anywhere, I guess."

"Goddammit! That's what the three of them said!" he shouted, jerking a thumb at Marys Dos and Tres and Miss Doone. "Do you all take me for an idiot? Ah, what the hell -- let's get out of this place!" And with that he snatched up the canvas wine bag he always kept between his legs in the car and started trudging back toward where the vehicles were parked. The rest of us gathered everything up and followed suit. I tried to edge over to Lorna to ask her some questions, but she avoided me deftly, attaching herself to others in the group.

When I got to the pink English Ford Bill Davis was storing baskets and blankets in the trunk (sorry, I mean the boot -- it was an *English* Ford) and Hem took the opportunity to pull me aside and growl *sotto voce* to me: "It was the Feds, wasn't it, Marlo? It was the goddamned Feds! I know it was, as well as if I'd seen them myself, clear and sharp at first light!"

"No, Papa," I said as soothingly as I could. "I swear to you it was not the Feds. It was *not*."

He looked at me as though I'd betrayed him. He didn't believe me. But at that moment Davis came around to the front of the car and Hem clammed up. Bill opened the hood -- er, the bonnet, rather -- and took a look at things.

"What are you looking for, Bill?" Papa asked.

"Oh, just checking the generator," Davis replied, poking around in the car's innards. "A few days ago it had a loose connection, and I just wanted to be sure it was still okay. Wouldn't want to lose that baby."

Papa watched the goings-on vacantly. "Gertrude Stein would've called it the Lost Generator," he mumbled to himself.

"Yeah," Davis went on, "without the generator functioning properly, this car's engine would be as good as dead."

"Death in the afternoon," Papa muttered.

I kicked a front tire of the English Ford and said, "You rented this car in Gibraltar, Papa. Am I right?"

"Yes," Hem replied.

"Know how I knew that?" I asked. "A little detective work. Look at this." I opened the right rear door of the car and leaned inside, scooping up some material from off the floor mat. I held it out in the palm of my hand for Papa to see: a few grains of grayish-colored, clay-like substance.

"Dirt," Papa said. "So what?"

"Not dirt, Papa," I replied, rolling the rough texture of the stuff between my thumb and forefinger. "Claybutt."

"What?" Papa asked, frowning and squinting.

"Claybutt," I repeated. "Don't know what that is, huh? Well, I'm sure you remember the line from the song *Our Love is Here to Stay* which goes,

The Rockies may crumble,
Gibraltar may tumble,
They're only made of claybutt . . .

"Now, I doubt very seriously that this car has been in the Rocky Mountains recently. On the other hand, we started out from the south of Spain, not all that far from Gibraltar -- where your ship from the U.S. put you ashore a few weeks ago, in fact. And somebody with claybutt on their shoes got in this car at one time. *Ergo,* this car came fom Gibraltar."

Papa looked at the stuff in my hand, then at me, a puzzled expression on his face. Finally he said, "Wouldn't it have been easier to just look at the license plates on the car? They're GBZ Gibraltar plates, not Spanish plates. Anybody can see that."

"Uh, yeah," I said, tossing the claybutt to the ground and dusting off my hands.

Davis finished his poking around and we all got in the car and pulled away from our picnic grounds and the Pass of Roncesvalles.

Back on the paved highway, route number C-135 down to Burguete, I tried to talk to Papa but he was in a foul mood. Then I remembered the horn. That would interest him and cheer him up. After all, he had been telling us those stories about Roland on the way up. I reached into my soiled white trenchcoat pocket and extracted the historical artifact. It was bent up, but it was still the Horn of Roland.

"Papa," I said, shoving the bronze instrument over his shoulder to where he sat in the left front passenger seat, "take a look at this."

He gave it about a tenth of a second's worth of viewing time, then snatched it out of my hand and threw it out the window, over the Ford. "Don't try to humor me with junk!" he snarled.

The horn hit the back side of a traffic sign alongside the road and bounced back over the car into the oncoming lane. I frantically twisted around in the back seat, looking out the rear window. I saw the priceless horn lying there on the asphalt -- until a semi-tractor-trailer grinding its way up the mountain road and bound for France ran over it with its left front tire, flattening half of the thing completely. Then the first set of double wheels crunched the remnant between the tires and deftly picked it up. The last I saw of the Horn of Roland -- or what was left of it -- it was revolving over and over between two huge Euzkadi tires of a Pegaso big rig which was hauling cojones de toro to the kitchens of La Belle France.

Chapter 9

Trenchcoats In Madrid

It was midafternoon and I was on my bed in Madrid's Hotel Suecia, propped up with pillows behind my back and head so I could do some reading, my legs stretched out on top of the bedspread. My Irish mother Kathleen Shamus, que en paz descance, would've been shaking her finger at me had she been present, lecturing me in her County Cork brogue: "You'll be a-gettin' your filthy shoes off that nice coverlet right this minute, Felipe Marlo Shamus!" Yeah, I still had my shoes on, and maybe they were messing up the spread, but I was a private dick and nobody told Marlo what to do nowadays. Unless he had a gun in his hand and I didn't, that is.

I picked up a book Papa had given me to read -- *The Best of Hemingway* or some such title, a collection of short stories. I was glad to have it, because otherwise I guess I'd have been staring at the walls. The Suecia was a pretty nice place but it didn't have TV like good hotels in the U.S. did. And even if it had, what would there have been to look at on the tube? Spanish television ran for four hours or so each evening, from about seven until eleven p.m., there was one government channel and it showed stuff that was so boring it'd make you puke. Some guy sitting at a desk, reading from a stack of papers the same news you could hear on the radio: *Los Estados Unidos has increased in size dramatically with the admission into its union of the huge, former colonial territory of Alaska, which is near the North Pole.* No pictures -- still or motion -- to accompany it, just the guy sitting behind the desk, with a curtain in the background. Or maybe a scratchy film about how to grow sunflowers. Or another biography of Generalísimo Francisco Franco, Caudillo de España por la Gracia de Dios, with lots of fuzzy old newsreel footage from the Spanish Civil War. Aiiiiieeeeeee! That was why nobody in Spain owned a TV set except Franco.

I hefted the book. Yeah, I was lucky to have this. I had plenty of time on my hands right now. Hem and Miss Mary were just crashing here in Madrid for a few days, trying to recover from Pamplona. Papa was picking up my tab, of course, so I could be nearby to watch for the Feds. Bill and Annie Davis were in the hotel, too. The Pamplona crew had dispersed at the end of los sanfermines, although Marys Dos and Tres and Lorna Doone were supposed to rejoin us at the Davis place in Malaga in a few days.

The last full corrida of the sanfermines, which had taken place the day before the shootout on the Irati, had been a good one, a fine way to close out the feria. The bulls were from the Vizconde de Garcigrande, of Salamanca. I've never been a big fan of salmantino toros, but this lot just about converted me. Every last one of them was applauded and one got a vuelta. Luis Segura and Diego Puerta each cut two ears and Miguelín cut one. And at feria's end Curro Girón led the pack with five ears and a tail -- his exact tally of last year, 1958.

We hadn't seen Ordóñez since he left Pamplona to go fight in El Puerto de Santa María on July twelfth with Dominguín and the Benítez Cuberos. For the first time of the temporada, Dominguín had really and truly bested Hem's boy, and that news had not been well received, prompting an even longer hibernation at this hotel, away from the bulls. For a while.

I sighed and opened the book, and I read:

The road dropped sharply from the heavily forested top of the ridge and down the dry hillside and through some high grass to the little stone bridge spanning the rushing stream which tumbled over great black rocks that looked like the bloated corpses of bull hippos felled by 6.5 Mannlichers where they had bathed in the early morning sun, and it was already getting hot as they lay waiting to kill the men who had betrayed their honor.

"They are late," Il Tigre said.

"Yes, they are late," Rick Norton said. The sun was climbing now.

"But at least we have the valpolicella. It is very good valpolicella." Il Tigre tilted the long bottle to his lips and drank deeply. His manhood had been shot away in the war, but he could still drink like a man.

"It is good valpolicella." Norton said.

"It is the very best valpolicella. It comes from the hills behind that ridge. The

contadini know how to make good wine there. It is the best."

"It is very good. It is excellent." But Norton thought, *it is not good, it is unspeakably bad, certainly not as good as the rioja of Logroño, where the vines grow in chalky soil and sheep's dung and the grapes taste of the musty Spanish earth and the dung, and the first drops on your tongue are like the sweet mother's milk of a young and dark-eyed vasca with a face of burned gold suckling her firstborn, and you follow the wine with a mouthful of hard chorizo made from the cojones of wild boars and fresh from the smokehouse. But it was good enough valpolicella.*

"Why are they so late?" Il Tigre drank again from the long bottle, wiping his mouth with a coarse woolen sleeve of his heavy coat, which was stiff with the dried blood of the first of those who had forsaken their honor. The sun was higher now, and it was getting hot, but in the shade of the fir trees it was still cool, and their heavy coats stiff with the dried blood felt good.

"It makes no difference to me if they are late," Norton lied. "We will take them whenever they come, and while we wait we will enjoy this excellent valpolicella." But his dry mouth tasting of copper coins told him that he did want them to come soon, and then he and Il Tigre would kill them, and afterward they would return to the town and sit in Harry's Bar and have some truly good valpolicella and talk of women and bulls and the war.

I put the book down. It was okay, I supposed, but too wordy for a real man of action. Not enough *biff, bam, hiya babe* -- know what I mean? I stretched and got off the bed. I looked out the window, down into the Calle Marqués de Casa Riera. The day was sunny without a cloud in the sky, and it was hot. July in Madrid. Franco and his government had long since packed up and moved north to San Sebastián with its cooling sea breezes for the hot months, leaving Madrid half closed down. I walked over to the chest of drawers, pulled out the top one and took out a bottle of Magno. I uncorked it and downed a slug, then put it back. I stood there for a minute in front of the mirror doing Bogey grimaces with my mouth, then went to the closet and got my hat and trenchcoat -- I was back to the standard khaki color, thank goodness -- put them on, and left the room.

Outside Papa's room I paused and listened. I could hear him snoring away in there. I looked at my watch: two thirty-five. Old Hem would be out until at least five. I checked his doorknob: locked. Hell, I might as well use the time, I told myself. I went to the elevator and pressed the call button. In a minute the doors opened and the uniformed elevator boy with the little pillbox hat held them ajar until I was in, then let them close and pushed his lever down. Abajo, Pancho, and don't spare the caballos, I thought. We descended.

I walked to the corner of the Calle de Alcalá then took a left and continued west a few blocks. Before I got to the Puerta del Sol I turned to the left up the Calle

Victoria, Madrid's business center of taurine activity. At number nine I walked under the orange and blue striped awning and entered the building, taking the steps to the third floor two at a time, passing don Lavinio Stuyck's second floor offices as I went up. Soon I reached the frosted glass-paneled door with the peeling imitation gold leaf letters which now barely spelled out:

FELIPE MARLO SHAMUS
INVESTIGADOR PRIVADO
PARA EL MUNDILLO TAURINO

I took my keys from my pocket and let myself in.

The office was hot, stuffy, airless. Motes floated in the sunlight streaming in the window facing the Calle Victoria. I looked around. Why had I come here, I asked myself. Probably, I thought, because this was my querencia; I felt safer, more at home here. Then I heard the outer office door open and two men come in. A bad sign.

I opened the door connecting my private office, where I was now, to the outer office with its ratty sofa and a couple of chairs which served as a waiting room during business hours and my bedroom at night -- when I wasn't away on a case, that was. Standing there were two trenchcoated men with faces familiar enough to make me groan inwardly. Capitán Gilipollas and his goon Bálthazar of the Madrid police.

"So they let you out, huh, Marlo?" Gilipollas said, sneering. "Or did you bust out? How do I know you ain't on the run? Yeah -- he could be on the run, huh, Bálthazar? Maybe some of his Red buddies sprung him." Bálthazar was doing his usual imitation of a Cro-Magnon Man, flexing his big hamhock fists and drooling down the front of his coat; he smiled a gap-toothed smile and grunted.

"Whattaya want, Gilipollas?" I snarled. I didn't have time for these idiots. But I had to be careful; they could be dangerous.

The captain looked at me, head cocked to one side, and spoke. "I want to know what you're up to, Marlo. Talk!"

"Nothing that concerns you," I said, turning to go back into my inner office until Gilipollas grabbed my arm.

"Not so fast, Marlo," he said. "Now, before I set Bálthazar here on you . . ."

I held up a hand in the "halt" position. "Gilipollas, can't you get it through your thick skull that the only real role you have to play in the saga of Felipe Marlo, Taurine P.I., is one of a provider of comic relief in the guise of a brutish character? You and your laboratory creature here." I indicated Bálthazar. "You have no real bearing on the development of this case I'm working on. None."

The captain's mouth was gaping open as he tried to assimilate what I'd said. Finally he decided it hadn't been good and I could see him getting ready to explode.

"Why, you, you . . ." he began, then growled, "Get him, Bálthazar!" The beast began to lumber toward me, a grin spreading across his lantern jaw. Oh, hell, I said to myself; I might as well say adiós to a couple of teeth.

At that moment the outer office door opened again and this time the mustachioed and trenchcoated men I'd last seen in that narrow street in Pamplona came in. They shut the door. Captain Gilipollas and Bálthazar turned and looked at the newcomers.

"I don't know who you two mugs are," Gilipollas said, "but I want you out of here. We're police, see?" The other two men didn't move and didn't say anything.

"I told you -- " the captain began, only to shut up fast when the smaller of the newcomers produced an I.D. card identifying him as Seguridad.

"Capitán Gilipollas," said the state security agent calmly, "you're looking more and more like a tool of the Reds to me. If you are not out of this office in five seconds I will take it to mean that you are volunteering for service in one of our internment camps for enemies of the state. Perhaps that popular one outside of Albacete. Do I make myself clear?"

After only a moment's pause, without another word and without looking back, the captain and his thug exited. The two remaining men walked closer to me. The talkative one spoke again.

"Now, Señor Marlo, with those two bufones gone we can talk. I don't believe I have to remind you what we want to know. And that this is your last chance."

I thought fast. If I told them the truth -- that I knew plenty about their rivals, the Sección Trece boys, trying to bump off Papa -- but one of them buying the farm instead -- and said nothing about any Reds in the mix, that would probably mean a return trip to la cárcel for me, since I was obviously being nonproductive. I'd been out for about three weeks now, but I hadn't yet fingered a single commie. I'd better make something up, and do it fast. I took a deep breath and plunged in.

"Yeah. Okay," I said, "here's what I've turned up so far. I can't prove anything yet, but I'm convinced I'm on the scent and you'll be able to haul in a big batch of Reds soon."

The two security agents looked at each other, then back to me. The silent one produced a notepad and pen and both stood there, waiting for me to go on.

"Hemingway started supporting the Reds back in 1936," I said, "but . . ."

"We know that, Marlo!" barked the talker, "Por Dios -- "

"Wait a minute, wait a minute!" I interrupted. "Gimme a chance, willya? I was going to say, *but* in recent years he has become disenchanted with them and is now, in fact, a secret agent of the CIA."

"The CIA!" both security men blurted simultaneously.

"Correcto," I said, "now just keep listening and writing. Yes, Hemingway is now a secret CIA agent, but his greatest enemy is . . . the FBI."

"The FBI!" the two men shouted in unison, then looked at each other with baffled expressions.

"El Mismo," I confirmed, then continued: "The CIA has been infiltrated by Reds, and they're out to get Hemingway, too."

The writer agent was scribbling furiously but the talker was eyeing me warily.

"It sounds crazy but it's true," I rushed out, before the talker could say anything. "And that's not all. The Reds in the CIA are linking up with the Reds in Spain, the link being a Spanish torero."

"A Spanish torero!" the two shouted together, stunned expressions on their faces. Then: "Who?" This from the talker.

I grabbed at the first name that came to mind. "That kid from Sevilla who took his alternativa in March. What's his name? Oh, yeah -- Curro!"

"Curro!" they cried.

"Right. Curro." I confirmed. "But, look, that's all I know right now. I'll get more for you, but it may take a few days. You've got to give me more time, está bién?"

The agents looked at each other, then retreated to the other side of the room for a whispered conference. When they came back the talker spoke.

"We will give you a bit longer, Marlo. In the meantime, we will be checking out what you have told us. We will be back in touch with you." And with that they left.

I puffed out my cheeks and blew out a big sigh, then collapsed in my squeaky swivel chair, removed my hat and put my feet up on the desk. I was sweating profusely. How the hell was I going to get out of this?

Usually, I thought to myself, putting my feet on the desk was enough to make the phone ring. Just then the phone rang.

I removed my feet from the desk, snatched the receiver from its dangling position on the hook and put it up to my left ear while I choked the phone's long neck with my right hand. "Marlo," I growled into the mouthpiece.

"Señor Marlo," a basso voice boomed out of the black bakelite earpiece, "I think maybe you've run into a couple of my pals already, even if we haven't been introduced properly."

"Whattaya wearing?" I shot back.

A pause. Then, "¿Qué?"

"I said what are you wearing? That's a simple enough question."

"Uh, well, uh, I'm wearing a trenchcoat," the deep voice replied, "and a fedora. Both black leather."

Jesus! Black leather! This was really bad! "Okay," I said, deciding to play it cool, "let's have your threats, warnings or questions, or all of the above, and make it snappy -- I don't have all day."

Another pause, followed by, "Señor Marlo, you are running in dangerous company. Enemies of España --"

"Yeah, yeah, I know all about it," I cut the voice off. "Hemingway the Red plotting against la patria, and so on. Am I correct?"

Silence, then, "Um, sí. Sí, correcto. But be warned, Señor Marlo. We of Sección Trece -- ¡Muerte a los Rojos! -- are not as lax as Coronel Medidas and his fools. We know that the Red Hemingway is in contact with other Reds who get their orders direct from Moscow, and we are --"

"How's about I kill Hemingway for you?" I said, cutting to the chase. "Will you guys back off if I guarantee that?"

More silence. Then, "Kill the Red Hemingway? You?"

"Sure, why not?" I said with a confidence I did not feel. In for a penny, in for a pound.

From the muffled sounds, I could tell the guy had his hand over the mouthpiece to his telephone and was talking to someone else. Finally the hand was removed and he said to me, "Very well, Señor Marlo. We will see if you can put your mouth where your money is, as you norteamericanos say. You have until, shall we say, August twenty-fourth to kill the Red Hemingway. Or we kill you. ¿Está bién?"

"Why August twenty-fourth?" I asked.

"Because Coronel Descolorado goes on vacation the day after that," the deep voice told me, "and he would like to have everything resolved before he does so."

"I see," I replied. "Okay, you've got a deal. Oh -- uh, muerte a los Rojos to you, too. 'Bye." I placed the earpiece back on its hook and broke the connection. Oh, brother. As William Bendix, who plays Chester A. Riley on that popular TV comedy show back in the states, *The Life of Riley*, is always saying, "What a revoltin' development dis is!"

I left my office and started walking down the Calle Victoria toward San Jerónimo, past colorful carteles announcing Sunday's novillada at Las Ventas. Of more interest, however, was the one touting the upcoming feria in Valencia, starting in a few days, which we'd all be going to: in addition to Ordóñez and Dominguín, we'd have the two top contenders for the escalafón número uno spot, Curro Girón and Jaime Ostos. We'd also have the escalafón leader of '57, Gregorio Sánchez. And Bienvenida of course. My eyes zeroed in on the last day, the biggy, the mano a mano with Antonio and Luís Miguel and bulls of Ignacio Sánchez and Báltazar Iban.

My train of thought was interrupted by blaring, fuzzy-sounding pasodoble music and blurred, metallic shouting which was getting louder and louder. I looked to my right, up the Calle Victoria, and saw one of those small vans with huge loudspeakers on the top edging its way down the street. There were two men in the cab and one of them was holding a microphone and bellowing into it from so close up that the result was guaranteed to be virtually indecipherable noise booming out of the speakers, in addition to the music. I surmised that they were promoting Sunday's novillada, but who could know? When the van drew even with me it stopped and the two men got out, leaving the pasodoble music -- *El Gato Montés* -- playing. Oh, my God, I thought: they were wearing trenchcoats and fedoras. The Taurine Police. Damn! At least the fabric of their clothing was not black leather.

"Señor Marlo?" the announcer asked me. He was a small, wiry guy who might have been a mayoral. The other fellow, the driver, looked more like a retired picador.

"That's me," I said, waiting. *El Gato Montés* was still going full blast.

"Señor Marlo, we are to remind you that although you are on temporary parole, you are still officially in the hands of la Policía Taurina."

"Yeah," I said, "and I'm grateful to you for reminding me. I might have forgotten."

"Just follow the Reglamento, Señor Marlo, and you will be fine."

"Yeah," I replied, "sure."

And that was it. They got back in their little van, which I now saw had pictures of bulls and toreros painted on its sides, and the small man resumed shouting into the microphone. Maybe they were moonlighting, I said to myself -- or maybe all cops of the Taurine Police had to put in some time in the trenches now and then. Who'd be next to call on me? I wondered. The dogcatcher?

The raucous music and the blurry shouting receded as the van turned the corner, and I lit a fag and headed back to the Suecia. As far as I was concerned, we couldn't leave for Malaga, our next stop, soon enough. There were too many cops in Madrid. I looked forward to another slug of Magno from that bottle in my room.

Chapter 10

Papa Vows to Torear

"Papa's sixtieth birthday is going to be one he will never forget!" Miss Mary said, as we stood next to the swimming pool in the morning sunshine at La Consula, the Davises' fabulous place at Churriana, in the hills just outside Malaga. She appeared to be in much better spirits now and her broken toe seemed to be healing. Tomorrow, July twenty-first, was the big day; the invited guests would begin arriving later this afternoon, the rest coming in the next morning. There would be so many of them that Miss Mary had blocked out a whole bunch of rooms and suites at the new Hotel Pez Espada at Torremolinos, a couple of miles down the coast where the beaches began.

Beyond Torremolinos was a long, empty coastline of nothing but vacant beaches and little unheard-of fishing villages with names like Marbella, Fuengirola and Estepona. The Spanish Ministry of Tourism had grandly dubbed the seventy-five-mile stretch ending at the port of Algeciras "La Costa del Sol," announcing plans for tourist development there, but that was clearly a screwy idea. The long, deserted coastline was just too out of the way for foreigners to come in any numbers -- even if there were any hotels there, which, except for the Pez Espada, there weren't -- and the Spaniards themselves didn't have enough money to go to beach resorts, anyway. No, the strip would always, I was convinced, remain pretty much what it was today: an unimportant bit of virtually uninhabited coast at the tail end of Europe, dotted here and there with old stone atalayas, or Moorish watchtowers, and not much else.

But back to Miss Mary's party for Papa. It would take place at La Consula, a walled and gated estate with extensive gardens centered around a colonnaded mansion in the moorish style and the aforementioned swimming pool. One feature Davis's place did not have, however, was telephones. Weird, huh?

Hem's devoted spouse had ordered huge quantities of champagne from Paris, Chinese food from London, and bacalao from Madrid. There would be fireworks under the auspices of a pirotécnico from Valencia and flamenco dancers from Malaga, plus armies of musicians, waiters, barmen and cooks. She even rented a shooting gallery from a traveling carnival and had it set up on the grounds. For all I knew, maybe she'd hired Lawrence Welk and his bubble-music orchestra as well, complete with that dancing goof Bobby, Myron the grimacing accordionist and the Little Lemon Sisters or whatever their names were.

In addition to our usual cuadrilla, guests would include two real, live, Indian maharajahs with their maharanis, a U.S. Army general, lots of Ordóñez's friends, a guy who was bringing Hem a brand new Lancia from Italy, and the American ambassador to Germany. Papa subsequently boasted that he and the ambassador had "fought together" in World War II; I reasoned that maybe they'd gotten into a brawl in the Hotel Ritz bar at liberation time.

The whole thing was scheduled to begin at noon today, July twenty-first, and run until noon the following day. I checked my watch: Only a couple of hours away. I left Miss Mary to her last minute organizing and began wandering casually around the grounds, looking for Hemingway. I moseyed over to the as yet unmanned carnival shooting gallery, which had been set up the day before, and walked inside the tacky little shed-like affair. I froze in my tracks. Sitting alone in the place on a little stool in the corner was Papa, pointing a shotgun barrel at his own forehead, clumsily gripping the weapon with outstretched arms. The weapon was wobbling around unsteadily in the air.

"Whoa!" I cried, finally willing my feet to move and rushing up to him, grabbing the double-barreled hunting gun. "What the hell's going on here?" I said testily.

"Ah, Marlo," Hem said sheepishly. "Just out of curiosity I was trying to figure out how a person could shoot himself with a shotgun. With a pistol it'd be a snap, but a shotgun's pretty unwieldy, for that sort of thing, anyway. A writer needs to know things like that, after all. I might want to describe it in one of my stories. Do you know how it's done?"

I hesitated. "Uh, well, sure. You, ah . . . here, let me sit on that stool and I'll show you."

Papa got up and I sat down, putting the butt of the gun on the ground between

106

my feet and reaching down with my left hand until my thumb was on the first of the double triggers. "See," I said, "first you've got to support the gun by anchoring the stock like this. Then, once you've done that and you've got a finger -- or thumb -- on the trigger, you can put the end of the barrel into your mouth --" I demonstrated, trying to continue to talk but now emitting only "wumf wumf wumf" sounds until I leaned back, freeing my mouth which now tasted faintly of gun oil. "Anyway, as I was trying to say, if you do it like that, the trajectory of the shot goes up through the roof of your mouth and blows your brains out. If you did it the way you were holding it a minute ago, you might succeed only in giving yourself a lobotomy. And like the song says, I'd rather have a bottle in front of me, than have to have a frontal lobotomy." I chuckled, but Papa just stared at me with a strange look in his eye. Finally he seemed to snap out of it and tried to manage a laugh of his own, although it didn't really come off.

"Thanks, Marlo," he said. "I really mean that. You don't know how much help you've been. That's good information. Worth fifty grand."

"Ah, think nothin' of it, pops," I said, standing up and propping the shotgun against the wall. "Whenever I can --"

"Marlo," he interrupted me as though he hadn't even heard me talking, "do you remember that snotnosed kid in Pamplona, the one who ragged me about never having fought a bull?" He looked at me, a desperate expression on his face.

I waited a moment, then said, "Yeah. I remember. What about him?"

"He was right, you know. I've never faced a bull. Not even a little calf. I've wanted to, but . . . I just can't."

"Well, what the hell?" I said. "Plenty of people feel the same way. It's no big deal."

"But Marlo!" he cried. "I'm not just some guy off the street! I'm the macho Papa Hemingway! I know all about bullfighting, or at least I'm supposed to. You don't know what it's like. You write and talk to the point where the people out there think you really know all there is to know, but you can't actually *do* it. The feeling is not that good, clean and true feeling you get that comes after a good and fine thing is done. It's hell, Marlo,"

"Yeah," I conceded. "I guess so. A real pisser."

"But even so," he said, straightening up a little now as he spoke, "I am el Número Uno of the bullfight writers, don't you think? In English, I mean. Don't you think so, Marlo?"

"Yeah, sure," I said. "Of course. Claro que sí."

"Who's next best, Marlo? When you're on top, somebody's always nipping at your heels, trying to take your place. Who's my biggest threat? You're a taurine P.I., you know what I'm talking about. Who is it? Angus McNabb? Tom Lea? Vince Kehoe? Who?"

"Oh, Papa," I said, "why don't we just let it drop? There's no --"

"No, no, Marlo, I mean it!" he shouted, a bit wild-eyed. "Who is my most dangerous rival? And why? I must know. I must know, Marlo!"

"All right, all right, calm down," I said, patting him on the shoulder. Should I really answer his question honestly? I wondered. Then I said to myself, why not level with the man? Maybe the truth is what he needs. I sighed, then let it all hang out.

"Look, Papa," I said, "those writers you mentioned are good, but they're not your rivals. There's only one who can have any hopes along those lines, and there's a good reason why that's the case." I dug a cigarette out of a pocket and lit up, blowing a Rafael halo over Hem's head.

"Who? Who is it, Marlo? For God's sake, who -- and what is this 'good reason' you talk about?"

I blew another Rafael halo. Now Papa had two rings over his head, one on top of the other. But he wasn't aware of it. "Barnaby Conrad," I finally said.

"Bar -- " he began, but didn't finish. "Oh, no! You mean that phony who wrote *Matador* and *The Death of Manolete*?"

"Among other things, yes," I replied. "That's him."

"Why, that rat! That . . . that . . . *obscenity*! That Manolete ass-kisser! That . . . that . . . " Froth actually appeared in the corners of his mouth.

"Wait a minute," I said. "I heard somebody say you've got copies of a couple of his books in your house in Cuba."

Hemingway's eyes bulged. "Yes, but . . . but . . . " he sputtered, "by God, they were put there by the Feds!" Then, suddenly, he seemed to calm down a bit and asked me, "But why -- why is Conrad more of a challenge to me than the others?"

"Simple, Papa," I said. "Because he has fought bulls. He not only writes about them, he's fought them. And he's not only fought bulls, he's appeared on a cartel, here in Spain, with none other than Juan Belmonte. It gives him credibility." I took another drag on my weed and looked at Hemingway.

"Oh, Jesus, yes," he whispered. "Of course. The ultimate certification, good, clean and true. I think maybe I'd heard that but I'd forgotten it." I didn't say anything.

"But, Marlo!" he suddenly cried out, desperately. "What can I do to salvage things? There must be something I can do!"

"Sure," I said. "Beat Conrad at his own game. Write about the bulls *and* appear with one on a cartel with a matador as well known as Belmonte."

"But . . . fight a *bull*? In a real bullfight? Marlo, I'm sixty years old! It's too late for that!" His eyes pleaded with me to understand.

"Hell, I'm not talking about facing a Miura at Las Ventas," I said. "A becerro or some young vaquilla at a little festival in some small place. It could be a charity affair. One animal for you. Plus a famous matador on the cartel with you: Ordóñez.

He'd be happy to do it. Or, hell, maybe *several* famous matadors on the bill with you. Luis Miguel'd go along. And his brother Pepe. Maybe Antonio's brother Cayetano, too. Damn, that'd be quite a show!"

Hemingway's face had changed dramatically. Now there was a faraway look in his eyes mixed with excitement and anticipation. "Yes!" he cried. "What a coup that would be! They'd be talking about that for years -- decades -- to come!"

"You can sound out Antonio on the idea this afternoon," I said. "But I can tell you now I'm sure he'll agree."

"But wait, Marlo," Papa said, uncertainty creeping back into his voice and countenence. "I can't just go out there and face a bull, or even a becerro, without training. I'm in Spain now, where training facilities are available, but I'm not here most of the time. The date for the festival would have to be a long way off, to give me time to train."

"Okay," I said, "that makes sense. Hey, we're celebrating your birthday today; why not say one year from today, on your sixty-first birthday?"

Hem pursed his lips and thought about it, then shook his head. "No, not enough time. Within the coming year I doubt I'll have more than a couple of months in Spain, and I can't spend all my time training.

"Two years from today, then," I suggested. "That ought to be plenty. Just go ahead and commit to it on a one hundred percent basis, and you'll be set."

Papa stared into space, his jaw jutted out, then he turned and looked at me. "By God, Marlo, I'll do it!" he said, proferring his hand for me to shake. I took it and we shook on it, man to man, looking each other in the eye. "I swear to you on the grave of my poor old suicided father," he cried, "that if I am still alive two years from today, on July twenty-first, 1961, I will fight a bull! As the Great Whore is my witness, Marlo, I'll never be a chickenshit again!" I thought I could hear Max Steiner scene-ending music in the background. Too bad we weren't silhouetted against a purple and orange sunset.

Chapter 11

Hem's Party Blast

Miss Mary's party for Papa was a swell bash. Everybody showed up as scheduled and a good time was had by all: Ordóñez, the maharajahs and maharanis, the U.S. brass, Lorna Doone and the two "prisoners of war," Mary Dos and Mary Tres. Bill and Annie Davis, of course. Plus many more. Old Hem danced, sang, popped champagne corks and proposed funny toasts, led riau-riau conga lines over the grounds and shot off fireworks. And all the while, waiters served endless drinks, musicians played without stopping, and people got drunk, sobered up and got drunk again. At one point the pyrotechnics set fire to the top of a big palm tree and the Malaga fire department despatched a pumper to put it out while everybody cheered and agreed that "the burning bush" act was a masterwork of theatre.

The shooting gallery Miss Mary had borrowed from the carnival proved very popular. Antonio and Papa took turns shooting cigarettes out of each other's mouths, and out of one of the maharajahs' mugs, too. I suppose I should have gone on the wagon for the entire time, seeing as how I was on a case, but I confess I got caught up in the swirl of the gaiety and had a few belts of my own from the passing trays of drinks. Pretty soon I was letting our esteemed marksmen shoot weeds out of my mouth, too -- and they'd had lots more to drink than I had. Locura.

But I had plenty, believe me, especially as the night went on. In fact, thinking back on it, I'm not sure where reality left off and hallucination began. At some point approaching dawn I seemed to be making out with Marys Dos and Tres under the counter of the shooting gallery -- and then they were gone and I was constructing "pyramids" with the junk from their purses, which they'd left behind, including items which in retrospect seemed so incredible that I figured this part had to be a dream, a fantasy or otherwise some product of a booze-fueled imagination: for a while there I honestly thought some of the stuff from their handbags that I'd been playing with had counted two snubnosed Colt Cobra .38s and CIA I.D. cards for both of them. Funny the tricks the mind can play.

And in the meantime, leaning on the rickety wooden counter of the shooting gallery directly above my head, Papa and Ordóñez continued blasting away at anything and everything. Finally the flimsy back wall of the shed collapsed and we could all see, illuminated by the many lights strung up throughout the gardens, at least two dozen guys in trenchcoats -- both khaki and black leather -- crawling through the grass toward us with drawn pistols. Some of them wore red and yellow hammer-and-sickle armbands, others Falange-blue neckerchiefs, and still others the big, white stencilled letters *FBI* on their trenchcoats' breast pockets. Hemingway and Ordóñez never let up their firing, now directing their fusillades at the ominous agents slithering in our direction.

I joined in, pulling out my Moxley and blasting away, and I shortly realized that Marys Dos and Tres and Lorna Doone were now here and all firing nonstop at the encroachers, as well. The screams of the wounded and dying filled the air. Pretty soon there was so much smoke that I couldn't see anybody or anything any more, so I decided to take a nap.

I woke up with the noonday sun hot on my back. I finally opened my eyes and realized I was lying face down in the grass behind the shooting gallery shed, which had completely fallen down sometime along the way. My rod was in my shoulder holster and a cursory inspection revealed that none of its bullets had been fired. And there were no bodies of trenchcoated agents lying in the grass, either -- although Hem's and Antonio's were, their shooting gallery .22 rifles beside them. Papa's eyes were shut and his glasses were askew, but I knew he was okay because his lips were moving.

"Just like in Ronda," I heard him mumble.

I got shakily to my feet and went off in search of some hair of the dog, which I soon located. I sank into a chaise at poolside and nursed my drink while observing a few of the somewhat worse for wear guests staggering toward their cars. What a blast. Hem subsequently proclaimed it "the best party that ever was."

And now it was just about time to head for Valencia and los toros.

Chapter 12

Great Balls of Fire

Our entourage drove up to Valencia from Malaga the day before the first corrida of the July feria and got settled in at our hotel. Then we all went out to the beachfront estate of Juan Luis somebody, an acquaintance of Papa's, and frolicked on the beach and had a few drinks, enjoying the calm before the storm, so to speak. It really wasn't trenchcoat and hat weather, so I tried to stay in the shade of a beach umbrella while I checked out Mary Dos and Mary Tres in their swimsuits. Too bad Franco had long ago decreed anything other than full, one-piece bathing attire to be illegal for ladies in España; those two babes would've looked mighty fine in bikinis of the type they were said to be wearing now on the French Riviera.

I looked around for the dark-haired and sultry Lorna Doone, but I couldn't spot her. I wondered if she was really a Scottish reporter like she said. Maybe she was -- in addition to something else. I did see Miss Mary and the Davises sitting in some beach chairs some way off, while Papa bounced around in the surf up to his barrel chest. Then I noticed him doing backstrokes out to sea.

Our host Juan Luis, a pleasant enough fellow who was also dressed in swimming attire, saw Hem going further and further out to sea and he got up from his beach chair and shielded his eyes with a hand, watching. Papa kept on heading out -- he must have been between one and two hundred yards distant by now -- and I sat up

112

in my own folding chair. Then he was gone. Disappeared.

Both Juan Luis and I shouted "Papa!" at the same time, running down to the water line together. But whereas I stopped there, clad in my P.I. outfit and packing my gat, Juan Luis charged into the surf and high-stepped it through the water until it was deep enough for him to make a shallow dive and start swimming ninety miles an hour out to sea. Even so, I said to myself, if Papa remained submerged there was no way Juan Luis could make it all the way out to where we'd last seen him before it was too late. Damn! Why hadn't I kept a rein on him? That was my job!

Juan Luis was maybe sixty yards out now, swimming like mad toward the spot where we'd seen Papa last. I kept looking to see if I could spot his white-haired head surfacing anywhere, but all I could see was an occasional spurt of water here and there, followed by faint thumping sounds. At first I thought they might be caused by Papa's hands breaking the surface and flailing the greenish sea, but I never actually saw any hands or arms -- or anything else. Oh, Jesus! I felt so helpless!

And then suddenly there it was: a tiny pink head topped by matted white hair, bobbing in the water! Papa! And then his other head surfaced, and it seemed to be -- wait a minute! That was somebody else's head, a head with long, dark hair and wearing a diver's mask. Then as Juan Luis closed in on Hem, the other head disappeared and did not resurface.

Everyone in our cuadrilla -- well, everyone except Lorna Doone -- was there to try to be of help when our host finally had Papa far enough in to shore for him to be able to stand up and stagger onto the beach, supported on one side by Juan Luis and on the other by me. Miss Mary was frantic, but although Hem was obviously exhausted and coughing up water, he made light of the whole thing and kept saying that he'd never really been in any real trouble -- he'd just had a slight cramp, that's all.

Later, however, when he'd been helped to the beach house and tucked into bed for awhile, he signalled for me to stay when all the others finally left his temporary bedroom so he could get some rest.

"Marlo!" he said in a stage whisper, his eyes big and round.

I pulled a straight-backed wooden chair up to his bed, reversed it and straddled it, leaning my chin on my hands which were on the top of the chair's back. "Yeah, pops?" I said.

"It was the Feds, Marlo!" he babbled, a terrified look on his face. "The goddam Feds were out there under the water, waiting for me! And they almost had me!"

"Wait a minute, wait a minute, Papa," I said as soothingly as I could. "Whattaya mean the Feds were under the water waiting for you? That's impossible."

"I obscenity on thy impossibilities!" he cried. "They were there, I tell you! When they dragged me under I could see them -- two men in diving gear. With pistols!"

"Pistols!" I echoed, pushing my hat brim back a tad with the tip of my thumb. "Under water?"

"Hell, yes!" he retorted heatedly. "And they used them, too! Or tried to. Not on me, but on whoever it was who came swimming up from out of nowhere and started shooting. They returned fire, but then they broke and swam away, leaving me there. They were wearing swim fins, so they moved out pretty quick. At first I thought it was you who was saving me, Marlo, but then I remembered that you always wear that dumbass coat and hat. And besides, even if you hadn't been wearing them, it couldn't have been you because you don't have tits."

"Because I don't have -- what?"

"Yes, Marlo," he said, a bit calmer now, "it was a woman who was my rescuer. A woman in a red bathing suit and wearing an oxygen tank, fighting an underwater gun battle with the Feds! Over me!" He laid his head back on the pillow.

Holy Akron, I thought to myself. Damn! I meant Holy Toledo -- see how confused I was? A gun battle under water? Yeah, it was possible; bullets can usually be fired under water, especially if they haven't been submerged for too long, although you can't count on them going in a straight line. That would account for those spurts of water and thumping sounds: bullets exiting the water, fired from below. But who were the attackers? Not Feds, surely. Who was the mermaid, and where had she come from? How had she known to be there?

Even though I didn't know what was going on, I figured I'd better make Papa feel like I had things under control. I sure as hell didn't want him to can me; that'd be my ticket back to the pokey. I thought fast.

"Ah, yeah, well, I guess I might as well come clean, Papa," I said. "That lady works for me. I knew about those guys and so I sent her out there to keep an eye on you. If I'd done it myself, the opposition would've missed me on the beach and been prepared for me. But they didn't know about my secret weapon. What I don't know, though, is who your attackers were. You say Feds; I don't think so."

Hem looked at me, a bit dubiously I thought, and then he spoke again. "Whoever that girl is, Marlo, she's first rate. I liked her from the moment I saw her. I tried to talk to her, to say, 'Daughter. I will call thee daughter.' But as we were under water it just came out as 'glub, glub, glub.' But it was like when you were young and in love and everything was good and clean."

"Well, after all, you *were* in the water," I pointed out.

"I don't mean *that* kind of clean, you moron!" he snapped at me.

After a while we all returned to our hotel in downtown Valencia, located just off the Plaza del Caudillo, the main square faced onto by the Ayuntamiento. Papa and Miss Mary decided to have a quiet evening with room service dinner, so I went to my own room and dug my fifth of Magno out of my suitcase. I was taking a slug of it straight from the bottle when I heard a tapping on my door.

I put the Magno on the dresser and walked over and opened the door. Holy Moley! It was Mary Dos and Mary Tres, both of them wearing U.S.-style short shorts and halter tops -- no shoes -- and carrying what looked like a phonograph and a cardboard box full of 45 rpm records.

"Trick or treat!" they squealed in unison.

"Huh?" I said. Finally I recovered enough to invite them in. If these two chicks left the hotel dressed like this, I thought, they'd be arrested in no time flat.

"Look what we've got, Hotch!" the blonde Mary Dos said. Her halter was red and her shorts white, while the brunette Mary Tres's outfit was blue and white. Their gorgeous bods were now well tanned and just oozed sex. "In Madrid we found a record player in a store and it runs on this stupid Spanish electrical system, so we can play our records! We brought our own record player from home, but it blew up when we plugged it in back in Paris, when we first arrived from the U.S."

"And it blew out all the electricity on the whole floor of the Chez Grenouille, our hotel, too!" Mary Tres chimed in excitedly.

"We decided we haven't gotten to know you well enough, Hotch," said Mary Dos, giving me a big Ipana smile and rubbing her well-stuffed red halter on my arm as she spoke. "So we brought our rock and roll records to play for you. Including the latest hits from back home. We can have a party!"

"Er, swell," I said, loosening my tie. "Say, care for a belt?" I reached over and got the bottle of Magno off the dresser.

Well, they did, and before too long the previously full bottle was empty. In the meantime, the two Marys played their records and we got to know each other. Some of the tunes I knew, like *At the Hop, Get a Job, Bird Dog, Yackety Yak* and *Great Balls of Fire*. Others had come out while I was in jail and were new to me: *Venus, Stagger Lee, Kansas City, Charlie Brown* and *Sixteen Candles*.

We rolled up the rug and danced on the tile floor. I was feeling no pain by this time, and so when the girls insisted that I leave my trenchcoat and hat on and dance dressed like that "because I looked so cute," I went along with it. I must have looked a sight, doing my jitterbug rock-and-roll dance steps to *Great Balls of Fire* while dressed up in my P.I. outfit.

After a while the people in the rooms on both sides were pounding on the walls, so the girls finally turned off the record player. Actually, I confess that the only reason I know this is because an irate hotel manager upbraided me for it the next morning. All I really remember was trying to make time with the two babes on the bed, and them giggling and saying that I could do *this* if I'd tell them *that*. And then I could do *that* if I'd tell them *this*. Unfortunately, I just couldn't recall later what all those thises and thats were that I told them. But I think I had a good time.

Chapter 13

Stupid Looking Bulls

In Papa's words, the first corrida of the Valencia feria was "a modified disaster." Antonio Bienvenida, Luis Miguel and Jaime Ostos faced a string of Pablo Romeros. Ostos was brave with a bull Hem referred to as "stupid." Maybe he'd seen the toro's SAT scores or something; to me the animal just lacked nobleza, but what do I know? Bienvenida didn't show us anything worth mentioning, other than his rictus smile.

Dominguín placed his own banderillas in his inimitable style, sort of dragging his right toe in the sand toward the end, in a more or less signature adorno, I guess you could say. He looked like he might have something going with one of his two enemigos but then the animal ran out of gas and died with a media estocada. He took a vuelta on each bull, but the smile aimed at el público looked phony. Papa commented that Luis Miguel was "becoming sad" because he was beginning to realize that he was going downhill. Not that Papa was biased, of course.

At the hotel that night after the corrida I heard a big commotion in the hallway, down toward where I knew Luis Miguel's room was. A woman was screaming furiously and other voices joined the fray. I opened my door and saw some men dragging a hysterical Ava Gardner down the corridor. She was cursing like a sailor and kicking everybody within reach in the shins or stomping toes with her stiletto heels. I tapped a bellboy on the shoulder and asked him what was going on.

"The Señorita Gardner was insisting we unlock the door to the room of the matador," he explained, "but we of course could not do that. He asked earlier that he not be disturbed."

"Why do you suppose he wouldn't want a babe like that in his room?" I mused, rubbing my chin.

"Because the Señorita Rhonda Fleming is already in his room, señor," the kid replied, winking and smiling at me, then moving on down the hall. I puffed out my cheeks and blew, shaking my head. Some people had all the luck.

I walked down the hall past the room of Mary Dos and Mary Tres. Their door was cracked open and I could hear music coming from their record player, although I could've sworn I'd seen them leaving the hotel only a short while earlier. I was going to continue on my way when something made me stop and listen closer to the music. Then I peeked through the crack in the almost-closed door and saw not the two Marys but Lorna Doone, dancing by herself to the song coming from the victrola, and silently mouthing the words. Hmm, I said to myself, this answers a lot of questions. I withdrew quietly and went on my way.

The second day of the feria saw Ordóñez on the cartel, but not Dominguín. The other matadors were Curro Girón and, once again, Jaime Ostos. I was beginning to learn more about Hemingway's interest in the Fiesta Nacional; to me, he was clearly a torerista, not a torista. For that matter, he was an ordoñecista and not really an aficionado. At least that's the way he came across to me.

Day two was hot and windy and the Valencia ring was only half full, something which irritated Papa in light of the fact that Antonio Ordóñez was on the bill. But once the thing got under way he forgot about all that. After the corrida he told me he thought that with his first bull Antonio had performed the "finest, most erect, most beautiful, complete and classical faena" he'd ever seen him make. On the kill, however, he had problems, requiring four pinchazos and one estocada. Papa shook his head and commented to me, "What they would've given him if he'd not hit bone on his first trip in, no one can say."

After the corrida Antonio and his men left town for Tudela, where they had a fight scheduled for the next day with Luis Miguel and Jaime Ostos, but Papa decided to stay in Valencia. After all, another corrida with Ordóñez and Dominguín -- plus Gregorio Sánchez -- was to take place right where we were, two days away. That one, we knew, would be lleno hasta la bandera. Hem pontificated that with the astronomical prices the empresarios were charging for the big corridas these days -- up to seven bucks American for the best barrera seats -- it now took both Ordóñez and Dominguín on a cartel to fill a plaza.

That night the cuadrilla -- Papa's gang -- went out to La Pepica for dinner. I kept a close watch for more black leather trenchcoat types, but nothing undue transpired.

The next day dawned cloudy and hot and remained that way through the corrida. At the plaza we said hello to Dr. Tapapas; he was usually present for any corrida in which both Ordóñez and Dominguín took part, and sometimes when only one of them was on the cartel. As an old friend of both, he had a personal interest.

A packed house was on hand for a change, to see what was arguably the best cartel of three matadors one could possibly compile, facing bulls of the respected ranch of Samuel Flores. But as far as Papa was concerned, Sánchez might as well have stayed home; while he was performing Hem seemed to spend all his time either talking to Ordóñez in the callejón, or trying to do so, ignoring the toledano in the ring completely. He did watch Dominguín perform, however; I could only guess at what he was thinking at those times.

Luis Miguel's first bull was un duro but the elegant matador stayed with it pretty well, killing it on his second try with the sword, for which he received an ovation. Then Ordóñez's first came out and he did a beautiful, classic job, cutting two ears. Papa was ecstatic.

Dominguín's second started out as though it was going to give us a good show, but the animal ran out of steam fast and Luis Miguel started doing "the telephone" and other such flashy stuff, trying to keep the crowd interested. But five pinchazos and a descabello made sure it all turned to doodoo.

Antonio's second toro was garbage and he killed it fast. End of corrida. The rondeño still went out a hombros.

We had another day between corridas, because neither Luis Miguel nor Antonio were on the cartel and Papa didn't want to go. Instead, we went out to a hunting lodge on the beach about thirty miles from Valencia and played American touch football -- that's a bitch in a trenchcoat, let me tell you -- and swam some, although Papa didn't venture out past the waves this time. On all our minds was only one thing: the big mano a mano the next day.

Day six of the feria: another hot, cloudy day was on hand, but the difference this time was that it was also very windy. Papa cursed like a sailor, saying, "Goddammit, Marlo (the two of us were alone at the time), I swear I'd take the torrents of spring over this obscenitying wind!"

The bulls were of Ignacio Sánchez and Báltazar Iban and proved to be a mixed bag. But even if they'd all been those "bulls on rails" Papa was always talking about it wouldn't have been easy, thanks to that horrible wind which blew off and on all day. And we saw it all at close hand, from the callejón. Luis Miguel's first bull gave him a decent faena in spite of it all, and the kill was okay. Antonio's leadoff toro provided an excellent faena, thanks in part to a lull in the breeze; good kill, one ear. Clearly, this was a competition of the first water, and Ordóñez was ahead at this point.

Dominguín, now up again with a Báltazar Iban, refused to place his own

118

banderillas but went on to perform a meritorious faena which, according to Papa, he then negated by doing "Manolete tricks." He killed with four pinchazos and one entera. While Luis Miguel was acknowledging his applause afterward, I asked Papa how many times he'd seen Manolete fight. He ignored me.

The sky had grown darker and the wind had picked up. "It's barbarous," Hem said, his eyes scanning the heavens. Then Antonio's second bull exited the toril. I thought it had casta and a fine set of horns, as well; Papa thought it "looked stupid." Those damned SAT scores again.

The sobresaliente for today's mano a mano was a young kid I'd never seen before, but by golly, there he'd been in the paseillo with Ordóñez and Dominguín, wearing a traje de luces that made him at least *look* like he might be on a par with the other two matadors. And that reminded me that Antonio had talked about me dressing out as the sobresaliente for one of these two-man shows; maybe I will after all, I said to myself. Then the kid asked Antonio if he could do a quite and was given permission. He went out into the ring and within seconds was flying through the air, horror on his face. I decided to rethink my future as a sobresaliente.

The near-gale made any artistic work by Ordóñez impossible. It was a tough faena and Antonio looked scared; he finished with the bull as soon as he could.

Dominguín's third and last toro of the day, a big red one, now appeared and the man who reckoned himself to still be el Número Uno went out into the arena. His brother-in-law was clearly worried, watching every move from the barrera. The first two tercios were carried out with a minimum of capework, and then it was muleta time.

About now the wind suddenly died for a few moments, and I used the opportunity to light up and blow a Rafael halo which, purely by chance, settled just over Antonio's head as he leaned on the barrera, looking out into the ring. Luis Miguel had just executed his first muleta pass, a derechazo, and was turning about for a second one when he happened to glance for just an instant at where we stood in the callejón. For some reason, he did a "double take," looking our way again -- at Antonio, it seemed -- and at that moment the bull's horn caught him in the belly. Up into the air he went, coming down with his crotch landing on the same horn. Screams and pandemonium. Antonio was over the barrera and running to Luis Miguel's aid, as was the cuadrilla. Within seconds the frantic rush through the callejón to the enfermería was on.

In the small, hot and humid room which served as the plaza's emergency hospital, chaos reigned. Dr. Tapapas was already in his white operating coat, but there were too many people in the place. Dominguín was placed on the operating table and Papa rushed up and bent over him. And while he was like that, leaning over Luis Miguel's prone form, Dr. Tapapas suddenly raised a scalpel high and came down with it fast, like someone preparing to chip away at a block of ice with an icepick. I reached out and yanked Papa back, holding him by the waist, with Dr.

Tapapas's knife barely missing Papa and plunging into the operating table between Luis Miguel's legs, only an inch from his bloody crotch.

"Move aside!" screamed a disturbingly frantic looking Dr. Tapapas. "I am trying to cut away the taleguilla so I can attend to the wounds!" He began doing just that. "And get all these people out of here!"

Papa looked rather shellshocked, so I approached a Guardia Civil and told him to clear the room. I guess he thought that I, in my trenchcoat and hat, was from Seguridad, because he obeyed without hesitation. Hem and I exited, too -- in time, as it turned out, to see the last part of Antonio's faena with Luis Miguel's bull.

The crowd was roaring as Ordóñez gave the red bull one pass after another, each one more beautiful than the one before. The horns were passing so close to his body as to appear to be touching it. Hem was quickly shouting that this was the most beautiful work he'd ever seen. Finally one pinchazo and one entera gave Ordóñez two ears.

Afterward we went to see Luis Miguel in the infirmary. We were relieved to find him awake and alert, despite the terrible pain. Dr. Tapapas, I noticed, wouldn't make eye contact with us.

Papa wished suerte to Luis Miguel, then told him we had to go, but the matador reached out toward him with his right hand. "Ernethto," he thaid -- I mean, said. "I -- I must ask you something."

Hem went closer. "What is it, Luis Miguel?" he asked.

"Ernethto --" he grimaced in pain, then went on -- "when I was beginning my faena, something caused me to look at Antonio behind the barrera. I do not know if my eyes were playing tricks on me, or what, but above his head I could clearly see a . . . a . . . *halo!* As though he were an angel!"

"Now, Luis Miguel . . ." Papa began, but he was cut off.

"No, no, I saw it! I could not help but stare at it. That is why the bull caught me. Ernethto, do you think this means . . . that God prefers Antonio to be el Número Uno? That he has somehow become the Annointed One?" The normally aloof, even arrogant man was frightened, beseeching Hem to say something that would make sense of his strange experience.

Papa looked down and shook his head. "A way you'll never be," he muttered, more to himself than to Luis Miguel.

Dominguín was taken to Madrid and the Hospital Ruber, the taurine medical facility, while Ordóñez flew off to Palma, Mallorca, for a corrida the following day. Some of our cuadrilla who had been together since Pamplona prepared to depart, including Mary Dos and Mary Tres. They came to my room to say goodbye, but this time we kept it a little calmer.

Chapter 14

Ordóñez the Hoofer

Three days later Papa and I were in the Ruber, visiting not just Luis Miguel on the first floor, but Antonio on the third floor, as well. The rondeño had been gored in the thigh in Palma, according to Antonio at a moment when his mind had wandered to a strange tale someone had told him shortly after Luis Miguel's goring -- that his brother-in-law was insisting that he'd seen a halo over his, Antonio's, head just before the cogida occurred. While Antonio's mind was distracted by this thought the bull caught him. So, really, this strange halo phenomenon was responsible for both of them being in the Ruber. What could it all mean? Ordóñez asked Papa. I looked at my shoes and didn't say anything, but I thought to myself: Damn that Rafael de Polo or Pahla or whatever it was the gypsy kid called himself, and his flat smoke rings!

We eventually said our goodbyes and left Antonio's private room, then passed through an open ward of wounded toreros in side-by-side beds. I saw an old banderillero I knew who called himself El Pulmón because he had only one lung, and damned if he hadn't been gored in it. Pale and gasping as he was, I stopped by his bed to cheer him up. I pulled out a pack of Camels and offered him one, but he weakly shook his head no, so I lit up, myself. I couldn't learn much from him, however, as he was coughing so much, so finally I just patted him on the arm and we left.

In the outer hall we saw Dr. Tapapas coming our way and Papa called out to him. The doc looked a bit shaken and stopped, then continued toward us, fumbling in his white coat pocket for something. We waited for him, and while we did, I blew a Rafael halo which settled over Papa's head.

Dr. Tapapas was looking down, trying to find something in his pocket, which he finally did, producing a gleaming scalpel. Then, moving quickly, as though he had finally made up his mind about something, he looked up at us and suddenly shot his right hand out -- the one with the scalpel in it -- straight toward Hemingway's throat. But at the last second he saw the halo above Papa's head and he froze, the point of the knife only inches from Hem's neck. Papa automatically recoiled with a stunned expression on his face, but it would've been too late had the doc not abruptly halted his lunge. Then Dr. Tapapas, still mesmerized by the smoke halo, began crossing himself and moving his lips, and he backed off, rather wild-eyed. He dropped the scalpel back into his pocket.

"What -- what's going on, Dr. Tapapas?" Hem asked somewhat shakily.

The doc seemed to "snap out of it" and put a hasty smile on his face, his hands clutching and opening nervously. "Oh, ah, Señor Papa, ha, ha," he said uncertainly, "I, ah, I -- I saw what I thought was a thread hanging from your collar, and I was going to cut it off for you. But I see now that there is no thread -- it was just a trick of the eyes." He then mumbled something and scurried away.

"A trick," Hem repeated. "A trick. Yes, Marlo, that's very possible. There are an awful lot of tricks to be seen these days." And with that we left the Ruber.

The mano a manos were supposed to resume in Malaga on August fourteenth, if the two matadors felt up to it. When Antonio got out of the hospital he came down to join us at the Davis's place in Malaga. He trained and regained his strength while Hem worked on some Paris "sketches" he was doing for *Life* magazine. Ordóñez saw me reading a paperback western called *Killers of the Pecos* and he started joking about it, calling me *El Pecas* ("Freckles"). Then he resumed talk of making me a sobresaliente, now insisting that I call myself that -- El Pecas -- and saying that we would "pull it off" on August seventeenth at the mano a mano in Ciudad Real, only four days away. "We probably couldn't get away with it in Malaga," Antonio said, "but I think we can in Ciudad Real." I quickly fished out a fag and lit it up. My hands were already shaking.

The following day was a mano a mano, as well, and from what I saw and what folks have been saying about the thing since it happened, it just may go down in the books as one of the greatest corridas of all time. Papa said it was just that and so did lots of others. The bulls were juampedros and four of them were superb. Even one of the not-so-good ones let itself be drawn out by Ordóñez and turned into something capable of taking part in a beautiful faena.

Dominguín's first was the worst of the entire lot. The less said, the better.

Ordóñez then went out and put on a performance with his own first bull which was textbook perfect in every respect, with sculptured passes and a screaming public. He cut two ears and saw a petition for the tail denied.

Luis Miguel was now playing catchup -- and he caught up. Beautiful naturales highlighted his faena, and a single entera assured him of two ears of his own. Then Antonio upped the ante by putting on a show that outdid his first and had the crowd going insane; this time he came away with nothing less than two ears and the tail -- and a hoof! My God, the place was a manicomio, and Antonio took his vuelta with both Luis Miguel and don Juan Pedro Domecq.

La Malagueta was still rocking when Dominguín's third bull exited the toril. He greeted it with a larga cambiada and the muchedumbre roared. With the muleta he sat on the estribo and passed the animal back and forth with his right hand, in a tanda which looked dangerous as hell to me but which Papa brushed aside with the comment, "It looks suicidal but it's only a trick." Yeah, sure. I've got a feeling that if Jesus had returned to earth and it turned out he looked like Luis Miguel, Hemingway would've said, "It all looks impressive, but it's just a trick."

Next Dominguín showed us eight spectacular naturales and he really had el público going. Ensconced behind a burladero in the callejón marked *Prensa*, I lit up and without thinking blew a Rafael halo which settled over Ordóñez' head, just like last time. ¡Carajo! I said to myself, then thought: Please don't look this way, Luis Miguel! But he did, right after his great tanda of naturales. When he should've been making sure the bull was fixed for the moment, he locked his gaze on Antonio behind the barrera, and that damned halo of smoke sitting just above his head. Dominguín's eyes grew wide and his mouth dropped open -- and the bull charged and hurled him into the air. Oh, no! I cried silently, covering my face with one hand and hurling my cigarette to the ground with the other.

When I heard a huge collective sigh and then applause, I peeked through my fingers. ¡Gracias a Dios! He wasn't hurt! Okay, I asked myself, what'll it be now? Molinetes or manoletinas? Because I knew that ninety percent of the time, when a matador comes through a cogida in good enough shape to continue his faena, the first pass he's going to do is either a molinete or a manoletina. It may not be great art, but it gets the crowd back into it and on his side fast. Well, Luis Miguel did molinetes *and* manoletinas and the spectators went wild. All except Papa, that is, who muttered something about cheap tricks. At sword time he went in hasta el puño and the bull fell. Pandemonium. Two ears, tail -- and hoof. Vuelta for the bull.

Holy Toledo, I thought, five bulls down and the score at his point was Dominguín: four ears and two tails -- Ordóñez: four ears, one tail and one hoof. I tried to remember: did two tails beat a tail and a hoof? Come on, I thought; this wasn't poker. Anyway, there was still one toro to go. It was of course Antonio's and after it had been in the ring for two or three minutes you could feel the disappointment setting in; the toro was a piece of crap. But instead of either demonstrating to the crowd how useless it was or just killing it to be done with it, as most would have done, Ordóñez went out there and taught it to be a bull. The faena developed beautifully and the crowd came back to life and was soon just as enthusiastic as before. The muletazos got better and better and el público got louder and louder. And then Antonio took the sword and went in all the way to the hilt, without even using his special Rincón de Ordóñez. The pandemonium we'd had earlier was doubled, if that was possible. The presidente ordered two ears cut. Then the tail. And then a hoof!

At corrida's end both matadors went out a hombros with Domecq's mayoral. The final total of appendages cut was ten ears, four tails and two hooves. Holy mother of God!

Chapter 15

Bulls in Frogland

I felt a little out of place in Bayonne. Unlike Papa, I was no good at frogspeak. Hell, I even had problems trying to read restaurant menus, so I just took Hem's suggestions, noting that he tended to avoid things from the menu's fifth column. He shrugged off my complaints with the words, "In another country."

But the corrida was the same. Not the crowd, but everything in the ring. And the two matadors on the cartel were the same: Luis Miguel Dominguín and Antonio Ordóñez, with a mixed bag of toros bravos. Or whatever the French call them.

Luis Miguel's first bull was difficult, and when he killed it -- in an okay manner, it seemed to me -- Papa commented that he had "faked a proper kill." Maybe so, but if he did, the bull went along with it and faked a proper death. In any case, he did a great job on his second and cut two ears; Papa said nothing. With his third toro Luis Miguel had no luck and Hem allowed as how he had "lost his security" and was "rapidly becoming tragic."

Antonio, on the other hand, had a superb afternoon, cutting six ears. Papa proclaimed that Ordóñez had "destroyed Luis Miguel mercilessly," describing the rondeño's display as "a performance no one fighting bulls could equal."

Thankfully, we left Bayonne and France immediately after the corrida and headed back to Spain. Upon arrival, the billboard with the big double-yoke-

and-bunched-arrows symbol of el Partido Falangista and the ejército español's sprawling motto *Todo por la Patria* actually looked welcoming after twenty-four hours in Frogland.

Chapter 16

Marlo, Sobresaliente

This was the day I'd been dreading. August seventeenth. Ciudad Real. Believe me, I tried everything I could think of to get out of the sobresaliente bit, but Antonio was cheerfully adamant. It was to be something like a bar mitzvah; I was to become mucho hombre this afternoon. In Ordóñez's hotel room beforehand, Miguelillo helped me get dressed in the ivory and black traje de luces Antonio had provided. I wasn't a thick type by any means, but I sure felt like I was, trying to wiggle into that outfit. Miguelillo gave me a rolled-up pair of medias to stuff into my taleguilla for my bulto, but I'd come prepared: I jammed a huge salami I'd picked up at a bar down in there. Finally I was ready and Antonio and Papa pronounced me to be as professional looking as any great matador de toros. Considering my spectacular bulto, maybe even better.

"A year in jail," was the answer to my question as to what the penalty was if I got caught masquerading as a torero. I swallowed hard.

At the bullring I kept to the shadows until the noises from the plaza told even me that the paseillo was upon us. Everybody else had already formed up -- Antonio and Luis Miguel in front, the cuadrillas, mounted picadors and the mozos behind -- leaving room for me three steps to the rear and between the two matadors. At the next-to-the-last second I appeared and took my place, not looking anywhere except at the ground. Suddenly I heard a sharp intake of breath from just in front of me, to the left.

"Hotch! You fool! You can't wear that!" Luis Miguel was shouting at me. Oh, crap, I thought, I knew it wouldn't work. He had turned and seen that while in the shadows I had donned my trenchcoat, putting it on over my traje de luces and topping my head with my fedora; I had to carry my montera in my hand, anyway, so there was room on my head for my usual hat. Antonio looked over his left shoulder at me and started laughing.

The gates were already swinging open, so it was with no time to spare that Dominguín's cuadrilla, responding to their boss's angry shouts of instruction, wrestled the coat and hat off me and tossed them aside. And then Luis Miguel saw that I had earlier, in the hotel room, slipped on my shoulder holster filled with my trusty Moxley .38. It made the right side of my chaquetilla bulge out and unless I held the embroidered seam close to my chest the gun butt was apparently easily visible.

"¡Una pistola!" Dominguín cried. "¡Díos y los santos! What in the name of -- Never mind! Hold your chaquetilla shut, for God's sake! And let's go!" And with that, as the banda taurina was already playing *Pan y Toros*, we commenced marching out into the plaza de toros de Ciudad Real.

I did as Luis Miguel told me and grasped my embroidered, vest-like attire together as best I could. Once the parade was over and I was behind the burladero I held my capote up in front of my chest. I was already sweating; I didn't like this torero business -- not from this side of the barrera, anyway. All I had to do now was pray that at least one of them, Luis Miguel or Antonio, made it through to the end. I kept cutting my eyes this way and that, looking for the fastest way out, in case neither of them did.

I'll be honest with you. I had my mind on things other than the artistic points of each bull, faena and kill -- at least until it was all over. I do remember that of six Gamero Cívicos, Dominguín cut one ear, while Ordóñez cut five ears, two tails and a hoof. At the end he invited his cuadrilla -- and me -- to take the vuelta with him. My relief was so great that I was grinning like an idiot as we circled the ring. At one point I almost pulled out my .38 and fired celebratory shots into the air, but, mercifully, I restrained myself.

Antonio instructed me to throw back all hats, coats, canes, etc., thrown into the ring during the vuelta, but to keep all ladies' handbags and shoes so that they would have to be reclaimed by their owners at the hotel later. The problem was that all the real babes throwing stuff into the ring threw flowers. I happened to *see* the three or four women who threw purses and shoes, so, unbeknownst to Antonio in front of me, I threw them back and saved him some agony.

Back at the hotel the dames in the lobby were all fighting to try to see Antonio and Luis Miguel, and one of them even played up to me. Still in my traje de luces, I was naturally taken for a real live torero, and the babe asked to see my scars. What the hell, I thought; I said okay and tried to undo my pants, but the taleguilla was on so tight I realized I couldn't get it off without Miguelillo's help. The chick seemed real disappointed and she kept staring at the bulge of the salami I'd jammed down in there earlier. "Too bad," I said, forgetting she didn't know it was a sausage, "we could've eaten it together." She gasped and hurried away. Probably just as well, I mused. When she'd seen my scar she probably would've asked where I'd received my goring or what ganadería the bull was from, and I'd've had to tell her the cicatriz was from a Jap bayonet on Guadalcanal. And that would no doubt have really confused her. That Jap's not confused, though; he's pushing up cherry blossoms these days.

Chapter 17

What Does Picasso Know?

From Ciudad Real we drove to Bilbao for the August feria. No more godawful flamingo pink English Ford: now we were really traveling in style, burning up the carretera in Hem's new Lancia with an Eyetie driver named Mario behind the wheel. I told myself, I guess if you buy a car this fancy, they throw in a driver. Bill Davis sat in the back with me, relieved of his chauffeur duties, while Papa sat up front. The powerful blue car had a horn to match, and Mario cheerfully blasted everything else off the road. Like Papa, Mario just talked, he never listened.

When we got to Bilbao it was a sizzler. Papa commented that it was "hot but not too hot and clear and the wide streets are beautiful." I muttered to myself that it was hot, yes -- too hot. And steamy. And to hell with the beautiful wide streets. My euphoria from having survived as a sobresaliente was wearing off.

We went to the corrida and had to sit in barrera seats instead of standing in the callejón, as Bilbao is a strict place. Hem didn't like that. Ordóñez was on the bill, but not Dominguín; the rondeño cut two ears per bull, which is the trophy maximum in this town.

The next day Luis Miguel was on the cartel while Antonio sat this one out. The fight was a disappointment and Papa kept talking about how Dominguín looked sad. "If he continues, he will be destroyed," Hem said.

Dr. Tapapas was there and I resolved to have a chat with him -- and to try to keep Papa away from him. Too many weird things had already happened in the kindly old doc's presence. If Hem had been alert to it, he'd have sworn the doc was a Fed. I didn't think so.

Ordóñez had another date without Dominguín booked for the feria, but it's not worth mentioning. The bulls were nada and so was the afternoon. Even Papa seemed distracted; he'd heard that Pablo Picasso still considered Luis Miguel to be el Número Uno and that really bugged him. "Goddammit, Marlo, what does Picasso know?" Hem growled. "He hasn't seen a bullfight in twenty-five years." Yeah, I thought, and it's probably been about that long since he last saw a woman he thought didn't have both eyes on the same side of her head, too. How on earth could anybody who perceived things that way possibly be in a position to judge who was Number One in bullfighting? Did you ever see that bull in his *Guernica* painting? Holy moley! Do you think that thing could ever have made it into Las Ventas? Or even into some hick town portátil, for that matter? Unh-uh.

On August 20th the last corrida of the temporada with both Dominguín and Ordóñez was scheduled; Jaime Ostos would be the third matador, and the bulls would be Palhas. The day started out rainy but later the sun came out and it was hot and muggy. Doña Carmen Polo de Franco, el Caudillo's old lady, was there in the president's box to see the show.

The first three toros were despatched, with Ordóñez and Ostos cutting one ear apiece. Dominguín did a bunch of desplantes and killed with a single estocada but won no trophy. Then at the break all three matadors went up to the prez's box and paid homage to Doña Carmen. I idly wondered what would've happened if the old bag had been taking a few nips and, just as a joke, pointed to the three toreros and squawked, "Off with their heads!"

I was still chuckling to myself at the thought while lighting up a Camel as Luis Miguel took on his second Palha. Off with their heads, I thought mischievously, unconsciously blowing a Rafael halo out toward the barrera from my front row seat next to Papa. Wait a minute! A Rafael halo! I looked for the smoke ring and saw it drifting out toward where Antonio was leaning on the fence watching his brother-in-law. Frantic, I jumped up and leaned out over the callejón, waving a hand at the receding circle of smoke, trying to break it up, but it was already too far out -- headed inexorably for the space just above Ordóñez's head. Damn!

Hemingway, not understanding, barked at me to sit down, and I reluctantly did so. Out in the ring Luis Miguel was performing a quite during the first tercio, and in the middle of it he glanced over at Antonio and saw the Rafael halo hovering over his head. Luis Miguel's face displayed that now-familiar look of shock and he neglected to refocus on the bull in time. A horn plunged into his groin and the bull tossed him high into the air. He came down on the same horn, and then the toro was chopping at his body on the sand as the cuadrilla rushed out to help.

Cursing silently, I yanked the pack of Camels from my pocket and threw it onto the concrete floor below my seat, where I stomped the thing flat in a fit of frustration. I'd give up weeds starting right now, so help me Hannah.

Luis Miguel was hauled off to the infirmary and Antonio finished the bull after an excellent faena. With his second scheduled toro, Ordóñez gave us a great show and then attempted to kill recibiendo but hit bone. He repeated, with the same result. His third recibiendo try went in hasta el puño.

That evening Hem wanted to visit Luis Miguel in the local hospital, prior to his being transferred to the Ruber in Madrid. When we got there we found him in great pain and feverishly babbling about Antonio being God's new favorite, and so we didn't stay long. On our way out we encountered Dr. Tapapas, who stopped in his tracks upon spotting us and cast a glance at a fire axe on the wall. As Papa rushed up to ask questions of the surgeon, I pulled back the right flaps of my trenchcoat and jacket, letting the doc get a glimpse of my rod in its shoulder holster. Dr. Tapapa's eyes bulged. He then answered Papa's questions rather absentmindedly, casting wary glances in my direction as he did so.

"He's a brave man and a beautiful matador," Papa said of Dominguín. "Why the hell do the good and the brave have to die before everyone else?" I figured Hem was speaking rhetorically, since Luis Miguel wasn't going to die. In fact, I figured he'd probably outlive Papa by thirty years or so. Maybe in his second sentence Hemingway was talking about himself.

I walked out of the hospital with Papa, then made up some tale about an errand I had to do. I said I'd meet him back at the hotel shortly. As Hem climbed into a taxi I went back into the hospital. I was going to have a little talk with old Doc Tapapas -- whether he wanted one or not.

I took a left, toward the doctors' private offices. As I did so I heard a commotion in the hallway going the other way, toward the patients' wards. I turned and saw two white-coated interns trying to restrain an hysterically screaming and thrashing auburn-haired woman.

"I'm here to take him home, dammit!" she screamed in American English. Ah, I thought, little Ava has arrived. I turned back the other way and proceeded to seek out Dr. Tapapas.

Chapter 18

Mario Gets His Pink Slip

On August 22nd Papa and Bill Davis packed Miss Mary and Annie off to the Davis place outside Malaga. Then Papa and Bill, along with Lorna Doone and me, were rocketed from Bilbao to St.-Jean-de-Luz in the Lancia, Mario behind the wheel, in what seemed like no more than a couple of minutes of driving time. There was, however, a lengthy stop at the border, where the Guardia Civil made us open the car's trunk and checked it out. Once again, Mario sat on the eardrum-shattering horn and blew all competing traffic off the road like dead leaves facing an industrial leaf blower on an autumn sidewalk. Ordóñez had a corrida in Dax the following day, but we'd be staying in the nearby beach resort.

Once again I felt a little ill at ease being in the Land of Frogs, but I decided to make the best use of my time. We all put up at the Hotel Chantaco, located a little way inland and outside the pretty oceanfront town of St.-Jean. After a few minutes I got a cab and went shopping while the others unpacked and got settled in.

I was back before long, loaded down with a dozen red roses and a big bottle wrapped up in brown paper and tied with string, the way the Europeans always do. Wonder why they don't just use paper bags like they do in the U.S.? Anyway, I put the stuff in my pad, then walked down the hall to Papa's room to check on plans for the evening. Hem had been telling us during our rocket ride from Bilbao about

133

this favorite place of his called the Bar Basque, where he said we'd eat that night. "In the old days the best place to eat Basque food and hear the Basque tongue was at the Bar Basque," Papa had said. "There, no one minded if you ate Basque food or spoke Basque."

Papa confirmed the dinner arrangements, proclaiming, "We will go to the Bar Basque where you can get Basque chorizo made of the cojones of wild Basques and the barman permits the old bullfighters that have no money to sit against the back wall and watch the poules and their johns that are laughing and bragging, and the food and the drinks are good and true."

We went to the Bar Basque -- Papa, Bill Davis, Lorna Doone, me and the garrulous Mario -- but I didn't see any old bullfighters or hookers with their johns. And I damned well wasn't going to eat any of that chorizo. As far as people speaking Basque was concerned, maybe they were, but it could've been French, too. Hell, it was all Greek to me. And the food *was* good. True, too, I guess. It sure wasn't false.

During the dinner I managed a few private words with the raven-haired Lorna Doone, who looked particularly luscious on this night. She agreed to my suggestion. Then we turned back to the single source of conversation at the table and listened to Papa telling us about Gertrude Stein and F. Scott Fitzgerald and Ford Madox Ford and Ezra Pound and Nick Adams and a gambler and a nun and a radio.

Finally we finished and went back to the hotel. Once there Hemingway took me aside and told me that as the mano a mano season was finished and the Dax corrida would be the last of his stay, he would on the following day be going to Malaga and from there he and Miss Mary would return to the U.S. by ship. I had done a good job as a bodyguard, he said, but he wouldn't need me after Dax. He felt he'd be okay with Bill back to Malaga. I said fine.

I went straight to my room and collected the dozen roses and the bottle-shaped brown paper package, stuffing the latter into a pocket of my trenchcoat, then headed down the hallway toward Lorna Doone's room. As I walked, I did a little leap into the air and clicked my heels together. "Hoot, mon!" I cried. I was in good spirits, despite the fact that I would shortly be out of a job. And then . . . ?

Chapter 19

Papa Is Ambushed

The Dax corrida proved to be a big letdown. It was a lackluster affair and Antonio wasn't on his form. What a way to wind up a summer of corridas, I said to myself. Ordóñez left town immediately after the fight, first bidding Papa and the rest of us farewell. Papa now confirmed that my period of employment was over; he thanked me for my services and said he'd send a check to my Madrid office for what he owed me. He then leaned close and whispered in my ear, "Marlo, I know that if you hadn't been with me all the time as you have been, the Feds would've gotten me by now. I am in your debt." Turning to Bill Davis, he asked his old friend to drive me to the train station in Hendaye, on the French side of the border with Spain; I got my bag and Bill drove me the few miles in the Lancia; I asked what had happened to Mario.

"Papa canned him," Davis replied, his eyes on the road.

"Why?" I asked. "Because of his reckless driving?"

"Nope," Bill answered, still facing straight ahead as he drove. "He said he couldn't stand someone who talked all the time and tried to monopolize the conversation."

"Oh . . . yeah. Sure," I said. "I feel the same way."

Bill cast a glance at me but didn't say anything. Mario getting the boot didn't bother me one little bit. I didn't like his driving or his talking, but I also didn't trust him. While passing Hem's room at the hotel in Bilbao one evening, I had encountered Mario slipping out the door. He'd smiled big and babbled something about looking for some misplaced ravioli or something, then hurried off down the hall. Funny guy.

At the station Davis let me out, shook hands with me and bade me au revoir, then drove off. I waited a couple of minutes, then went into a car rental agency there at the station and hired the smallest job they had, a tiny Citroën 2cv, a car which I swear to God looked like it had been put together using flattened tuna fish cans. I put my bag in the back, then drove back to the hotel in St.-Jean, where Papa had said he'd be for another hour or so before leaving for Malaga.

Near the Hotel Chantaco I parked behind some bushes, backed in so I could tail the Lancia when it left. In about forty minutes it roared by, Davis at the wheel and Papa next to him. No one was in the back seat. I pulled out and followed, keeping a discreet distance. Thank God Davis was driving and not Mario, I said to myself. If the Eyetie had been behind the wheel, my little deux cheveaux would've been left behind like it was sitting still. My piece of junk had a lot of shortcomings, but one very big advantage it had was that it looked like every second or third car on the French highways. The real reason I'd chosen this model, however, was because I was cheap.

But even with the more mild-mannered Bill Davis behind the wheel of the Lancia, I started losing ground fast. About a kilometer or two before our small back road fed into Route 10, the main highway to Biarritz to the north and Hendaye to the south, I could still see the Lancia up ahead, but just barely. Well enough, though, to see that something had gone bad wrong. The big Italian car was fishtailing in the road, and then it appeared to come to a stop on the shoulder, maybe in a shallow ditch. Another car, black in color, was blocking the way just ahead of the Lancia, parked sideways across the two narrow lanes. I stomped the gas pedal of the Citroën and tried to narrow the gap as fast as I could. It looked to me like Papa had terminated my services a bit prematurely.

By the time I was maybe 200 yards away from the two cars I could hear gunshots. Lots of them. Four men in black leather trenchcoats had piled out of the black car and were shooting at what I thought at first was Papa and Bill in the Lancia but which turned out to be someone hidden in some trees and bushes off to the left side of the road. Whoever the guys in the bushes were, they were sure as hell good shots; a black trenchcoat stumbled and fell to the tarmac, then a second.

I stopped the 2cv and got out, pistol in hand, running for the cover of a low stone wall. I peeked over the top and took a gander in time to see a third black trenchcoat go down in the road. At that moment Papa's Lancia, obviously still driveable by Davis, lurched back onto the road, stopped, and roared off with loud squeals and a cloud of white smoke from burning tires, nicking the front end of the black car and bumping it aside as Papa and Davis passed it on the shoulder of the road and hightailed it for the main highway. The last remaining black trenchcoat guy raised his pistol and took aim at the retreating Lancia, but before he could squeeze off a shot he was knocked backward against his own car by yet another shot from the bushes to the left, dropping his gun and grabbing his shoulder. He then staggered to the driver's door of what I now recognized as a Spanish-built Seat with Madrid plates, got in and scratched off, also in the direction of the main highway. But I knew that without his gun and wounded as he was, he no longer posed a threat to Papa and Bill. And besides, that Seat could never catch the Lancia. He had to be a Sección Trece agent and he'd undoubtedly be running for cover back in Spain, only eight or nine kilometers away. Funny, I mused, but under that black leather fedora, that guy had resembled Papa's ex-driver, Mario. In any case, shot or not, if he could get past the French authorities at the border, *that* guy wouldn't have any trouble crossing into Spain.

I stood up from behind my stone wall cover and at that moment heard a loud engine start up. Lorna Doone, wearing a red jacket and pants outfit and goggles, her hair under a red scarf tied tightly beneath her chin, edged out onto the road astride a motorcycle. She was reloading, putting a fresh magazine into what looked like a 9mm Tokarev automatic. She smacked the clip into the gun's butt with the palm of her left hand and with her right hand waved the pistol at me in a sort of salute. Then she gunned the cycle and roared off in the direction of the others. I just stood there, my own rod hanging from my left hand down alongside my leg, my mouth dangling open like the village idiot's.

I got back in the 2cv, drove to the car rental place in Hendaye and turned it in, then walked across the border to Irun and boarded a train for Madrid.

Chapter 20

Hemingway Pays Off

I was in my office overlooking the Calle Victoria. The window was open but it was like an oven in there in late August, and under my trenchcoat I was sweating like hell. At least I'd taken my hat off, but when I'd tried to toss it onto the hat rack in the corner I'd missed, and the fedora was lying on the floor where it had landed, upside down. Crap, I thought: all my luck floating out and going up to the ceiling. I was taking a slug of Magno from a brand new bottle, but I resisted poking around in my desk drawer for a pack of fags, remembering the vow I'd made after blowing that Rafael halo in Bilbao. I went through my mail, pitching three or four long overdue bills into the trash can, unopened; then I came across a letter sent by Papa from Malaga two days earlier. Slitting it open with one of those little souvenir Toledo swords they sell all over Madrid, I extracted a letter and a check. I looked at the check first: it appeared to be made out for a lot more than I was actually due, based on my regular rate of 500 pesetas ($8.47 U.S.) per day, plus expenses. Then I read the letter:

Dear Marlo,

Even though you were no longer in my employ, I know it had to be you who

138

saved Bill and me at that ambush by the Feds outside St.-Jean. I am doubling the amount you said I owed you, as you will see from the enclosed check. Miss Mary and I are going home now. While this summer was good and clean and true, it certainly turned out to be dangerous as well. I will close now. Suerte to you there in the capital of the world.

Con abrazos,
Papa

P.S. Just like in Ronda.

I pitched the letter into the round file and slipped the check into a coat pocket, then propped my feet up on the desk. Maybe that'll make the phone ring, with a new client on the other end of the line, I thought wishfully. But the telephone didn't ring; instead, the door to my outer office opened and through the frosted glass in the top half of the door leading into my private office I could see the hulking shapes of two men in hats and trenchcoats. "Mierda," I mumbled.

I swung my legs off the desk just as the two mustachioed Seguridad men -- the same two who'd called on me before, here in my office -- let themselves into my inner sanctum without knocking. "Come in, señores," I said, rather superflously.

The one who had done all the talking before did so again. "Señor Marlo, you are to come with us. Coronel Medidas is waiting." I picked my hat up off the floor and we went.

Chapter 21

Marlo Reveals All

I'd never been in the colonel's own digs before, and they were pretty snappy, except for a big picture of a constipated-looking Generalísimo Franco hanging behind him on the wall. The colonel bade me sit down in a big chair covered with tooled cordoban leather; he remained seated behind his desk, which was only a tad smaller than the aircraft carrier *USS Yorktown.* He waved his two agents out of the room, then spoke to me, toying with a pencil as he did so.

"So, Señor Marlo Shamus, the Red Hemingway has left for los Estados Unidos. If he had any nefarious plans with España as his target, he apparently either failed or got cold feet, eh? Now tell me everything. Oh, and Señor Marlo" -- the colonel's eyebrows went up but his eyelids remained half shut, in an expression of weary tolerance -- "please do not waste my time and yours with any of those fanciful tales you told my men upon your return to Madrid from Pamplona. About Señor Hemingway being a CIA agent and the matador Curro heading up a spy ring, or whatever nonsense it was you gave them. When they reported it to me, I recognized it immediately for what it was: a clumsy attempt to get them to report back to me as fast they could, thus, at least temporarily, getting them off your back. Am I not correct?" His eyebrows went even further up, awaiting my answer.

"Ah, well, you see . . ." I began, leaning forward and searching for a cigarette pack which wasn't there.

"The truth, Marlo!" snapped the dapper colonel, now frowning.

"Uh . . . yeah," I said, squirming a bit. "Yeah, I needed more time, and I couldn't work with those mugs breathing down my neck."

"Yes, and I allowed you that time," replied Colonel Medidas. "Now please be so kind as to let me have your complete report here and now. At its conclusion I will decide whether to permit you to resume your amusing little private investigator job or to return you to the jail of the Policía Taurina. Or to have you shot. Or, even worse, to turn you over to the gentle care of Colonel Herculo Descolorado and his men of Sección Trece." He paused, then said, "Your report?"

"Yeah . . ." I said, my mouth involuntarily twitching, Bogey-style. "Okay, here it is, unvarnished. Just the facts. The truth. Good, clean and true, as Papa -- er, Hemingway -- would say."

I told him all about our various encounters with the black leather trenchcoated agents of Sección Trece -- even my telephone conversation with one of them -- and how I hadn't been responsible for any of their deaths, that as far as I knew, all of their casualties had been imposed by the mysterious babe we called Lorna Doone. I said it didn't take an Einstein to figure out that the Sección Trece boys were trying to rub out Hemingway, using methods left over from the days just prior to the outbreak of the Spanish Civil War in 1936, when anarchy ruled. Unfortunately for them, they were pitifully inept, failing repeatedly. "I guess that's what you would expect, though, when one does one's recruiting in Neanderthal country," I said.

A ghost of a smile flitted across Colonel Medidas's face, then he said, "Marlo, who is this mysterious Señorita Doone? What part did she play in all of this? I believe I know, but I would like to hear what you have to say."

I cleared my throat and told him. "The so-called 'Lorna Doone' is a Communist agent working for the new Castro regime in Cuba. You see, Castro doesn't give a flip, personally, for Hemingway, but he sees him as being very valuable to the newly emerging socialist state in the Caribbean. He wants him to be associated with Cuba; he's a part-time resident of Cuba, a great international figure, a famous writer, a Nobel Prize winner -- *and* a highly-touted anti-Fascist, based on his days pushing the republican cause during your civil war. Somehow Castro got wind of a plot by Sección Trece -- loose mouths among Colonel Descolorado's goons, surely, maybe communicating with friends or relatives living in Cuba -- to kill Hemingway when he came to Spain for the Dominguín-Ordóñez mano a manos this summer. He sent his best agent, this 'Lorna Doone' chick, to protect him. And, brother, did she! She's a true professional, colonel. She probably shadowed Hemingway until he boarded his ship back to the U.S. My fedora's off to her."

Colonel Medidas frowned and toyed with his pencil some more. "How do you know all this, Marlo Shamus?" he asked.

141

"Simple," I replied. "She told me. Told me everything. Her real name's Chiquita Fiona Urqfart. Cuban mother, Scottish father, born in Scotland but has lived in both countries, back and forth, all her life. When Castro started making big noise as a utopian revolutionary, this idealistic girl joined up with his guerilla bunch while ostensibly continuing her professional work, that of the Caribbean "stringer" for a Scottish newspaper, *The Daily Haggis*, I think it is. Castro took her on and gave her a second job as an undercover agent for revolutionary Cuba."

"How, when did you suspect her, Marlo?" the colonel asked, obviously fascinated.

"Oh, lots of things didn't wash," I said, "and I was already kind of suspicous. But the clincher was one night at the hotel in Valencia. I was walking down the hall, past the door of two girls in Hemingway's entourage everybody called Mary Dos and Mary Tres -- I'll come to them in a minute -- and heard music coming from their room. I knew the two Marys weren't in the hotel at that particular moment. I also knew they had a record player and a bunch of American pop records, but the record I heard being played was of a song sung in *Russian*. I peeked through a crack in the door and saw 'Lorna' singing and dancing in there, all by herself, and the record she was playing and enjoying so much was -- now get this, colonel -- the song I just happen to know was -- and still is -- the number one hit in the Soviet Union: *Wake the Town and Kill the People!*"

Colonel Medidas sat back in his chair, horror on his face. "No!" he protested.

"Yes, colonel," I said. "Yes, I'm afraid so. Well, anybody who could get hold of *that* record -- and would actually *listen* to it, and sing and *dance* to it -- *had* to be a Red, wouldn't you say?"

"*¡Ay! ¡Por supuesto!*" the security boss gasped, pulling a handkerchief from his coat pocket and mopping his forehead and the back of his neck with it. Then he frowned, put away the handkerchief and said, "But, look here, Marlo, I can understand you eavesdropping and learning something about this . . . this 'Lorna' creature. But you said she *told* you all those other things. How is this possible? Why would she do that?"

My mouth twitched and I said, "The last night we were in St.-Jean, the night before the Sección Trece bozos tried their ambush, I went to Lorna's room with a dozen roses and a bottle of hooch. I'd started to get champagne but then remembered *Wake the Town and Kill the People* in Russian and instead got a liter of vodka. Like that American writer dame Dorothy Parker said, 'Candy is dandy but liquor is quicker.' One thing led to another. And, huh, huh . . . another. Yeah, she spilled the beans, all right. And more." I smiled and closed my eyes at the thought.

"But, Marlo!" Medidas almost shouted. "If this 'Lorna Doone' was such a highly trained, professional Red agent as you say, why would she give in to your rather obvious ploy? Flowers? Liquor? With a nation's secrets at stake?"

I smiled an even bigger smile. "She's still a dame, colonel. I just turned on the old Marlo charm, you see." I winked at him.

The colonel exhaled loudly and slowly. "Yes," he finally said, "I see. And now she has no doubt gone back to Scotland or Cuba. Well, that's probably the end of her, as far as we're concerned, although we'll keep a lookout for her. What about those two other women you mentioned?

"Mary Dos and Mary Tres?" I asked, feeling on safer ground now that the colonel seemed to be accepting my story, which was of course true. "I suspected them from pretty early on as being a couple of CIA agents, and Lorna confirmed that to me on -- er -- our big night. Apparently they were just a couple of bimbos and they blabbed all their secrets to their 'new friend,' while playing rock-n-roll records and drinking brandy. Lorna told me she'd learned they had a twofold mission: to keep an eye on the ex-commie sympathizer Hemingway during this touchy period of the Cold War, and to check out reports that a commie agent -- Lorna Doone herself, unbeknownst to them -- had infiltrated Papa's -- er, Hemingway's -- retinue. This was correct, of course, and they even tried pumping me for info one night, but they ended up never really knowing what was going on or doing anything about it.

"Their 'chance' appearance in Pamplona," I went on, "was staged. They, or more likely their bosses, knew Hemingway would take two good-looking babes into his 'cuadrilla' in a New York minute, so when they saw Ordóñez 'passing' automobiles in the Plaza del Castillo, they made their move. They'd ridden down from Paris with another CIA agent, a temporarily unassigned spy plane pilot named Francis Gary Powers, and he was the one who drove the car and then gladly 'got lost' when Hemingway told him to beat it and took the two babes into his group. The same two girls later joined in on the shootout with the Sección Trece boys at the Irati River, but they didn't really know who was good or bad -- they just wanted to fire their new snubnose Colt .38s at somebody, and when Lorna started shooting, so did they, although they didn't hit anybody. Lorna told me on that last night that she'd heard the two have already quit the CIA and gone to Hollywood, where they're supposedly currently undergoing -- er -- probing discussions I guess you could say, with a TV producer about starring in a show about airhead chick secret agents or something like that, to be called *Charlie's Angels*. But those in the know say that such a development is really several years down the road, and in the meantime all Marys Dos y Tres will be doing is, uh, providing inspiration to the producer. By the way, I don't know how Lorna learned all this, but it probably came from Moscow by way of Havana." I sat back in my chair.

"There was something about the taurine surgeon, Dr. Tapapas," Colonel Medidas said, obviously disinterested in the Hollywood careers of the Mary bimbos.

"Yeah," I said, "there certainly was. I couldn't understand why every time

Hemingway went near the guy there seemed to be a near miss with an accident involving a scalpel. I paid a visit to the doc in Bilbao and, uh, shall we say, encouraged him to talk. Dr. Tapapas, I confirmed, is not a brave man. What he did was out of desperation. It seems our old buddy Colonel Descolorado had the doc's son, a university student, picked up recently and put in one of the Generalísimo's detention camps for Reds. He told the doc that if he ever wanted to see his son again, he'd have to see that an 'accident' resulted in Hemingway's death. Descolorado knew that Tapapas and Hemingway would be coming into contact with each other several times during the summer of mano a manos since the doc followed Ordóñez and Dominguín around, and he used the situation to his own advantage. But the taurine surgeon's attempts were clumsy; he was scared out of his wits and worried sick. Maybe the jefe of Sección Trece will let the Tapapas kid go, now that Hemingway's left the country and the doc can't stage any more of his goofy scalpel tricks.

"The bottom line, colonel," I continued, "is that Ernest Hemingway is no threat to Spain or anybody else -- except maybe himself. He may have spouted a lot of republican propaganda in the past, but I can tell you he's about as political these days as a picador's horse. He really was here in Spain only to see the mano a manos -- that and to try to relive some things from his past. His only involvement with any government agents are with those of his own country, the FBI, and that's imagined. He's paranoid, colonel. But, like they say, just because you're paranoid, it doesn't mean they're *not* out to get you, ha, ha."

Medidas didn't even smile.

"There's only one person in this whole equation I'm not sure about," I said, getting serious again, "and that's the Italian driver who came with that new Lancia Hemingway had delivered from Milano recently. He got fired right there at the end, but I'd been suspicious about him."

Colonel Medidas was silent for a moment, then said, "Señor Marlo, I will tell you something I probably shouldn't. In any case, even if you did repeat it, we would deny it -- and then see that you paid for your indiscretion. The driver Mario was working for Sección Trece. His father was among the Italian troops sent to Spain by Mussolini during our war, to fight the Reds. The son has spent much time here in our country and was enlisted by Colonel Descolorado. We know that his assignment was to deliver the Red Hemingway to Sección Trece, which he was going to do upon your return to Spain from France. But when his position was abruptly terminated, Colonel Descolorado decided to stage an ambush in France and assassinate the Red Hemingway there, beyond the borders of Spain, to avoid any tie-in with the Spanish authorities. Obviously, the attempt failed."

"Um," I mumbled. "Obviously."

Colonel Medidas sat pensively for a few moments, holding his hands together, Dürer style. Then he spoke. "Señor Marlo Shamus, I am letting you go. There is nothing you have done which has harmed España and you have, in fact, actually helped us by revealing what you know. There is little we can do about Sección Trece at this time, but we will remain vigilant. I will see to it that your previous sentence by the Taurine Police is expunged from the official records. You can return to your work as a private investigator. Of course, if you get yourself in trouble in the future as the result of some other actions you perpetrate, I cannot help you."

"Of course," I said, getting up out of the tooled leather chair and trying not to show the immense relief I felt. I shook hands with the colonel and left the Seguridad offices, whistling *Get a Job*.

Chapter 22

A Despedida for Marlo

I took another slug of Magno and put my feet on my desk, then groped around in my pockets for a pack of cigarettes until I again remembered the vow I'd made after Dominguín's last goring. I sighed.

All in all, it had been a good summer for Felipe Marlo Shamus, Private Investigator for the Mundillo Taurino. I'd gotten out of the jail of the Taurine Police and gone back to work, earning good money. I'd eaten and drunk well, thanks to Papa. Also thanks to him, I'd hobnobbed with a famous taurine writer and top level matadors and seen a lot of corridas from the callejón or barrera sombra seats. I'd ended my celibacy period, had my earlier jail sentence wiped out, and I was back in business, free and clear, with a nice little roll of U.S. greenbacks as a stash. Yeah, things could be worse.

I thought about Papa. I honestly didn't believe he'd forget his promise to face a bull of some sort by his 62nd birthday on July 21, 1961. He'd sworn to me on the grave of his father that he'd do it if he was still alive. Fear of that pending deadline wouldn't push him into doing something stupid, would it? Nah, surely not. But in the back of my mind was a nagging worry that maybe I shouldn't have shown him that bit with the shotgun. Oh, hell, I then said to myself, that's silly. I took another belt of Magno.

Then I heard the outer office door open. Hey, business maybe, I thought. I got out of the squeaky swivel chair and went to the connecting door, opening it. I groaned. Two guys in trenchcoats. The same two that had been driving that loudspeaker van down the Calle Victoria promoting the novillada a few weeks back. One a little mayoral type, the other a big, ex-picador type. No mustaches. The Taurine Police.

"Señor Marlo," the little guy addressed me.

"Yeah?" I said warily.

"Señor Marlo, the last time we spoke, you were told you would have no trouble as long as you followed the Reglamento."

"That's right," I replied. I didn't like this.

"Señor Marlo, it has come to our attention that on the 17th of August you participated illegally in a corrida de toros, a mano a mano, in Ciudad Real, dressed as a torero and taking part in the paseillo and, in fact, passing yourself off as the sobresaliente. Do you know what the penalty is for masquerading as a torero, Señor Marlo?"

"A year in jail," I murmured to myself. "Oh, Jesus."

"Come with us, please, Señor Marlo," said the small guy, as the big one came around and with a huge meathook gripped my left arm like a vise.

We walked out of my office, the three of us.

Acknowledgments

Thanks to Gil Arruda and Judy Nadelson, as well as Beatriz Itoiz Chartón of the Archivo Casa Misericordia de Pamplona, for invaluable help in researching the factual Pamplona corrida portions of this piece; the old gray matter can only retain so much without help. The faux Hemingway story of the valpolicella killers is by Hugh Hosch and is taken from *The Best of Bad Hemingway, Volume II*, copyright 1991 by Harcourt Brace Jovanovich, New York. Oh, by the way, while I have tried to make the corrida reports presented herein essentially accurate, as well as the dates, the chronology of events and places visited, much of *Felipe Marlo's Dangerous Summer* is fictional and any resemblance to actual persons living or dead is -- ha, ha -- purely coincidental.

Felipe Marlo in Blood and Carmen

Editor's Note

Just as the following story was being prepared for publication, some disturbing reports of a seemingly metaphysical nature were made public, indicating that Prosper Mérimée and Georges Bizet, writer and composer of *Carmen*, and Vicente Blasco Ibáñez, author of *Blood and Sand*, had all three actually rolled over in their graves. It is not known if the pending publication of this story had any bearing on these developments.

Chapter 1

Marlo's Arrival in Sevilla

I stood in front of Sevilla's Estación de Córdoba, the main railroad station, my beat-up B-4 bag in hand, and gazed around at the busy scene. It was Monday, April 25, 1960, and the city's Feria de Abril was in full swing. Although the fairgrounds were a little way off to the south and across the river, a few people in feria dress could be seen here and there; a caballero in black traje corto and a snazzy dame in a frilly manola dress of white with red polkadots rode their horses amidst the tiny Seat 600s -- the Spanish-built Fiats -- the black Mercedes taxis and the flower-garlanded horsedrawn carriages. Beyond and to my right, beyond la Plaza de la Legión, the bridge spanning the Guadalquivir to the Triana side and the road to Huelva was busy with both vehicular and pedestrian traffic, the usual rush before the siesta hour set in and shut everything down like the slamming of the toril gate. It was good to be back in Sevilla.

Best of all, of course, it was good to be walking the sidewalks of a Spanish city as a free man again. And for Spain's only taurine private investigator, being there in the número uno city of Andalucía at feria time -- with all my expenses covered and a temporary income, to boot -- was especially gratifying.

Plastered onto the reddish-brown brick facade of the station was a colorful cartel promoting the corridas for this year's spring feria at La Maestranza. I stopped and studied the poster for a minute or so, noting that the schedule called for appearances by bulls of Miura, Concha y Sierra, Nuñez Manso, Benítez Cubero, Sánchez Cobaleda, Pinohermoso, and Albamadera. Appearing in some of the seven corridas de toros would be Antonio Ordóñez, generally recognized as Spain's top dog these days, as well as the Venezuelan phenomenon Curro Girón, Diego Puerta, and Sevilla's controversial young Curro Romero. Also scheduled to be seen were the rejóneador brothers Angel and Rafael Peralta, plus foot soldiers Chicuelo, Manuel Vázquez, José Julio, Mondeño and Antonio Cobos. Most were scheduled for two appearances each. There were two other matadors, neither of whom I'd seen, both of them with recent alternativas. The junior of the two, with two appearances (including the one on the final day of the feria) was the somewhat brutish-looking -- yet at the same time not unattractive -- Quinn Helado, known by his apodo, Escamopayo, while the only diestro with four corridas this feria was the current toast of Sevilla, the darkly handsome Tirón Poder. Indeed, it was the movie-star-like countenance of Poder which dominated the cartel pasted to the station's wall. As I say, I'd never seen him, but I planned to while I was in town.

Sometimes Spanish ferias ended with a performance of toreros enanitos, and I was glad to note that this year there'd be no such event staged; I've always felt that putting on a show with dwarf bullfighters is somehow belittling. In addition to the seven corridas referred to, however, there was one other event on the program, a novillada, but I'd already missed it, as it had taken place the day before. It had featured the gypsy kid from Jerez de la Frontera, Rafael de Paula.

I checked my watch: a little before one. After siesta I had a meeting with my new employer, Don Pedro Albamadera Semental, to discuss the job I'd come to do. I had plenty of time to find a place to stay before looking up Don Pedro. I turned left and headed east into the center, noting a few more foreign tourists than I'd been expecting to see. Old Félix, my turnkey at the taurine prison, had told me that with Franco's latest devaluation of the peseta, a Spain which had already been incredibly cheap for foreigners -- and especially estadounidenses -- was now virtually free for them: a modest room for the night for twenty-five cents U.S. , a good enough meal with wine and dessert, forty cents. Not bad. Unfortunately, any dough I earned was in pesetas.

Walking along the Avenida Generalísimo Franco I saw a group of college-age girls who were unmistakably American: cashmere sweaters, tight skirts to the knees, white socks rolled up past the ankles and -- the clincher -- freshly-shaved, well-tanned legs. Only U.S. chicks had those tanned, smooth gams; European babes hadn't discovered the wonders of Gillette yet and remained fuzzy to behold below the hemline -- and under the arms, as well. Well, what the hell, they were all still dames, weren't they? And after the better part of a year in the pokey, believe me, I wasn't picky.

I found a cheap pensión just off Sierpes and checked in. Yeah, and I'd occupied a hard, wooden seat in Third Class on the train down from Madrid, too. Me and nine other people, including three screaming brats, all crammed into the eight-seat compartment. I still had a little of Don Pedro's advance money left, and while I figured to get more, it seemed to me that being frugal for a while yet would be playing it smart. It'd leave me enough pesetas to eat and drink in a style to which I sincerely hoped I'd once again become accustomed.

I unpacked my bag in my tiny room with its single lightbulb hanging by a cord from the ceiling and a view of some tiled rooftops from its only window, then cleaned up as best I could at the washstand with its white-enameled bowl of galvanized iron and water pitcher to match, including the dents and blue-black chipped edges. It was good to get the black grit off the back of my neck, a reminder of the soot-bellowing locomotive which had pulled the train down from the capital at a speed of at least thirty miles an hour over an uneven, bouncing track, and with some of the cars' windows at least partially open.

Now, sporting a fresh white shirt under my trenchcoat and with my fedora perched on my head at a properly jaunty angle, brim pulled down, I went out again into the streets of Sevilla. It was time for nourishment. At a corner news kiosk adjacent to a souvenir shop for tourists on Sierpes I noted several foreign newspapers. This was generally the case these days, although once in a while the news reported from outside España was not to the Generalísimo's liking and the foreign editions would disappear for a spell. Spanish papers were of course always heavily censored. I smiled when I saw the airmail edition of the *Daily Telegraph* from London, as this was my favorite paper. Not for its news content, but because its tissue-weight pages (fewer ounces for its shipment via air) served as a far more comfortable source of toilet paper than did that awful gray crepe paper stuff you found on rolls in Spanish bathrooms -- if you found anything at all, that is. This item, at least, was no deal: I paid the newsdealer the import price of fifteen pesetas, well in excess of its thruppence cost back in Old Blighty. I folded it and slipped it into a pocket of my trenchcoat for future use. Who knew? I might even read part of it. I also looked for a copy of today's *ABC*, fresh off an earlier train from Madrid; even there, I knew, the Sevilla feria would be of interest and would be written up in the *Toros* section. Then the vendor reminded me that *ABC* didn't publish on Mondays.

I went into a small taurine bodega on Calle Alvarez Quintero, leaned against the bar with a Magno in front of me and opened up my copy of the *Daily Telegraph.* There was a photograph of the Queen with twelve-year-old Bonnie Prince Charlie at some event, but I found I couldn't concentrate on the printed words, as my mind kept calling up mental images of the past few days.

Chapter 2

Marlo Is Sprung

Maybe I'd better give you a little background before I go any further. Only a few days earlier, yours truly, Felipe Marlo Shamus, the world's only private investigator for the mundillo taurino, born in Mexico as the son of a Mexican torero cómico and an Irish washerwoman named Kathleen Shamus Marlo, but raised from age thirteen onward in L.A., subsequently a "bullfight P. I." in the Bogey style, after following -- although somewhat obliquely -- in the joint footsteps of father and screen idol, had been Prisionero Número 3665 Marlo, Felipe, of La Prisión Taurina de la Virgen de la Macarena in Madrid. I'd been there since the previous August, eight months past, jailed by the taurine police -- or rejailed, to be more precise -- this time for impersonating a torero during a caper while I was on the payroll of "Papa" Hemingway during the so-called "Dangerous Summer" of 1959, when I saved old Hem's posterior on several occasions. Since the penalty mandated for such an offense was a year in the can, I still had four more months to go when old Félix the ex-picador appeared at my cell door on Good Friday, April 15, and unexpectedly unlocked it, swung it open and, with a sort of crude derechazo gesture indicated that I was to come out.

"¿Qué pasa, Félix?" I asked, sitting up on my bunk.

"Getcha hat 'n' coat, shamus," he growled. "You're outa here!"

"Huh?" I flipped my cigarette away and stood up.

"Sí, no mierda, cuate," shrugged the big guy, who really wasn't a bad sort. "The Generalísimo's granted an Easter amnesty to lots of guys all over España who're servin' time, to show el público what a sweet old guy he is. No Reds, o'course, and no really tough types, neither. But guys like you -- pimps, brawlers, deadbeats, torero impersonators -- olé! You're free to go!"

And so I grabbed my trenchcoat and fedora from off the single peg in my cell wall and, after a mess of paperwork in an office, walked out into the April sunshine, a free man. I had collected my previous belongings, which consisted of my keys, my wallet still with the 2,000 pesetas in it (worth $34.00 U.S. when I went in, but only a little over $29.00 now, after the recent devaluation), and, amazingly, my Spanish Moxley .38 revolver and shoulder holster, for which I had a permit -- still good, I noted, for two more months. The only reason I was able to get the permit in the first place -- for that matter, to become a taurine P.I. in Spain -- was because Franco, like his old buddy Adolf, liked American movies (only Franco liked los toros, too), and my resemblance to Humphrey Bogart prompted him to have all the usual barriers removed, allowing me to set myself up in business in Madrid in 1958. Except that I'd spent more time in the taurine hoosegow, for two separate fiascos, than I'd spent actually plying my trade. Ah, well. I wasn't surprised that my money hadn't been filched from my wallet -- nobody, not even prison guards, stole money in Franco's Spain, not petty cash, anyway -- but about my rod, yeah. I wasn't a felon, so I guess they figured it was okay. Well, by managing my stash carefully, I mused, I ought to be able to get by for a couple of weeks. After that . . .?

I thought I'd probably be wasting my time, but I headed for my old office in the Calle Victoria, just off the Puerta del Sol, anyway. The building at No. 9 looked the same: seedy as ever, the orange and blue striped awning still out over the sidewalk, Las Ventas empresario Don Lavinio Stuyck's offices still on the second floor, taurine cartels still posted on the edifice's front wall. I climbed the dark stairwell to the third floor and walked down the dingy corridor to my old office door. The lettering, even more peeling than was the case the last time I'd seen it, still read,

FELIPE MARLO SHAMUS
INVESTIGADOR PRIVADO
PARA EL MUNDILLO TAURINO

I tried my key in the lock and it opened with a creaking of hinges. Yet unrented, huh? Well, I knew the economy had been bad and that the devaluation was supposed to pull in more tourist money for the country, but I guessed the new good times hadn't penetrated this far yet. I walked to the door to my inner office, went in and sat down in my squeaky swivel chair. I hefted a new half liter bottle of Magno out of my trenchcoat pocket and uncorked it. Then, as I'd been pounding the pavements and my dogs were killing me, I put them up on the dust-covered desk and tipped the brim of my fedora back a little with the mouth of the bottle and looked at the old fashioned stand-up telephone with its earpiece hanging on its hook, just to the right of my crossed ankles. In the old days, when I was lucky, this was when it would ring and there'd be somebody on the other end who needed my services.

The telephone rang shrilly. It startled me so much I tipped over backward in the loose-springed swivel chair and crashed to the floor, spilling brandy all over me. I scrambled to my feet, hastily setting the now half-empty bottle on the desk and grabbing for the phone like a suddenly capote-less banderillero lunging for a burladero with a Miura in hot pursuit. I was dumbfounded: the thing was still hooked up! I supposed the Telefónica -- never known for its speed -- had just never gotten around to cutting off my service since I'd paid my last bill.

I gripped the shaft of the instrument with my right hand and ripped the earpiece from its hook with my left, jamming the black bakelite receiver to my ear.

"Marlo!" I snarled.

A cultured servant's voice on the other end of a crackly wire advised me that he was calling from Sevilla on behalf of Don Pedro Albamadera Semental, the ganadero. Don Pedro understood that I was -- ah -- now at liberty to possibly offer my services in a delicate matter involving the mundillo taurino, and would I be available to come to Sevilla and do some work for him? If I agreed, he would have a Madrid associate call on me next Tuesday, the day after Easter Monday, and provide me with an advance of funds sufficient for me to make the trip and get checked in at a hotel, preparatory to being interviewed by the rancher himself. As Don Pedro would be entertaining a number of relatives and guests from out of town during Easter Week, the first opportunity for our meeting would be just over a week away, on Monday the twenty-fifth. My standard fee and any reasonable expenses would be guaranteed. Was I interested?

"You bet your sweet --" I shouted, then coughed and, modulating my voice, cooed, "Why, yes, that would be most acceptable." We murmured our goodbyes and I gently replaced the receiver on its hook. Then I threw out my arms and cried, "Whoooooeeeee!"

Marlo was back in business!

Chapter 3

Marlo Meets Don Pedro

Hombre, you're on top of the mundo, I told myself as I walked down Sevilla's broad, tree-lined Avenida José Antonio. The fresh, yellow-green leaves proclaimed spring to be here -- as did the sunny and mild weather. It was still okay for a trenchcoat and hat at this time of the year; it was the heat of summertime I hated, when my, er, official togs, I guess you could say, made me sweat like a picador's horse in the ring of Ecija, "the frying pan of Spain."

I walked alongside the huge old cathedral and headed into the Barrio Santa Cruz, the oldest part of Sevilla, bound for Don Pedro's city house. My appointment was for six p.m. I understood from the well-heeled young señorito who had delivered my cash advance to me at my office in Madrid the past Tuesday -- enough, incidentally, for me to pay my back rent and another month on top, as well as settle my overdue phone bill -- that his employer normally spent most of his time at his ranch outside Sevilla, where he raised toros bravos of the celebrated Albamadera hierro, but that during Semana Santa, Easter and the Feria de Abril he came into town for a few weeks.

I checked the address once more, noting yet again that it was near the Church of San Esteban. As I walked through the narrow, winding streets of Santa Cruz, now almost completely in shadow, I took in the ornate, grilled windows and geranium-filled flower pots everywhere, and from the occasional open door or window -- the majority were shut tight -- I could hear the languid strumming of a guitar or the gurgling of a patio fountain. Once I heard a young woman singing about corazones y amor. Everything was so still and quiet and peaceful that it seemed like a Sunday afternoon. Yeah -- but if I'd been back in L.A. at this time on a Sunday, I would've had my radio tuned in to Mandell Kramer in *Yours Truly, Johnny Dollar*. Johnny was a good "eye," he was hip -- he wore a trenchcoat, too. Or maybe I would've been sitting in the bleachers in the top of the ninth inning of a Dodgers game, with Larry Sherry pitching a no-hitter. I'd gone to the park a few times since the Bums had moved out from Brooklyn, just before I left the U.S. and came to Spain two years earlier. Hey, they'd won the World Series last year, hadn't they?

Snap out of it, Marlo, I said to myself, Sherlockingly adding, the game is afoot! Then I mused: what game? Baseball? Football? Afoot: must be football. Ah, to hell with it. I walked on.

Don Pedro's city house, when I found it with the help of a white-jacketed traffic cop with a pith helmet to match, looked more like an archbishopric than a private home. While almost all houses in Sevilla face directly onto the street, with unseen courtyards beyond, Don Pedro's place had a ten-foot wall along the street side, covered with bougainvillea and with a fancy grilled gate in the center. Behind the wall a small garden preceded the big house itself, a whopper built of yellowish stone with barred windows and flower boxes, and a red tile roof. Beside the front gate was a button to press. It was hooked up to an electric line, I supposed, but it was so old it looked as though it might have operated one of Torquemada's auto-da-fé machines in the sixteenth century. If Spain had electricity then, that is. I pushed it.

In a minute or so a distinguished looking old bird with silver hair and wearing a black frocktailed coat opened the big front door of the house and came out to the gate. I identified myself and, obviously expecting me, he showed me inside and led me through the very dark and cool interior to a bright inner patio filled with ferns, potted palms and flowers. An old man, very thin but ramrod straight, was sitting in a wheelchair, his legs covered with a laprobe. Beside him was a small table of wrought iron, covered with medicine bottles and drinking glasses.

"Señor Marlo, Don Pedro," the manservant said to his boss. I now recognized his voice as the person I'd first spoken with by telephone about the job.

The geezer in the wheelchair gestured toward a wrought iron chair opposite him and spoke to me without offering me a smile. "Por favor, Señor Marlo, take a seat. Can I offer you an aperativo?"

I sat down, twirling my fedora in my hands. "Uh, yeah, sure," I said. "How about a Magno?"

Don Pedro's mouth twitched and he looked at the butler or valet or whatever he was. "Bring Señor Marlo a Napoleon brandy, Recto," he commanded. Recto bowed and left, presumably for the 144-kilometer underground labyrinth of cellars filled with wine and coñac storage racks, or wherever it was the Napoleon brandy was kept. I was starting to like this job already. I pulled out a Camel and lit up.

Almost before I could clear my throat and venture some small talk, Recto was back with my drink on a silver tray. I accepted it with a "Say . . . thanks, pal!" I lifted the snifter in a toast to Don Pedro, then froze.

"Ah . . . you're not drinking, Don Pedro?" I asked.

He tossed his head in a gesture of resignation. "Alas, my dear Marlo," he said, "my doctors no longer permit me any pleasures. No alcohol, no tobacco, no rich foods. Women -- I speak of sexual partners -- are also in the past for me. Sometimes I think that if it were not for my concern for Carmen, I should prefer to go on to my reward -- whatever it might be. But please go ahead and indulge yourself; at least I can try to enjoy such things vicariously." I shrugged and blew smoke in his face, then chugged down the Nappy in one go.

"Not bad," I said, putting my glass on a small table next to my chair. Don Pedro signalled to a nearby Recto to bring me a refill. I was in hog heaven, having a swell time; I wasn't sure why, but I felt almost like I was really Bogey in a flick of a Raymond Chandler story. But I had to satisfy my curiosity about something.

Leaning forward as I sat on the iron chair, still twiddling with my fedora, I looked at Don Pedro and posed a question. "Uh, if I might ask, sir, how exactly did you hear about me?"

Don Pedro looked me in the eyes and said, "You come highly recommended to me by an American I happen to know and respect through our mutual interest in the bulls -- one Señor Bill Davis of La Consula, near Málaga. He told me of the fine job you did last year, protecting the writer Hemingway during his so-called verano peligroso. He also explained to me how the antics of Antonio Ordóñez -- insisting you dress in a traje de luces and appear as the supposed sobresaliente in the ring at Ciudad Real during his mano a mano there with Luís Miguel -- resulted in your being arested and jailed by the taurine police, for impersonating a torero. When I had Recto check into your status some days back, shortly after speaking with my friend Davis, I learned that you had just been released from the taurine prison. I delayed your arrival here in Sevilla until now as I have had Easter guests -- but also because someone I want you to keep an eye on for me has been away fulfilling contracts and has only today returned to Sevilla for the feria.

"I see," I said. "But why did you want me for this job? A half Mex, half gringo? There must be local guys you could hire."

Don Pedro looked at me sternly. "No one I could trust," he said. "At least none with your skills and knowledge of el mundillo taurino -- and who is truly neutral, with no ties to anyone or any government agency. No, Señor Marlo, you are the man I want for the job at hand."

"Yeah," I finally said, then went on: "Say, Don Pedro, who is this Carmen you mentioned a minute ago?"

He smiled a small smile and nodded, his thin hands forming a steeple. "Ah yes. Carmen. Carmen is why you are here, Marlo. Sit back and I will tell you all about it." And he commenced to do just that.

But first he told me about himself and his family. The name Albamadera, he said, was almost as old as Spain itself, absolutely reeking with pundonor and all that kind of stuff. His grandfather's great-great grandfather (I think I got that right), also named Pedro, is supposed to have been a hero of the Peninsular War against Napoleon in the early nineteenth century, personally shooting dead the infamous French aristocrat Jurque de Bonaparte, a cousin of Napoleon, sent to rule over Southern Spain from Sevilla.

The modern day Don Pedro was acknowledged as one of the country's leading ganaderos, his ranch called, simply, Albamadera, located some kilometers out of Sevilla, on the banks of the Guadalquivir. There Don Pedro and his late lamented esposa Doña Dolores Hachabatalla de Albamadera had lived quasiblissfully until her death some twelve years earlier. They had not been blessed with loving children, Don Pedro said. Then he frowned and cleared his throat. There was something he supposed he'd better clarify for me, he said.

It seems that Señora Albamadera and he *had* had a child many years ago, a son whom they named Bajamadera -- apparently a related family name -- and who grew up wanting to become a stage actor in the classic mold, doing serious stuff like Lope de Vega, Tirso de Molina, and so on. But before too long the thespian wannabee was considered by most theatre-goers to be nothing but a "ham," and the young man grew aware of this. Shortly thereafter, adding to his parents' concerns, Bajamadera Albamadera became possessed by the Devil. Don Pedro and his wife, both very devout Catholics, were beside themselves.

Don Pedro had his own contacts among the clerical hierarchy, and he had a full-time exorcist brought in from Rome. The special priest performed an elaborate exorcism ceremony and the son was shortly declared to be free of possession. Everybody was happy, and the imported priest returned to the Vatican.

And then the unthinkable happened. The Devil came back and, like a car dealer working with a deadbeat, repossessed the ham actor. The kid then disappeared-- ran off to spread his deviltry elsewhere, apparently -- and Don Pedro and his wife chose to let the matter drop, writing their son off as a lost cause, a nonperson, though they were desolate.

I thought about what Don Pedro had told me. What a pisser, I said to myself. You got a kid with a stupid first name to start with -- Bajamadera means Underwood in English -- who turns out to be nothing more than a ham actor, and he gets possessed by the Devil. Not only possessed, but exorcised and then repossessed! Who would've ever thought of the Devil as a repo man? But he sure was in the case of poor old Underwood, the bedeviled ham.

Anyway, as a result of all that and Doña Dolores passing away soon afterward, Don Pedro was left all alone. There was of course Recto and the household staff, as well as his mayoral and the ranch hands, but . . .

Then one day ten years ago Don Pedro was at a horse auction and he saw a delightful little gypsy girl of some nine years, who was being mistreated terribly by her most disreputable parents. Wanting to spare the child the misery and brutality she was obviously experiencing, and desirous of filling a void in his own life, Don Pedro over a period of time -- with the aid of money, of course -- persuaded the niña's parents to let him adopt her. Thus Carmen, the little gypsy girl, came into his life. Don Pedro was a happy man.

But not for long. By the time Carmen was twelve, he found he was having to watch her like a hawk, lest she -- well, do the wrong things. But try as he did, he could not make the girl do his bidding. From the very beginning, clothing proper for a young señorita of an upstanding family was eschewed by Carmen in favor of gypsy attire and no shoes. She slipped out of school, or, if guarded, simply daydreamed through classes or made eyes with boys. Soon cigarettes were being smoked, at first surreptitiously, then openly. Then came Coca-Cola. And finally -- here Don Pedro covered his face with a hand for a moment -- that estadounidense abomination, chewing gum! I clucked and shook my head in sympathy for the old coot.

But, wait! There was more. Oh, yes. Carmen had always flirted with the young men, but Don Pedro had thus far been able to control them through threats or money. But now she had met one with whom those tactics would not work, for he was famous and supposedly had plenty of his own money. If it were someone who could be bought off, why, he would be willing to spend any sum to be rid of the fellow. Regrettably, the muchacho in question, while indisputably handsome, was an ignoramus who was totally without culture and who could not, in fact, even read or write his own name. Why, he actually thought a blistering opinion of him written by that fat blowhard critic Faraón -- the one who was always saying, "I, Faraón, say it!", was a flattering piece -- until Carmen read it correctly to him.

And what *was* this matador's name? I asked. (Here Don Pedro sighed and paused before continuing.) He was the newest taurine sensation, the recently alternativa-ed hotshot, Tirón Poder, who would be appearing in not two, not three, but *four* corridas during this year's spring feria at La Maestranza -- more than anyone else. He had a large house there in Sevilla, of which he had taken possession recently. He lived there with his mother, whom he referred to as "Mama." Carmen had stars in her eyes, and nothing Don Pedro could say or do would sway her from her infatuation with this torero.

At this point I interrupted to ask how she happened to meet this Poder character. I was told the relationship dated back a long time, to a period about two years after Don Pedro had adopted Carmen. Young Tirón, then a lad of fourteen and thus some three years her senior, was already determined to become a matador de toros. Sometimes at night he would swim the river and pass Don Pedro's prize Miuras with an old cloth for a while before the ranch hands could arrive on the scene and break it up, seizing and pummeling the kid. On other nights, he would serenade Carmen from below the balcony of her room, sending her into swoons with promises that he would go off to Madrid as a maletilla, along with some other little would-be torero ruffians he called "his cuadrilla," to return as a matador and to marry her. And return as a matador he did, although the process took eight years, during which time Carmen heard nothing from him. When he did come back earlier this month, after taking his alternativa in some pueblo outside Madrid and with a few startling triumphs already under his faja, it was as a conquering hero: local boy makes good, returns to his home town to conquer it, as well. His former "cuadrilla" returned with him, and one of them, Quinn Helado, Escamopayo, did so as a full matador, as well. Poder looked up Carmen and she fell for him all over again.

I held up a hand as Don Pedro paused to swallow a pill, followed by some water. "Uh, just a question, Don Pedro," I said. "What's this about the kid swimming the river and then caping *Miuras* on your ranch? What were you doing with Miuras? Your hierro is Albamadera."

The old one looked somewhat perplexed and shrugged, mumbling something about it all being Blasco Ibáñez's idea, or words to that effect. Before I could say anything further, he had resumed his tale, catalogueing the many times of late during which Carmen had slipped out of the house -- despite all his precautions against such behavior -- to join young Poder in activity which was almost assuredly unsavory and a degradation to the name of Albamadera.

Now Don Pedro paused and smacked the arm of his wheelchair with the palm of his right hand, causing Recto to take a step or two in his direction, before retreating to his post behind a potted palm. Not noticing, el viejo recommenced his monologue. He'd lived around toreros all his life, he said, and damned if he wanted his adopted daughter ruining her life with one of that lot. Life with a torero was sure to bring her only grief, in any one of many forms -- possibly all.

The old don was silent a moment, then went on. But that wasn't everything, he sighed. No, there was more. I was of course aware of the Spanish government's ongoing battle with Red subversives, he stated, looking at me for confirmation. Sure, I replied; who wasn't? Well, Don Pedro continued, it seemed that this Poder character was mixed up with a bad lot. And why not? His family had been Red sympathizers during the civil war, just as had been the families of his "cuadrilla" and his other close friends. Despite the smiting down of the Red rabble in the war by the hand of Dios -- as carried out by his servant Francisco Franco -- there were still ingrates to be found in España, many of them actively plotting against the regime. It was Don Pedro's belief that Tirón Poder and, most likely, his entire cuadrilla, were active supporters of the Red underground movement. Poder -- and, he acknowledged with resignation -- Carmen as well, tended to hang out at the big tobacco factory there in the middle of Sevilla, and Don Pedro had it on good authority that many of the factory workers were Reds involved in some kind of illegal activities and/or incipient plot. If Poder got hauled in by the police as a result of his connection with these Reds, fine. But Don Pedro was terrified that Carmen would be taken in with him, and this he would not tolerate.

In the meantime, the police could not be counted on to just be sitting on their hands. They, too, must certainly be aware of the festering situation at the tobacco factory. If he, Don Pedro, knew of it, then they would, too. And with Carmen hanging out around the place like it was the corner soda shop or something -- well, Don Pedro was very concerned.

The old man began coughing and Recto instantly reappeared from behind his palm plant to assist him with pills and water. I used the break to sit back and mull things over. Yeah, I knew only too well from my experiences how touchy the Spanish cops were on the subject of Reds. Only the other day old Félix was laughing about the government changing the name of the kiddie story to *Little Blue Riding Hood.* Blue, of course, was the color of the Falangist Party, so it was okay. Then I imagined all story, song and movie titles "corrected" accordingly: *Blue Sails in the Sunset, The Blue Badge of Courage, Blue Planet Mars, The Blue Shoes, Blue Stallion, Blue River Valley, My Love Is Like a Blue, Blue Rose . . .* ah, the possibilities were endless.

I snapped out of my reverie as Recto withdrew once more. I spoke. "So as I understand it, Don Pedro, you are worried about your adopted daughter Carmen, age nineteen, deepening her involvement with this matador Tirón Poder."

"Correct, señor," the old guy confirmed.

"But what do you want me to do about it? If your words have little or no effect on her, what can I hope to acomplish?"

Don Pedro cleared his throat. "I want you to keep a close eye on her, Marlo," he said, frowning. "And I want you to try to break up her affair with young Poder, if that is possible. If it turns out after all that money will do it, go ahead and offer him whatever it takes. Be sure to report back to me what she and that scoundrel Poder -- and their disreputable associates -- are up to. If necessary, intervene to prevent her being apprehended by the police, should it come to that. I don't want to forcibly remove Carmen from the scene, but, por Dios, if that is what it takes to protect her . . . "

"Mmmm," I said, lighting another Camel and this time blowing the smoke up toward the purpling andaluz sky. Then I spoke to him about what was worrying me. "Look, Don Pedro, I want this job. I mean, I *really* want this job -- but, frankly, I don't see how I'm going to be able to keep an eye on Carmen and Poder without attracting the wrong kind of attention. I"m not exactly your typical sevillano."

"I have thought that one out," said the don. "Señor Davis outlined to me the ruse you used in the Hemingway case last year. As I understand it, you explained your presence among the writer's entourage as being another author who was a friend of Señor Papa. Your, er, somewhat unorthodox -- for España, at any rate -- attire was attributed to the strange whims of an eccentric foreign writer. Am I correct?"

"Uh, yeah, I guess so," I said, a little uncomfortable with the way in which he had made my P.I. outfit of trenchcoat and fedora sound sort of goofy.

"Fine," said Don Pedro. "Then I do not see why you should not do the same this time, too. But use a different false name, in case anyone in the mundillo remembers reading anything from last year with the other name in it. This time you can be an American correspondent interested in writing about Tirón Poder, the great new sensation. A reporter, perhaps for the newsletter of Los Aficionados de Los Angeles, a California peña I have heard about. And I believe Hollywood is a part of that city. That should help to explain your taste in clothing. You know Los Angeles; it should be very easy for you."

"Yeah," I mumbled, thinking. He was right. "But like you say, I'll need a new monicker. Name."

"May I suggest something which will, to sevillanos, sound like a Hollywood name? That should complete the ruse."

"Uh, like what?" I asked guardedly.

"I was thinking of something like . . . Rock Dean," Don Pedro said. At long last, a big smile creased his face.

Chapter 4

Garbaje Info

Business was moderate a bit later that evening in the cavernous old taurine bar called El Bodegón Torre Ador, two or three blocks from La Maestranza in the Calle Santander. A good stone's throw down the street was the river and one of Sevilla's landmarks, the ancient Moorish structure known as the Golden Tower. A vastly larger crowd would be on hand about this time tomorrow night, I knew, since "an extraordinary corrida de toros" -- one outside the abono but still part of the general feria scene -- would have ended shortly before. And hundreds of aficionados would proceed directly here from the bullring, at somewhere between eight and eight-thirty, since all the corridas began at five-thirty.

I got a Magno at the long bar made of dark wood and took it to a small table off to the side. I was fixed for geetus now, as Don Pedro had instructed Recto to give me a thick envelope which contained not only a substantial advance in pesetas, but also entradas for all six of the remaining corridas. In fact, I had missed only one corrida, an Easter Sunday affair with seven bulls of Concha y Sierra for the horseman Don Rafael Peralta, Curro Girón, Chicuelo and Antonio Cobos. This had been the first time since 1940 that toros of this ranch had appeared in the Feria de Abril, and I was told they'd looked good, although the only ear cut that day was by Peralta. Then there was the novillada on Sunday, the day of my arrival, with animals of Don Juan de Dios Pareja Obregón for Curro Montes, Limeño and the gypsy kid de Paula. No ears cut in that one, the local papers said. De Paula had complained of his last bull giving him the evil eye.

I pulled out the tickets and thumbed through the stack, once again shaking my head in wonder: all barrera sombra sobre los capotes, one of the best seats in the house. Not because Don Pedro wanted me to have the most enjoyable viewing of the corridas possible, Recto had explained to me; rather, I had the seat next to Carmen's, the tickets for which were similarly provided by Don Pedro, and she would surely be there on the four days Poder was on the cartel. This would make it easy for me to keep her in sight, as well as giving me the perfect opportunity to introduce myself to her. As to the other two corridas for which I was given tickets, the ones without Poder, well, as Recto said, I might as well have them, too, since they were after all part of the abono -- and his employer would not be attending any performances this year. In other words, I had Don Pedro's own tickets. Wow!

And now here I was at the joint Sevilla's most ardent taurinos patronized before and after corridas -- including, I was to learn, surprisingly large numbers of British and American aficionados who really knew their stuff. As for tonight, I was hoping a certain member of Poder's retinue, his mozo de estoques, would show up. As prompted earlier by Don Pedro, Recto gave me the man's name and suggested I tell Raúl, one of the bartenders here, that I was a reporter and would like to interview the fellow immediately, and that there were plenty of free drinks in it for him if he showed. Raúl obviously passed the word -- for which service I of course greased his palm -- and shortly after nine a little old fellow appeared in the bar and Raúl pointed me out to him. He came over, a sort of semi-ragamuffin twisting his gorra in his hands, and I recognized him from decades-old photos. This was the celebrated ex-matador de toros, the former gran figura known then, as now, by his apodo: Garbaje. Except that nowadays no one remembered his real name. From the looks of him, I wondered if he did, himself. Garbaje had seen better times.

"Señor Dean?" he asked, almost groveling. I looked over my shoulder to see who he was talking to, then remembered that I was Rock Dean, writer. I turned back around and said yes, that's me, and I shook his hand, bade him sit down, and bought him his first of many derechos of Gin Rivas. He bought my story of being a writer, without qualms.

"And what books has the señor written?" he asked obsequiously, between swallows. "Perhaps I would have heard of one or more of them."

Well, this took me by surprise, so I had to think fast. "Uh," I finally blurted, "are you familiar with, er, *Frijole Winds?*"

"Frijole Winds?" His face was blank. Then, suddenly, he was all grins. He had made a decision. "Oh! *Frijole Winds!* Of course! A wonderful book! Marvelous!" He kept nodding and smiling, and it was all I could do to keep a

straight face. Then, too late, I remembered that I was supposed to be a reporter for the Los Aficionados de Los Angeles newsletter. Oh, well. I bought him another gin and asked a few reporter-type questions before I ventured into other realms. Garbaje wanted to know if my book on Poder would include lots of pictures, explaining that his boss really liked pictures. I'll bet he does, I said to myself, if the klutz can't read.

A couple of hours later I was no longer able to understand what old Garbaje was saying -- if he was really speaking at all, and not just making barnyard-like noises. Then his forehead hit the table and even the grunts and whinnies ceased. But it was okay -- I'd gotten lots of good info, thanks to Don Pedro's expense funds. I now knew that Tirón Poder, the matador referred to these days by the great taurine critic Faraón as "the first man of the world" ("Just as he used to call me, long ago," Garbaje had whimpered) was, in fact, in the running for Meanest Man in the World -- in the dickensian sense of being cruelly cheap and stingy. Neither he, Garbaje, nor the cuadrilla had been paid their full wages for the past year, while Poder himself squandered money and ran up I.O.U.s for clothes, cars and women. His peón de confianza, the banderillero Carradino, was, Garbaje said, disgusted with it all and talking of leaving not just the cuadrilla, but the mundillo itself.

At one point during my "interview" with Garbaje, the present-day swordhandler grabbed my wrist across the small table and hissed at me to look toward the entrance of the bar. There, a stunningly beautiful, barefoot gypsy girl in a scarlet manola dress and with a red carnation in her long, blue-black hair was laughing, smoking and flirting with several rough-looking young hotdogs. The girl called out to the bartender Raúl, asking him if he'd seen Tirón this evening, to which the barman said no. Then the party swirled back out the door and disappeared down the street, their shouts and laughter growing fainter. Garbaje then explained to me that I had just seen Carmen Albamadera, the adopted daughter of Don Pedro and the novia of his jefe, Poder. Holy moley, I said to myself. What a dish! This Carmen chick compared to other Spanish women like an habanero pepper did to a garbanzo. ¡Carajo!

Chapter 5

Enter Doña Luna

At last: Tuesday, April twenty-sixth, my first corrida. Not just of the feria, but since I'd gotten out of jail. I was ready!

Today's espectáculo at La Maestranza was the one outside of the abono and would include the dons Angel and Rafael Peralta horsing around in what seemed to me a bully-boy act with a single toro, while Manolo Vázquez, Curro Romero and Tirón Poder were lined up to face two bulls each, with all seven of the astados being from the ranch of Don Carlos Núñez Manso of Sevilla. What a crappy deal for a ganadero, I said to myself, to have Manso as part of your herd's handle. I hoped the bulls didn't live up to their name.

I cursed myself for not having kept a closer eye on the time, as the magic hour of 5:30 approached. I'd gone by the chapel where the toreros go to pray prior to all corridas, and there I'd seen and heard the firecracker Carmen, in a similar yet different red gypsy dress to that of last night, standing rather than kneeling before the statue of la Virgen de la Macarena. Her lovely legs were akimbo and she was shaking a pointing index finger at the figure and shouting that she -- la Virgen -- had damned well better protect her Tirón this afternoon, or there'd be hell to pay. Whew! Tough babe, I thought. I crossed myself, just for insurance, and backed out of the place.

168

At a little bar tucked under the tendidos I became embroiled in a conversation with a short, almost rotund young fellow from Granada who called himself Diamante Rubio, and who told me he was a novillero, but peddling canes and other souvenirs at the moment. He looked and sounded like a big bullfrog with choppers. He had blondish hair, teeth like a picket fence and a voice like a foghorn, which he employed to tell me he worked all the ferias of Andalucía -- when he wasn't appearing in novilladas, that was. He was looking forward to seeing Poder today. As long as I kept buying him Magnos -- with the help, of course, of Don Pedro's expense money -- he kept socializing with me. When I looked at my watch and saw it was 5:25, I groaned. I knew the challenge which surely awaited me, trying to get to my asiento in this ancient bullring boasting the tiniest seats (and leg room) in Christendom -- and no aisles. And on a day when the plaza would be full hasta la bandera. Aiiiieeee!

Peering over the crush of latecomers at the top-of-the-stairs doorway opening onto the plaza -- which already appeared to be totally filled -- I could see where my seat should be, down below and to the left. But how the hell was I going to get to it? People who had been savvy enough to come early had been seated a long time and were now P.-O.'ed at all those who had already climbed all over them while trying to get to *their* seats. By this stage, with the toque sounded -- exclusively by clarines, in the sevillana tradition (no timbales are used for toques in La Maestranza) -- announcing the commencement of the event, nobody was willing to move any more. Not one centimeter.

"Nuts!" I shouted, pushing my way between two seated sevillanos wearing suits and ties. This wasn't just a pleasure outing for me, this was my job! I had to get to my seat! The señores began yelling at me that I'd waited too late, and for me to get the hell out of there; they pushed back against my attempts to get through and said some pretty lousy things about my dear, departed mother. Finally, in frustration, I reached under the flap of my trenchcoat and pulled out my .38, shoving it up one of the guys' noses and barking for him and his pal to get the hell out of my way or I'd blow their obscenitying brains to las Islas Canarias. Well, that worked. Men yelled at me -- until they saw the gun -- and women screamed, as I shoved people aside and tromped on feet, but the racket was pretty well covered up by the applause for the alguacilillos, now in the ring, and I heard no complaints. Nobody shouted for the cops or the Guardia Civil (seated as a bloc on the sol side); almost assuredly, they thought I was one of Franco's boys from Seguridad, since those guys favored the same form of dress as me.

Finally jamming myself down into my microseat, I was struck by two realizations. First, I was the only spectator in the plaza wearing a trenchcoat and fedora, and, second, on my left side I was tightly but pleasantly squeezed against Carmen. Cheek to cheek, I guess you could say. She turned and glared at me, first in the face, then taking in my hat and coat, and finally back to my face.

I lifted my fedora to her. "Hiya, babe." I said, in what I hoped was my most charming and debonair manner. She frowned and looked away, throwing her head back and sniffing disdainfully. She loves me, I told myself.

On the other side of Carmen was a mustachioed fat guy whose face I recognized from one of the local newspapers: Faraón, the taurine critic for said rag. Wearing a derby hat, he was puffing on a big stogie and was acknowledging with waves of a plump, ring-festooned hand the greetings being shouted to him from here and there

Then I noticed that the two barrera seats on the other side of Faraón were empty -- on this day of "no hay billetes!" What on earth? At that moment two things happened: the paseillo began, and She made her grand entrance.

The crowd was applauding the toreros and the banda taurina was playing the ring's traditional pasodoble *La Giralda*, but, even so, I became aware of something else going on, off to my left. An incredibly gorgeous blonde with a fixed smile on her face and her shoulders draped with a coat two thousand minks had given their pelts for was somehow miraculously approaching, the mass of humanity magically parting like the Red Sea before Moses and the Israelites. Damn! I said to myself. I had to pull a gun to get through this megasized sardine can, yet here this dame comes through the packed humanity like a hot knife through butter! She glided along the front row with the greatest of ease, followed by a foppish looking prick in a gray silk suit who reminded me of that guy who plays Superman on TV. He was stumbling and having a much harder time of it than was the broad. All around me I could hear people whispering and gasping a single name: "Doña Luna!" Carmen looked at her and frowned, sticking out a lovely lower lip.

Doña Luna Whoever-She-Was gracefully sank onto her postage-stamp-sized seat, as her escort sat with much more difficulty, the smarmy Faraón performing a mock bow with his cigar -- without standing -- and giving her what I'm sure he thought was a dazzling smile. She smiled back, then looked out into the ring, her expression one of feigned surprise at seeing that there was an approaching parade of toreros out there.

After the matadors and their cuadrillas had saluted el presidente, they came over to the barrera immediately in front of us. Carmen called out, "Tirón!" and waved wildly at him. Poder saw her, smiled a big smile and lifted a hand in recognition. Then he nodded to Faraón, causing that big bag of hot air to beam broadly in return and hold up an index finger, proclaiming in a loud voice to one and all, "Tirón Poder is the first man of the world! I, Faraón, say it!" He continued to beam. This was the same blowhard, I recalled, who had not so long ago disparaged Poder as a hopeless bum.

But now Poder was no longer paying any attention to the critic -- for he had spotted Doña Luna. And obviously for the very first time. First, his mouth dropped open like that of a street urchin from Extremadura suddenly plopped down in that new California amusement park, Disneyland. Then he put on a smile that I swear started and ended somewhere back behind his two ears. He hefted his montera and saluted her with it. Doña Luna just smiled her own, set, hypnotizing smile accentuated by lots of scarlet lip gloss. A diamond necklace sparkled, even in the shade. Next to me I could hear Carmen muttering unladylike curses under her breath.

"She is magnificent, no?" murmured a male voice to my right. I turned and looked at a little shrimp of a guy with steel-rimmed glasses and a gray, pencil-line mustache. He looked like a dentist or a banker, maybe.

"Yeah, quite a dish," I agreed. "Who is she?"

"You don't know?" he seemed aghast. "Oh, you are most certainly from out of town, señor! That, my friend, is none other than Doña Luna Jezebella de Avaricia, Sevilla's most celebrated collector of men. She 'brands' her possessions by having them wear a special ring; see the one that dandy with her is wearing? And now I note that young Poder is already enchanted!"

"Mmmmmm . . ." I mumbled. Say, I told myself, this could be the solution to Don Pedro's problem! Get Poder interested in this Doña Luna creature, and maybe he'd forget all about Carmen. And then maybe if I played my cards right . . . Hey, cut it out, Marlo! I reprimanded myself. What in hell was I even daydreaming about? I had a job to do; I didn't have time to go mooning over my client's adopted daughter. Yeah, but even so . . .

Poder was still staring at Doña Luna with that foot-wide grin on his face when his peón de confianza, the lean and lanky banderillero Carradino, came over and took his arm, more or less snapping him out of it -- for the moment. At last the corrida was getting underway.

I'm sorry to report that, for the most part, the bulls that afternoon lived up to their name. Manso, that is, not Núñez. I don't know what a Núñez-acting toro would be like. The Peraltas rode round and round, poking the bull with selections from their big bundle of sticks, but that was about it for them. Curro Vázquez could do little with his astados, either.

As for Curro Romero, except for one minor footnote, he was a disaster. I suppose I'm not remembering things correctly, but I swear to you it seemed that with at least one of his bulls he killed it while lying face-up on one of those little low-to-the-ground, wheeled trolley things automobile mechanics lie on to work on the undersides of cars, with Curro shooting out from the burladero on it and stabbing upward with his estoque as he passed under the bull. In any case, he earned a mighty bronca, and somehow I felt it wouldn't be his last. The footnote referred to was the fact that with his first bull he did perform a very nice rebolera with the capote during a quite, an act which -- very strangely, it seemed to me -- had many in the crowd screaming deliriously, as though he had just finished a marvelous faena. Even during the bronca given him on his departure from the ring, maybe a fourth of the people were applauding him.

His first time out, Poder dedicated his bull to Carmen, then went on to do a boringly routine job. On his second one -- the last of the day -- however, i was a different story. This time he walked over to the barrera and, ignoring a fuming Carmen, leaned over the fence toward Doña Luna, extending his montera and saying, "I dedicate this here bull to th' purdiest gal I done ever seed." Good looking guy, I mused, but no Olivier. Li'l Abner in Spain. Then he flipped the hat to her and she caught it. The crowd applauded. Doña Luna's smile, I noticed, never varied: it was always big, alluring and fixed.

Next to me, a Carmen insane with jealousy stamped her foot in anger. This *would* have to be one of the times she was wearing shoes -- and spike heels, to boot: her right heel came down on my left foot, just behind my toes, and even through the leather of my brown-and-white wingtip, I thought she'd broken the damned thing. Caramba! That hurt! I couldn't even reach my throbbing foot with my hand, so packed in were we, much less get it up to a position where I could put in in my mouth, to make it well. I had been getting ready to try to introduce myself to Carmen; that was clearly out of the question right now.

In the arena Poder was doing a beautiful job with this final bull. At least one of the string had proved workable. At the end, he dispatched it with a single entera and the crowd roared and leapt to its feet. Faraón tried to do so, too, but finally settled for sitting and shouting, over and over, "Tirón Poder is the first man of the world! I, Faraón, say it!"

Chapter 6

The U.S. Novillero

I'd been right: The Bodegón Torre Ador was jumping at nine p.m. The post-corrida crowd at the bar was three deep, and all the tables were full. I could hear plenty of English being spoken, in both American and limey accents, as well as Spanish. Some punk kid from the U.S. with a Southern drawl introduced himself to me as "Basugo el Verdugo" or something like that and professed to be a taurino, trying to hit me up for a drink, but I sent him packing. I didn't have time to waste on a young jerk who'd probably never see another corrida in his life.

But I did spot another young American who fascinated me, as I heard him telling someone something about his having fought a bull recently, and in a few minutes I was able to worm my way into his company. We played the obligatory sniffing-out game -- a sort of Can You Top That? contest -- that all taurinos must engage in upon meeting for the first time and which generally goes something like this:

TAURINO A: So, was this your first corrida?
TAURINO B: Oh, no. I go way back.
TAURINO A: Oh? How far back?
TAURINO B: X years. I saw my first corrida in 19--.

If this date is earlier than Taurino A's first year of seeing the bulls, A will most likely drop the subject, and B will be the undeclared winner. If not, the game will continue:

TAURINO A: I see. Well I saw my first one in 19 --.

Either way, a seniority of sorts is thus established. It may not hold up, of course, if it turns out that the taurino with the earliest date has nevertheless seen only some 500 corridas in the intervening years, whereas the other has witnessed over 9,000. But at least it's a starting point. Of course, if A or B is a práctico, that adds points. If one has actually worn a traje de luces and performed in the ring, well, that's it -- he's the winner.

The young American I met was thus the winner: He was an active novillero, originally from Philadelphia, named John Fulton Short, a tall, nice looking kid in his mid to late twenties. He said he'd been fighting bulls one way or another since '53, first in Mexico, and since '56 in Sevilla. He had a pad over in the Calle Hernando Colón, hard by the cathedral. He was trying to break into the big time, tauromaquially speaking; his dream was to someday take his alternativa here, in La Maestranza, and confirm it at Las Ventas. In the meantime, he sold some drawings and paintings to keep himself in pan y vino.

I gave him my line about my being a reporter for the Los Aficionados de Los Angeles newsletter, and then, to my horror, he started asking questions about some of that club's members, people he actually knew. Well, I frantically "danced" that subject for a minute or so, turning the talk as quickly as I could to Tirón Poder. Shortly the name of the figura's latest squeeze, Carmen, came up. John seemed fascinated with Don Pedro's adoption of a gypsy child and him raising her as his own. Then, studying the color of a fino I'd bought him, he said something interesting.

"Well, I just hope she watches her step," he said, now glancing around the crowded bar.

"Whattaya mean?" I asked him. It was good to be speaking English for a change.

He raised his eyebrows and said, "Well, I mean, I don't know anything for certain, but you can't live in this town without hearing things, and what I hear is that the bunch she hangs out with over there at the tobacco factory is pushing its luck."

"How so?" I queried, poking the brim of my hat back a notch with a thumbtip. I thought about Don Pedro's comments on probable Red activity among the factory workers.

"I can't really say," John replied, "but apparently some of the trabajadores at the factory are working on more than just cigarettes and cigars."

"Like?" I asked.

"Who knows? But the cops don't allow much leeway here, you know. If they *think* you're up to no good, you might as well be. The rumor is that something's about to happen. Hey, I gotta go -- got to meet somebody." He gulped down the last of the fino, thanked me for the drink and waved as he left.

And thus the subject was closed to me. I lingered awhile and turned over in my mind what the American novillero had told me.

Chapter 7

Carmen and the Cops

Wednesday, April twenty-seventh. Today was the second of six straight days of corridas, and Poder would be on the cartel again. But I had plenty to do before then.

I walked to the big square known as the Puerta de Jerez, stopped and looked around. Behind me was downtown Sevilla. To my right was el Puente de San Telmo, the bridge over the Guadalquivir to the side where all the feria's casetas were to be found, row after row. Every day, from the late morning until dawn the next day, the streets between the tented party places would be filled with humanity, including plenty of locals in costume: ladies in manola dresses, gents in traje corto, some on foot, some on horseback, others in carriages. I'd go over if I got the chance, I promised myself.

Meanwhile, from where I stood on the corner of the Puerta de Jerez, I looked across to the far side at the ornate, Moorish style hotel which was Sevilla's finest hostelry. A big framework sign on the roof declared it to be the Palacio Andaluz. But nobody called it that. The plush property had been built thirty-two years earlier, in 1928, during the reign of King Alfonso XIII, and it had been named after him. After Franco took over, the Caudillo didn't like all those references to the late monarchy -- still considered to be a threat -- so he went about changing the names of streets, parks, buildings, etc., which bore royal name tags. Thus the Hotel Alfonso XIII became the Palacio Andaluz -- officially, at least. In reality, nobody, not even the hotel staff, used the Franco name; to one and all, it had been and it still was the Alfonso Trece.

The last time I'd been inside that hotel had been two years earlier. I remembered my visit quite well, as I had heard a bizarre story in the big, dark and atmospheric bar which looks like something you might have found in King Farouk's pad. Obviously, I was splurging, since the Trece is the most expensive place in town. I was sitting at the bar, having a Magno, when the guy perched on the next stool struck up a conversation with me. He was incongrously dressed for someplace like this, wearing what looked like coveralls; a hammer and a chisel protruded from a big rear pocket. He'd obviously had a head start on me and was pretty well into his cups, and he wanted to talk. As it turned out, he was drowning his sorrows -- or trying to, anyway. With good reason, if you ask me.

The fellow was a big oaf with a wild, unruly mop of hair, maybe thirty, thirty-five years old, and he told me his name was Martillo Cincelero hijo. He looked at me as he said that, and when I didn't seem to register any name recognition, he went on to explain that his late father of the same name, a sevillano artisan, had been Spain's leading sculptor and had, in fact, created the well-known statue of the Galician matador Ventrudito Pocogrande in Pozo del Mundo, which is very near the northwestern port city of El Ferrol del Caudillo, Franco's home town. Galicia is not exactly renowned for its toreros or its afición, yet el Generalísimo himself is a big taurino, so the chief of state demonstrated particular interest in the Pocogrande statue.

It seems that after he saw it in Pozo del Mundo one day, Franco had his flunkies contact the sculptor, Cincelero padre, to commission him to do an equestrian statue of himself, the generalísimo, for the plaza mayor in El Ferrol. But Franco specified that the job would be Cincelero's only if he could guarantee that the finished statue would be somehow treated to prevent the usual hordes of pigeons from using it as a resting place, and fouling it, as he felt this was demeaning. The old sculptor, overjoyed at the prospect of having the honor of creating a statue of el Caudillo, to be placed in the main square of the leader's home town, immediately guaranteed that the work would be pigeon-proof, even though at the time he had no idea how to accomplish such a result. The whole time Cincelero worked on the great carving, using the finest Carrara marble shipped to Spain from Italy expressly for the project, he pondered the problem.

The son, telling me the story, went on to relate how his father even went to Amsterdam, a city with a long history of pigeon problems, where he studied a plan which involved the broadcasting of recorded cries of dying pigeons over a downtown P-A system. The death cries just sounded like ordinary pigeon cooing to humans, but to the feathered ones they warned of impending doom, and the birds stayed away in droves.

Cincelero senior knew the city of El Ferrol del Caudillo couldn't afford such a sophisticated system, but it did give the sculptor an idea. He checked with an ornipathologist friend of his and found that dying pigeons not only utter an identifiable cry, they also secrete a glandular fluid which, while undetectable by human beings, is smellable by other pigeons -- similar to the sex gland secretions of the same birds which are put into use at mating time. As with the death cries, this "death gland" smell made pigeons avoid the area in question. Why, Cincelero asked his bird doctor friend, could he not accumulate large quantities of this gland secretion and immerse his finished statue in it, thus guaranteeing that pigeons would steer clear of it? His friend said he saw no reason why the plan would not work, and so the sculptor proceeded accordingly.

Martillo hijo went on to describe how he and other family members were pressed into service, trapping pigeons for the project. Soon they had thousands of the birds in a huge pen outside Sevilla, and when the statue of Franco was finally completed, the sculptor, his son and all the assisting friends and relatives, working under the bird doctor's instructions, slaughtered the pigeons and drained their "death secretions" into a huge vat, finally "stretching" it with olive oil in order to completely fill the vat, which was big enough to "dip" the horse-and-rider statue -- with the help of a crane. The idea was that the oil would soak into the stone and the pigeon death gland solution would thus be impervious to rain.

All this was done and the now-marinated statue was placed on a huge flatbed truck, covered with a tarpaulin, and trucked from Sevilla to El Ferrol. Martillo hijo told me he and some of the others who were riding in cars behind the flatbed began to have concerns when they noticed entire air fleets of pigeons flying along behind the big truck. The sculptor himself, however, who was riding in the truck's cab, was unaware of this development.

When they arrived in El Ferrol and the statue was hoisted from the truck to its concrete pedestal in the presence of Generalísimo Franco and an army of national government officials and local Galician dignitaries, the sky became dark with thousands of circling and fluttering pigeons. Once the crane had done its job and backed off, the incredible mass of birds descended to the statue of el Caudillo on his horse and completely covered it with their writhing, flapping, feathery forms. Attempts to scare away the pigeons with gunshots were unsuccessful, and even a water cannon only drove them off for as long as the powerful spray was directed at the marble work; once it was diverted or turned off, the birds returned, seemingly in even greater numbers than before. What was not known then, but what the Cinceleros learned later, was that the bird doctor had erroneously instructed his pigeon-dissecting helpers to remove not the winged ones' "death glands," but their mating sex glands. The statue of el Generalísimo was being, uh, *loved* by sex-crazed pigeons. And always would be.

Needless to say, el Caudillo was furious beyond words, so exercised over the debacle that this physicians feared he might suffer a stroke, and he was whisked away to his nearby family home for two or three days of bed rest. When he was well enough to be back on his feet and had learned the whole story, Franco ordered sculptor Martillo Cincelero padre staked out, spead eagle fashion, in the same plaza mayor of El Ferrol, and soaked to the skin with an identical solution of pigeon sex gland secretions and olive oil. Once again, thousands of pigeons appeared in the sky overhead, then swooped down and completely covered the pinioned body of the screaming and futilely struggling sculptor until his form was still -- loved to death by the feathered horde. The writhing mass of pigeons was so great that even traditional birds of prey could not get to the lifeless body after some hours had passed.

"When did this happen?" I asked the young Cincelero, shaking my head in wonder. "The bit about your old man and the pigeons out there in the plaza mayor, I mean."

"Yesterday," the guy said. "Hey, how's about another snort, huh, pal?" He looked miserable.

"Sure," I said, "why not?" Carajo! I thought. What a pisser of a way for his old man to check out!

"Say, uh, I couldn't help noticing your sculpting tools in your back pocket," I said. "Are you going to continue your father's work?"

"No way, hombre," the drunken son had replied to me. "The life of a sculptor is for the birds." Then he broke down and wept.

I snapped out of my reverie and realized I was still standing there looking at the Hotel Alfonso Trece. To the left of the hotel and, in fact, running the whole remaining length of the Calle San Fernando, was the huge old tobacco factory, built in the baroque style, my goal this bright and sunny spring morning. I walked that way and checked my watch as I did so: almost eleven o'clock, when I understood the factory workers took a break and came outside to smoke and gossip. On my left as I walked down San Fernando were the walls enclosing los Jardines de Murillo, the extensive gardens behind the fourteenth century Alcázar. Hombre, I thought, this burg positively stinks of history.

The front of the tobacco factory was around the corner at the far end, facing onto the wide, treelined Avenida del Cid. In the distance beyond, the ornate, semicircular edifice of the Plaza de España and its curving lagoon overlooked the vast Parque de Maria Luisa. But the workers didn't use the factory's main entrance; rather, they went in and out of the series of doors on the Calle San Fernando side, where I was. I sauntered across the street to the tiny park-like area with a few benches and some low stone walls which would be convenient for sitting on, and I sat down, pulling from my pocket a morning paper. Turning to the *Toros* section,

I began reading Faraón's gushing description of yesterday's final faena by Poder. Along the sidewalk, half a block away, a strolling eight or ten piece banda taurina, its members dressed in blue uniforms with gold trim, stopped and began playing concert stuff: Lara and Albéniz. Nice touch.

Out of the corner of my eye I noticed a babe in a flouncy red dress coming my way. There was no tap-tap-tap of high heels, and a glance told me why: she was barefooted. It was Carmen Albamadera. I stood up, folded my paper and prepared to greet her as soon as she saw me. But just at that moment, during a pause in the band's mini-concert, our mutual attention was diverted by sounds from the street, where the clip-clopping of horses' hooves mingled with the loud laughter of a man and woman. We both automatically looked in the direction of the equine-borne gaiety and beheld Doña Luna and Tirón Poder riding beautiful horses -- a palomino and a white stallion, respectively -- man and woman alike dressed in impeccable traje corto. It was too far away to hear what they were saying, but their laughter carried easily. If they saw either of us, they didn't let on, and they continued on their way, headed in the direction of the feria grounds and the casetas. I now glanced back to Carmen, who had stopped and was staring at the twosome with a look of pure hatred. Her fists were balled up, her knuckles white. I decided to strike. I walked up to her, doing my best not to limp with the foot she'd speared with her stiletto heel on the previous afternoon at the plaza.

"Buenos días, Señorita Albamadera," I said, oozing charm as I doffed my hat.

She turned and looked at me, still frowning, then a sort of recognition seemed to dawn on her face. As before, she wore a red carnation in her hair.

"I was your neighbor yesterday at the corrida," I said. "I was just reading Señor Faraón's very complimentary account of Tirón Poder's work in the ring."

At my mention of the matador's name, Carmen's face once again took on a fierce expression. "Pah!" She actually spat on the pavement. "Tirón Poder! That chaser of . . . of . . . *putas!*" Hmmm, I thought. Hell hath no fury like, etc. And what an unfortunate description of the bedazzling Doña Luna. But I didn't say any of that. Instead, thinking of Don Pedro and my commission, I took another tack.

"Ah, sí," I agreed with her. "A most objectionable fellow. Look here, I didn't really get the opportunity to properly introduce myself yesterday, but as I have tickets for the same seat, next to you, for each of the remaining corridas, I think it might be a good idea if I did so now. The name's Mar-- er, Dean, Rock Dean. I'm an American writer and I'm here to write about, ah . . . Say, what are your main interests?"

"Interests?" she repeated, a baffled look on her pretty yet still frowning gypsy face. "Mine?"

"Yeah," I said, "you know, are you interested in, er, say, the movies? Or maybe pretty jewelry? Fuzzy animals?"

She tossed off my suggestions, just as she haughtily tossed her long, raven-black locks. "Ha!" she barked. "Such things are for the stupid little chicas -- the ones who will someday find themselves shunted into a convent -- to think about now, while they still have the chance! As for me, I am interested in men!" She looked at me straight on, a mischievous smile playing at the corner of her luscious red lips. "Real men," she added, "not cheap toreros."

"Oh, really?" I said, smiling what I hoped was an enigmatic smile and pushing my hat brim back a little with my thumb. "Do you like writers?"

"Pah!" she snorted. "Who wants to read boring old books?" Then she seemed to think of something. "Are you from New York? Are you rich?" Down the way, the band was now playing *Amapola.*

"Uh, no, not New York," I replied. "I'm from Hollywood. And yeah, I'm rich. Real rich. I write, uh, true life stories about beautiful damsels who are whisked away to great castles by handsome warrior kings."

Her expression went from wary to delighted. Her smile made my heart leap, and when she reached out and placed a lovely, soft, warm hand on my cheek, the taurine band suddenly began booming out the *Hallelujah Chorus.*

She cuddled up close to me and asked, "Is your name really Rock? What does that mean?" She looked soooo interested.

"Uh, it means, uh, Piedra," I said, smiling but trying to keep her from nestling against my rod in its lefthander's shoulder holster near my right armpit.

"Ooh!" She crooned. "Rock! Oh, I like it! It sounds so . . . so . . . hard!"

I gulped. "Ha! Yeah!" I laughed, a little uncomfortably. "Yeah, you know, you're absolutely right!" I stuck a finger inside my collar and tugged. Maybe I'd tied my tie too tight or something. Or maybe the temperature was climbing. Yeah, the temperature was definitely climbing.

At that moment the bells of the cathedral a few blocks away began tolling the hour. The tolling obviously served as a sort of factory whistle, because within seconds workers were streaming out the doors of the tobacco factory, lighting up cigarettes and laughing and calling to one another. Two gypsy dames in colorful, if cheap, dresses skipped our way, one of them calling out, "Carmen!" They came up to us, smiling, both of them looking from Carmen to me, and back to Carmen.

"Holá, chicas," Carmen said. Then, assuaging their curiosity, she introduced us. "Señor Dean, these are my friends Mercedes and Bimer. They work in the factory." Then to the babes: "This is Señor Rock Dean. Rock means Piedra. He is a norteamericano who writes wonderful stories and he is very -- er -- nice." The two chicks looked at me again and flashed big, toothy smiles, saying hello and giggling.

"Oomprey!" Mercedes said, pointing at me as she giggled.

"Huh?" I said, not understanding.

"You look like Oomprey Bogart!" she clarified. All three of the broads giggled at that.

"Uh, yeah," I said, trying to look a little embarrassed. "I've been told that before."

We were interrupted by a crowd of nearby workers shouting about something. Mercedes reached over and touched Carmen's arm and asked her, *sotto voce*, "Are they going to do it today?" Carmen shook her head quickly, putting a finger to her lips, then cutting her eyes in my direction.

"Perdónenos," she said to me, then grabbing the other two women by an arm each and steering them toward the crowd. I followed a few steps behind.

The workers were gathered in a circle, listening to a youngish, rough-looking guy talk. He needed a shave and his clothes were pretty bad. He was saying something about the "muy especial y muy importante" work they were doing there and how it would very soon begin to make an impact among the working people all over Spain. The crowd responded with cries of "Yeah!" and "Right!" and so on.

A squeal of brakes and car doors violently opening and slamming shut got the assembled lot's attention -- fast. Many started to furtively move away, and then police whistles were blown. I saw several cops disgorging from three Seats, two of them regular police cars, one of them unmarked.

"Alto!" shouted a couple of uniformed cops, as two or three ran to try to head off any workers attempting to slip away to either side of the factory. A burly, uniformed police captain wearing sunglasses beneath his Third-Reich-style peaked cap strode into the center of the crowd. The part of his face not covered by the big shades looked like it had caught fire and been put out with an icepick.

"You know me," he bellowed. "I am Capitán Zitcara. And this" -- he gestured to a weasely, similarly dressed cop with a lascivious leer on his face -- "is Teniente Inmoral. We are responsible for keeping the law in Sevilla. We have heard some things about goings-on inside the factory that we don't like. You people look like Reds. You smell like Reds! And por Dios, if I decide to haul any or all of you in, you'll *talk* like the Reds I catch always talk, and then if I have my way, you'll *die* like Reds, up against the wall!"

At this moment Carmen pushed her way into the center of the crowd, facing Capitán Zitcara, and, putting her hands on her hips, laughed in his face.

"You don't scare us, you big cabrón!" she cried defiantly. "You have nothing on anybody here! If you did, you wouldn't bother with speeches -- we'd all be in paddy wagons by now!"

The captain's lunar landscape face turned crimson, but he fought to maintain control. "Look here, Señorita Albamadera, this isn't your concern. I have no bones to pick with Don Pedro. Now you just run along and leave me to do my job."

"These are my friends, cabrón!" Carmen shot back. "They've done nothing wrong! Now why don't you and your thugs get out of here and leave us alone? Can't you see when you're not wanted?" The crowd tittered nervously.

I cringed inside when I heard her taunting the head cop thus. One of the things

Don Pedro had been crystal clear about was that he did not want Carmen hauled in by the police.

"You give me no choice, señorita!" Zitcara said. Then, to the leering lieutenant and three other officers standing beside him, he pointed at Carmen and cried, in the best Cecil B. DeMille tradition, "Seize her!"

Screams broke out in the crowd, and several voices urged Carmen to run -- which she did, fleeing through a narrow opening in the mass of workers, headed for the doors to the tobacco factory. As she ran, she turned and laughingly threw the flower from her hair toward me, where I stood between her and the cops.

"I'll catch her!" I yelled, running after Carmen. But then I suddenly stopped and bent over to pick up the flower, and all four of the pursuing cops crashed into me and we all went sprawling, just like we'd been in the Calle Estafeta in Pamplona on a morning when too many drunk frat boys had decided to run with the bulls. The workers then closed ranks, cutting off further pursuit of the gypsy girl. Once inside the huge, dark factory, I figured, she'd make for another door on a different side and be gone. A fuming Capitán Zitcara knew this and cursed even louder.

I got up and dusted off my trenchcoat, stuffing Carmen's red carnation into a pocket. The captain let fly with a few cuss words at me, but he knew I was not one of the factory employees and acted like he thought I was just a passerby who had been trying to help, so he let me go after asking a few questions. Then he angrily ordered the workers to go back to their jobs, which they gladly did; in the process, Mercedes brushed past me and whispered the name of a bar and added, "before the corrida," then went on her way. The cops returned to their cars and drove off, and soon I was once again alone outside the tobacco factory.

I pulled the slightly crushed flower from my pocket and sniffed it. It smelled like Carmen. I then realized I was smiling a sappy smile. I'd been wondering if Don Pedro would consider my assignment fulfilled if I substituted Poder's place in Carmen's life with -- me. Oh, no, I said to myself, I couldn't be falling . . . Could I? Holy moley, I sighed. The answer was painfully clear. I was.

And then I heard music from the banda taurina again -- only this time it wasn't the *Halleluja Chorus*. Instead, it was a sort of spooky-sounding bit I seemed to recall from some opera or another. Something I think was called the *Fate Theme*.

Chapter 8

At Lillas Pastia's Bar

What kind of a name is Lillas Pastia? I wondered. Sounded like Easter flowers and fettucini to me, but what did I know? Anyway, this was the place Mercedes had hurridly mentioned to me at the tobacco factory this morning. Turned out it was in Triana, across the river from La Maestranza, and it was a taurine bar. When I walked in at about four-thirty, a good hour before the start of the afternoon's corrida, the place was crowded and smiling gypsies were singing and dancing all over the place. Carajo, I thought: This looked like a hokey scene from an old Technicolor Hollywood movie. Well, I was supposed to be from Hollywood, wasn't I? So I should feel at home.

I walked up to the bar and ordered a Magno. I still had the flower and was smelling it, even if it was a bit the worse for wear. As the barkeep -- the owner, Lillas Pastia -- slid my glass to me across the zinc bar top, I was thinking about asking him how he came to be stuck with such a candyass name, when I saw Mercedes and Bimer come into the joint. They spotted me immediately -- I guess maybe a trenchcoat and fedora make one stand out a little in certain circumstances -- and came over to me.

"Holá!" cried Mercedes, all choppers. "It's Carmen's new novio! And look -- still with his flower! Buy us a trago, guapo?" I said sure and they shouted their orders at Señor Pastia. In a minute they had their drinks and we toasted each other.

Now two tough-looking characters came in, and I recognized one of them as the guy who'd been haranguing the workers at the factory that morning about the "muy especial y muy importante" work they were doing. They came up to the three of us, the number two man walking with a limp; the apparent leader spoke to me.

"Gracias for helping our camarada Carmencita to escape the fascist pigs this morning, señor," he said.

"De nada," I said, leaning back on the bar with my elbows, "that's my favorite pasttime, rescuing lovely señoritas from political pachyderms." Mercedes then introduced me to the two men. The jefe, a goodlooking type underneath the rough exterior, was one Daniel "Danny" Cairo; his whipcord lean pal was, simply, El Castrado, identified as an ex-novillero who'd had to quit the bulls when one of them robbed him of his family jewels. He had a glass of Magno in one hand, and later on somebody told me that while he'd lost his manhood in the bullring, he could, as they say, still drink like a man. Sounds like a character out of a Hemingway novel, I thought to myself.

Cairo asked me some questions, to which I responded with my reporter cover, but my actions at the factory this morning had in any case apparently convinced him that I was no stooge for the cops. I was inviting the men to join us in a drink when Carmen came through the doorway. I felt a surge in my chest, on the opposite side from my holstered gat.

Before Carmen could even make her way to the bar, yet another familiar face appeared. Holy Toledo, I muttered, because through the open doorway, getting out of a big purple Buick Roadmaster, I could see Tirón Poder, already dressed in his traje de luces and trailed by his cuadrilla. What the hell was he doing here, with a corrida coming up in an hour or so? Carmen, who hadn't yet seen Poder, came up to me, Mercedes and Bimer; Danny Cairo and El Castrado melted away, huddled in conversation. Carmen had a big smile on her face, and she threw her arms around me and planted a great big kiss on, er, my kisser. But before she could say much of anything, the bar erupted in cheering and applause as Poder walked through the entrance. Grinning from ear to ear, the matador held up a hand for silence, and got it.

"Gracias, mis amigos, gracias!" he cried. "I know it ain't normal for a matador t' do somethin' like this, right before a corrida and all, but hell, you're my real fans, right?" The crowd cheered again, and individual voices shouted "Olé, Poder!" and "Vayas, Tirón!" There were flashes of light, and behind Poder in the doorway I could see a couple of newspaper boys shooting pictures. Poder, matador of the people. Not bad PR, I thought.

Now the diestro was performing toreo de salón in the center of the bar, and his admirers were shouting "olé!" with each pass of the imaginary bull. His "faena" completed, he appeared to see Carmen for the first time, and he turned on the big smile again. On his left hand, observed by both Carmen and me, was a new ring -- Doña Luna's "brand."

"Holá, Carmencita!" he smilingly called out. "¿Qué tal, chica?"

But Poder had walked into a buzzsaw. Carmen sneered as she swaggered up to the matador, hands on her hips. She gave a two-handed shove to his chaquetilla forcing him back a step. "Don't 'Carmencita' me, you cabrón!" she yelled at him "I don't go with third-rate hacks!"

"Ooooooh!" said the crowd.

At this point, Carmen stalked back to the bar and took my arm, turning to glare at Poder and do a pretty good Mussolini impression, jutting out her chin, tilting her head back and jerking it down, then back up, like she was saying, "So there!"

Poder glowered as the onlookers tittered. Without a further word, he turned on his heel and stormed out the door. I saw old Garbaje out there, hurrying to open the Buick's back door for him. I also noticed the banderillero Carradino glancing over his shoulder and back into the bar as he followed Poder, a whimsical smile on his thin lips.

But Carmen wasn't finished with Poder yet. Running to the bar entrance, she stopped and shouted one last insult before he could climb into his car: "You will never be half the matador Escamopayo is!"

This barb obviously got under Poder's skin. Escamopayo, of course, was his boyhood friend, his fellow maletilla, who had walked and hitchhiked his way to Madrid with him and Carradino all those years ago, returning to Sevilla like Poder, as a matador de toros. Now they were the fiercest of rivals -- and the showdown would be the last corrida of the feria, on May first, when the two matadors would share the cartel with Curro Romero.

With one last glare back -- one which sent daggers so real in feeling that many of the bar patrons fell back in fear -- Poder got in the car and slammed the door shut, just as Garbaje, who had run around and gotten in the front to do the driving, stomped it and burned rubber, clearing the scene with a loud squealing of tires. The newspaper photographers were having a field day, snapping shots of the furious matador, the feisty gypsy girl and the purple Buick roaring down the narrow street, billowing clouds of white smoke from its screaming and burning tires.

Now the bar was really noisy, as everyone present was shouting about the just-completed scene. Then, above the clamor, someone shouted, "Policía!" and people stampeded for the door, only to find it blocked by the bulky Capitán Zitcara, the squirrely and leering Teniente Inmoral, and a bunch of lesser cops. Those guys, I figured, were looking for Carmen. But before I could say or do anything, Danny Cairo came over and grabbed both of us by our arms and pushed us through a storeroom doorway. El Castrado followed. Cairo rasped, "Follow me!" and led us on through the small room and out another door, which put us in a back alley filled with smelly garbage cans. The four of us ran down to the end of the callejón, turned the corner and split up into pairs. I hailed a cruising cab and told the driver, "La Maestranza!"

As we rode, despite my being distracted by Carmen hugging and kissing me in the taxi, I kept turning over in my mind all that had happened. Just how deep was Carmen in with these Reds, or whatever they were? And what about me?

Chapter 9

Two Ears for Poder

In less than five minutes we were at the Maestranza. The white walls with the yellow ochre trim gleamed in the late afternoon sun. Taking Carmen by the hand, I led her to the back entrance, the one the toreros use, and to the one-legged guy at the gate, one of the thousands of paraplegics from Spain's civil war, I flashed a phony Los Aficionados de Los Angeles membership card which I'd had made up earlier; it worked, and in a moment we were inside, mixing with the taurine in-crowd: bullring workers, picadors and their horses, newspapermen, promoters and general hangers-on of the mundillo. The purple Roadmaster was parked off to the side, against a wall, headed out for a quick getaway after the corrida. Rather than go back to his house, Poder and his cuadrilla had come directly to the plaza from the bar in Triana, and he and Carradino were arguing in the patio de caballos.

"That Doña Luna has drained you!" the banderillero was shouting at his jefe. "Dios mio, she even has you getting up before noon to go horseback riding with her! You are no more than a depleted farm animal! Well, no matter, this is my last season. You owe me a year's pay, and I've had it with you! In fact, I've had it with this whole, stinking business!"

Poder's face was a mask of rage. He backhanded a slap across Carradino's face, whereupon the peón just looked at his matador for a moment, then turned

188

and walked over to where Garbaje and the rest of the cuadrilla were standing and smoking in a far corner. Poder's jaw muscles worked and his hands were clenched fists.

At that moment little eight-year-old Pequeñito, a small urchin who pushed the carretón for Poder during backyard practice sessions at the matador's house, came up, propelling the strange contraption consisting of a bicycle wheel with handlebars, upon which a pair of toro bravo horns had been mounted. "Aja!" he cried to Poder, playfully making the carretón "charge" the matador.

But Poder was in no mood to play with Pequeñito. In his black rage, he pulled an estoque from its sheath and with two swift swipes of the blade cut the little kid's ears off. Everyone in the patio de caballos was horrified, but Poder just stalked off to brood on his own, as someone rushed little Pequeñito to the enfermería. Holy moley, I said to myself. Carmen cried out, then covered her face with her hands and sobbed uncontrollably. I hugged and consoled her, and tried to talk some sense into her.

"Hey, kid, buck up," I said, chucking her under the chin. "Look at it this way: This is just one of those little things we have to laugh off, huh?" She sobbed once more, then sheepishly smiled at me and rubbed an eye with a knuckle, nodding in agreement. She knew I was right.

"That's my girl!" I said, my arm around her shoulders. We started into the ring to find our seats, when I stopped suddenly. "Hold it!" I said. "What if the cops see you here?"

But Carmen just laughed and said that after Captain Zitcara'd had time to think things over, he wouldn't dare arrest the adopted daughter of Don Pedro Albamadera without any solid charge to back him up. I thought about that, shrugged, and guided Carmen on inside.

Today's corrida pitted toros of Don José Benítez Cubero against Antonio Ordóñez, Tirón Poder and Quinn Helado, better known as Escamopayo. Carmen and I were sitting in our barrera seats, with Faraón and Doña Luna and her herd of inert minks to our left, when things got under way. The band played and the matadors and their teams paraded across the sand, stopping in front of us. Only Escamopayo held the montera in his hand.

Ordóñez seemed to be in good spirits as he acknowledged the greetings shouted to him by numerous people in the crowd. Poder, on the other hand, ignored everyone except Doña Luna, whom he greeted effusively. Her ring branding him as her personal property gleamed on his left hand. Doña Luna just smiled that fixed smile of hers. The fop from yesterday wasn't sitting beside her today; his seat was left vacant.

The third matador on the cartel, Escamopayo, Poder's old fellow maletilla, was being totally ignored by his former buddy in the ring with him. But he looked pleased to be making his first appearance in La Maestranza.

And then I cringed at the sound of a dreaded name.

"Holá, Pecas!" Ordóñez called out, a big smile on his face. He was looking directly at me. Damn! I'd hoped he wouldn't recognize me, but then I suppose i was too much to expect that he wouldn't notice me sitting smack behind los capotes wearing my trenchcoat and fedora, which he knew so well. Last year, when I was working as Hemingway's bodyguard during "The Dangerous Summer," Antonio had even found a white trenchcoat and hat to match, so that I wouldn't have an excuse not to run with the bulls in Pamplona. And it was his bright idea, of course to have me dress as the sobresaliente in Ciudad Real, with the apodo "El Pecas," a gag which eventually resulted in my spending eight months in the taurine slammer He looked like he wanted to talk to me, but, thankfully, at that moment his first bul thundered out of the toril and he had to turn his attention elsewhere. Whew! He could blow my cover, I thought.

Antonio got with it and had the crowd going. At kill time, he went in and found el Rincón de Ordóñez, dropping the toro and cutting an ear. Poder didn't fare nearly as well on his first, appearing distracted and killing sloppily, earning a bronca. Escamopayo, on the other hand, was inspired, performing well with the capote and the muleta and gaining an ear from the third bull.

With his second toro Ordóñez did another good job, but the kill was slightly off, even for him, and he had to settle for a vuelta. Poder's next enemigo was a fine bull, but the frowning matador failed to take advantage of it and finished by blowing the bit with the steel big time, eliciting another bronca. Then Escamopayo put el público back into a good mood with a brilliant display of capework and a perfect entera: another ear.

As the toreros exited the ring at the end, with Poder receiving yet another huge bronca on his despedida, I glanced over at Doña Luna, sitting just beyond Faraón. The smile on her face seemed to have slipped a bit; it was beginning to look more like a grimace.

Chapter 10

An Unexpected Twist

The scene at El Bodegón Torre Ador was as lively as ever after the corrida. A guitarist was playing flamenco music on a corner stool, and the crowd was noisy. I was alone; Carmen had said she had to do something. As she had walked away from me, I'd noticed that she was looking at a flyer handout with Curro Romero's picture on it. How funny, I had thought at the time.

Across the room I saw the young American novillero John Fulton Short and nodded hello to him. At a table in the very center of the big joint sat the critic Faraón, holding court. He was waving his cigar around in the air and making proclamations.

"Escamopayo is the first man of the world!" he cried. "I, Faraón, say it!"

"What about Poder?" someone asked him.

The big man made a face. "Poder is washed up!" he bellowed. "Finished! Escamopayo has replaced him! I --"

Yeah, yeah, I thought, you, Faraón, say it. Until the next flash in the pan comes along, that is. But Faraón didn't finish his statement, for at that moment Tirón Poder and Doña Luna entered the bodegón, and everything suddenly went silent. The matador and the lady were both wearing smiles, but neither was convincing.

Dressed in a blue suit but wearing no tie, Poder led the dressed-to-the-nines

Doña Luna to a fully occupied table in the back corner of the tavern. At a snap o his fingers, all those who were sitting there grabbed their drinks, jumped to thei feet and vacated the table for him and his lady. The matador clapped his hand: for a waiter and demanded champaña. The two then sat and acknowledged the staring crowd with those wooden smiles, Poder toying with the ring on his hand obviously agitated. In a minute or so, the the guitarist resumed his playing and people started laughing and talking again.

Just then, over the noise of the tavern, came the screeching of tires braking hard on the cobblestones of the street outside. Through the open doorway I could see the rear fins of a red 1960 T-bird illegally parked, and then Quinn Helado Escamopayo himself, swaggered in, a cigarette in the corner of his mouth. He was wearing a black traje corto with cordoban hat and looked very smart. Severa people called his name, and he received some applause, to which he responded with a big smile and a wave. He looked around the big room and, seeing Poder and Doña Luna at the table in the back corner, strode purposefully in that direction casually flipping his cigarette away as he did so.

At the table he stopped and bowed to a smiling Doña Luna, accepting and kissing her proferred hand. Poder he ignored. The guitarist was playing a spirited flamenco number.

"Would you care to dance?" Escamopayo asked in his growling baritone voice, still holding the lady's hand. Without speaking, but her smile even bigger now, Doña Luna gracefully slid off her chair and stood up to face the junior matador. All eyes in the bodega were on the two of them.

The stunning couple proceeded to the center of the room, cleared for them by a retreating and ogling patronage, and there they began dancing flamenco beautifully, as though they had rehearsed a fully choreographed routine many times. Escamopayo clapped his hands loudly as they danced, and Doña Luna snapped her fingers like castanets, while both stamped their heels furiously in tune with the music. The guitarist strummed as if there were no tomorrow. And then it was over. Escamopayo posed, smilingly triumphant, frozen with one hand in the small of the back of a reclining Doña Luna, his other hand extended into the air. Both smiled gigantic smiles.

Their audience gave them a resounding ovation, applauding lustily and shouting words of praise to the dancers. I thought they'd sit down now, but not so. Instead, Doña Luna called out to the guitar player, "Hey, chico! Can you play *The Twist?*"

The musician, who looked like a weatherbeaten gypsy out of the classic mold, nodded seriously, rearranged his position on his stool, then began wildly strumming the new Chubby Checker tune which was supposed to be such a big hit back in the States right now. Doña Luna, a jet-setter if ever there was one -- and I'd bet duros to churros that she really had flown in one of those new BOAC Comet jets transatlantic -- even knew the words, and she sang them in English as she and her bullfighter danced frantically to the music, their arms bent and their torsos twisting back and forth:

> *"Come on baby . . . let's do the twist!*
> *Come on baaaaa-by, let's do the twist!*
> *Take my little hand . . . and go like this . . . "*

The couple twisted away, the guitar thrummed madly, and the bar patrons -- with the exception of Tirón Poder -- all smiling like idiots, clapped their hands and tapped their feet in time with the fast music. I looked around, halfway expecting to see baby-faced Dick Clark smiling from behind his *American Bandstand* rostrum. The Twist, I mused as I observed it for the first time, was a dance made for a torero who performed in the estilo sevillano, turning his upper body side to side from the waist while keeping his feet still. Bet Ordóñez the rondeño can't do that, I thought.

And then what had surely been Sevilla's premiere exposure to The Twist ended, the happy dancers collapsing in each other's arms. The bodega erupted in a roar of cheering and applause. The matador and the lady executed small bows of appreciation, then turned and walked back to the table. The crowd once again grew silent, anticipating a scene. And they got it. As the two approached, Poder leapt to his feet, his face twisted in rage. He shoved his chair back violently, sending it crashing over backward. Then he wrenched Doña Luna's ring from his finger, threw it onto the floor, and stomped out, pushing people aside as he did so. A smiling Escamopayo pulled out Doña Luna's chair and she sat, beaming at him with what appeared to be sixty-four porcelain-white teeth, each one of them on full display. For that matter, Escamopayo was all ivories, himself.

Now the guitar player resumed his job and everyone in the tavern began to excitedly talk about what they had just witnessed. Except me, that is. I followed Poder out the door and up the street. I was worried that as Doña Luna had now dumped him, he might try to go back to Carmen. I wanted to have a talk with him, but I didn't want it to be in the street, where we could be easily interrupted or distracted.

Poder walked and walked, never looking to his right or his left, headed east, toward the newer part of town. He's going to his house, I thought. And when he gets there, he's going to be in a really foul mood. He's lost face twice today, I told myself, once in Lillas Pastia's place, when Carmen taunted him in front of his core supporters, and again tonight at the bodegón, in front of Faraón and the rest of the world.

But at least loss of face was not the total disaster for a Spaniard -- or any occidental -- that it was for an oriental, I reasoned, when such could actually prove fatal. My mind automatically took me back to Guadalcanal, 1942. I was part of a squad which had been ordered to flush out a machinegun nest manned by some of the Rising Sun's finest. Crawling up a slope, I came across the body of one of our guys who hadn't made it, a flamethrower operator. I borrowed his cumbersome weapon and trained it on the slit high above me where a machinegun barrel was poking out, then squeezed the trigger. A spume of flaming jelly shot into the bunker and a moment later this son of Tojo came running out, screaming, his head on fire. A ball of flame with buck teeth. Now *that*, I told myself, was a good example of much loss of face.

But never mind all that, I told myself. Just talk to Poder and steer him away from Carmen.

I followed him through the Parque de Maria Luisa and into the area called E Porvenir. Finally he came to a new house of modern design, unlocked the door and went inside. Fortunately for me, he was so distracted he didn't bother to close the door, and I slipped in behind him.

I heard Poder speaking argumentively with someone. I looked around; the house was new and expensive enough, but it was pretty bare inside, and a lot of the furnishings were, to my surprise, pretty cheap stuff. Instead of paintings on the walls there were several fairly recent cartels, all with Poder's name listed, each of them held up by strips of tape. I walked through the entrance hall and living room, stopping at the top of a flight of some three steps leading down into a den of sorts, with the obligatory stuffed bull's head over a fireplace. Poder was standing, looking down at an old woman who was on all fours, scrubbing the tile floor with a brush. A pail of soapy water sat on the floor next to her.

"Mama!" Poder was angrily shouting. "I said why th' obscenity are you doin' this? You know you don't have to do nothin' like this no more!"

"I do it for practice, Tirón," his mother replied, calmly, continuing to scrub with great circular motions, "for when you are nobody again."

"Get up!" Poder cried. "Get up, I said!" But his old lady ignored him and kept cleaning the floor.

"Your time is almost over, Tirón," she went on, puffing a little. "You've lost your touch. You owe everybody money. They all hate you. Even this house is yet to be paid for. When you are finished, you'll be glad there is someone who can still bring in some money. You'd just better hope I can get a job doing this."

My heart went out to the old gal, and I felt I should not only make my presence known, I should say something to make this hardworking old dame feel better. "Hey, ma," I said, coming down the steps, "don't sweat it. I'll hire you. You can scrub *my* floors."

Poder wheeled about, a look of incredulity on his face. "Quién -- quién --?" he began. He sounded like a mallard quacking.

"Cut the duck imitations, pal," I said. "See if you can do a crow. You're gonna be eatin' plenty of it."

"Get out o' my damned house!" he roared. "I don't know who th' hell you are, but por Dios --" he pulled an estoque from the wall, where it hung by its pommel from a nail, and he began sliding the blade out of its sheath. "-- I'll stick you like a salchicha on an alambre!"

"Hold it, cuate!" I snarled, whipping my .38 from its shoulder holster and aiming it at him from waist level; hip guys, especially gumshoes, don't hold a pistol out straight and aim down the barrel like some kind of pantywaist. Poder froze for a moment, then shoved the sword back into its scabbard. Mama Poder stayed where she was on the floor, the knuckles of one hand now in her mouth.

"Whattaya want?" he growled. "You some kind o' cop or somethin'?"

"Naw, I'm no cop," I said, still covering him with my rod. Behind Poder, little Pequeñito came into the room from the yard out back, where I figured they practiced with the carretón. His head was all bandaged up where his ears used to be. He looked at my gun, all wide-eyed, then at Poder, an expression of concern for the matador on his small face.

"What, then?" Poder asked. He was leaning forward, sort of rocking back and forth, like a long distance runner waiting for the starting gun. But mine was a *stopping* gun.

"Take it easy," I said. Then I had an inspiration, and, based on what Don Pedro had told me earlier, I figured the old guy'd go along with it. "Look, I couldn't help hearing what your old lady just said about you oweing everybody money. How's about I tell you how you can get out of this hole you've dug for yourself? And do it easy and quick, with no pain on your part. Dinero, lots of it! Like . . ." I named a figure, big.

Poder looked at me suspiciously, his eyes slitted. "How? And, I'll say it again: Who are you?"

"Okay, the truth," I replied, letting my rod drop just a touch, so's not to look quite so menacing, but still ready. "I work for Don Pedro Albamadera. He wants you out of Carmen's life. And he's willing to make it worth your while if you don't try to resume your role as her novio, now that Doña Luna's obviously dumped you."

"Why, you -- !" he started for me, but I whipped my .38 back to attention, and he stopped. Mama Poder and little Pequeñito were watching all this, both of them goggle-eyed. The matador stood there, frozen in a sort of crouch, licking his lips and staring at my gat. Finally he seemed to come to a decision, and he relaxed and straightened up.

"Está bién," he said, quietly, adding, "Look, Carmen and me, we're also involved in -- in somethin' else. Strictly business, I guess you could say. But not monkey business, I promise. Just . . . business. And it'll be finished pretty quick." He sighed, then spoke again. "I guess it's just as good that this -- you comin' here

and all -- happened. As a matador, I been feelin' my nerves goin' -- know wha
I mean? Maybe with all that dough from old Don Pedro, I can buy all the stuff
need to make th' chicas still wanna go after me -- and I won't hafta risk my ass ou
there in th' ring all th' time. Y' know?"

"You say your nerve's gone, huh, kid?" I asked.

"Sí," he replied. "Just look. How can a matador kill with a hand that shakes?"
He held out a hand which was steady as a rock.

"Looks okay to me," I said.

"Yes, but I kill with *this* hand." He now stuck out his other hand, the right one
it was shaking like a leaf in a windstorm.

I just stared. I didn't know what to say, until I saw him smiling at me. I'c
been had.

"Jesus!" I cried. "That's the oldest gag in the book!"

Poder laughed out loud, then his expression grew worried again. "Yeah, yeah
I try to joke about it," he said, "but my nerve really ain't no good. And I got more
corridas comin' up -- includin' the one with Quinn and Curro on Sunday." He
cursed violently. Then he called out over his shoulder, "Pequeñito!"

The kid didn't react at all; he just continued to stand there and stare at the
matador with his mouth open.

"Pequeñito!!!" Poder was screaming now.

"Sí, matador?" the little earless kid suddenly piped up, rushing to Poder's
side, his expression that of one who is anxious to please. He'd finally heard his
maestro.

"Get the carretón!" Poder bellowed, extra loud. "We must practice!"

"Sí, matador!" the niño said, turning and running for the door leading to the
backyard. Practice? I said to myself. Now? This guy was a fruitcake. Maybe
he's really cracking up, I thought.

Poder picked up the sword he'd pulled on me earlier and went outside. I went
over to help Señora Poder to her feet, but she pushed my hand away.

"I still have to finish cleaning the floor!" she shouted. "I have not yet done this
area here by the steps."

I glanced around the big room, which had not even a throw rug anywhere on its
tile floor. "Well, okay," I said, "suit yourself." Then I saw something. "Hey, looks
like you missed a spot over there," I told her, pointing with my gun to an uncleaned
space beyond a coffee table covered with comic books. She groaned and began
crawling over to the area I'd shown her, scrub brush in hand.

I walked to the back door. Pequeñito already had the horns-mounted, one-
wheel device rolling about the yard. The only light came from windows of the
house, and in the gloom his white-bandaged head with the gauze holding the pads
where his ears used to be looked almost ghostly. Poder now had a muleta and was
doing ayudados, the sword in his right hand extending the cloth held in his left.

Then he finished off a tanda with a remate and spun about to acknowledge a make-believe público giving him a standing O. I don't know what got into Pequeñito right then, unless maybe he was secretly pissed about the ear business, but he made the carretón turn on a dime -- as bulls sometimes do -- and, as Poder was receiving his illusionary cheers, the kid pushed the contraption on and, with the tip of the righthand mounted horn, gave the matador a puntazo in his left cheek.

Poder screamed and turned to face the boy, fury on his countenance. Without so much as a how-do-you-do, he lined up his estoque with Pequeñito in its sights, and went in, over the horns. The niño was sort of hunched over, his hands on the handlebars of the carretón, and the sword caught him at the base of the back of his neck -- smack dab in the kid's withers, I noticed -- and the blade went all the way through, finally sticking into the ground. Poder quickly extracted the steel, thus the effect was that of a metisaca. Pequeñito fell to the earth like a -- well, not like a ton of bricks: he was too light for that. Like a ton of feathers, I guess would be more accurate.

A scream pierced the night air. Señora Poder, aghast, stumbled out into the yard and cradled the lifeless form of the muchacho. She unleashed a torrent of vindictives at her son, in response to which Poder yelled at her to shut up.

I grabbed the matador by the shirt front with my left hand, having holstered my rod, and with my right hand I twisted the estoque from his grip and threw it across the yard. "What the hell did you think you were doing?" I roared at him.

"Wha -- Wha --?" he babbled, his eyes rolling as I shook him, "Whattaya mean? Did what?"

"Speaking so disrespectfully to your mother, that's what I mean, you creep!" I shot back. "Don't you have any manners?"

Poder fell to his knees, sobbing, his hands over his face.

"So now you're remorseful!" I yelled. "Too late for that!"

"No, no . . ." Poder gasped. "It . . . it's just that . . . it was a perfect entera, but . . . but . . ." He sobbed some more.

I was baffled. "But what?" I shouted furiously. The matador looked up at me from his kneeling position. Tears were streaming down his distorted face.

"But I can't even cut a single ear, much less two -- he doesn't *have* any!" He then began sobbing uncontrollably.

"Holy moley!" I groaned, turning around and walking out of the house. This was more than I could handle. I had to get away from this piece of human garbage before I went nuts, too.

But as I walked through the darkened streets of Sevilla, headed back to my pensión off Sierpes, I had to grudgingly admit something to myself, whether I wanted to or not. It *had* been, like he said, a perfect entera.

Chapter 11

Marlo Needs Action

This job was getting to me, I thought. I hadn't counted on all the emotional stuff involving so many people. Why couldn't it just be a case of me nabbing the taquilla cashier who'd been pocketing wads of pesetas, or beating the negatives out of a torera's blackmailer? Something simple. But that's not the way it was.

At least I had a couple of days' breathing space. Poder had contracts to fight in San Martín de la Vega, south of Madrid, on Thursday, and in Tayuela, near Cáceres, on Friday; he'd be back in Sevilla in time for the Saturday corrida, and then on Sunday was the finale of the feria, the big one with Curro and Escamopayo. I got back to him by telephone and said I'd confirm the payoff deal with Don Pedro.

On Thursday I used my abono ticket to go to the day's event at La Maestranza, figuring what the hell, why not make use of it? Niether Carmen nor Doña Luna were there, but Faraón was, of course. The two dames' barrera seats remained empty; the people in higher-up seats who would've moved down to occupy them in most rings couldn't make it through the packed crowd at this plaza. It bugged me that Carmen had vanished; maybe she'd reappear the next day, I told myself.

The cartel offered bulls of Don Manuel Sánchez Cobaleda of Salamanca for Ordóñez, Manolo Vázquez and José Julio. This was the first day of the feria in which toros bravos of a ranch other than that of a local sevillano ganadero had been featured. I wasn't much on salmantinos, myself, and the day proved me right in my doubts: all were "nada," and during the proceedings Julio suffered a cogida while placing his own sticks. Fortunately, he was not badly injured and would appear again the next day. Thankfully, Ordóñez left me alone this time.

I dropped by Don Pedro's place after the corrida and brought him up to date. As I'd figured, he was ready to go with the buyoff of Poder, but he told me to hold off paying him the cash until after the last corrida on Sunday, May first. That way, he said, it gave him four chances -- the corridas scheduled for Thursday through Sunday -- for Poder to "pull a Manolete" in the ring and thus relieve him, Don Pedro, of the necessity of parting with the moolah. Hey, made sense to me.

Friday morning I woke up but just lay there in bed, under the wooden crucifix on the pensión's wall, thinking about Carmen and her dubious factory worker friends. People kept whispering and hinting about something going on there. Since whatever it was would almost assuredly be illegal, there'd be no mention of it on the radio or in the papers. And certainly not on television. Spain wasn't like the U.S. -- there wasn't any morning TV, anyway. Back in L.A., I could've tuned in to Dave Garroway's *Today* show, to see if Frank Blair had any news to report on the subject, but not here in España.

Carmen didn't show at La Maestranza Friday afternoon, either, although I did happen to run into Bimer outside the Bodegón Torre Ador, and she flirtingly hinted that "my novía," as she put it, was off someplace with her pals from the tobacco factory, setting something up. She wouldn't tell me any more, except to say she was sure I'd see Carmen at the corrida on Saturday.

In the meantime, the Friday event pitted Diego Puerta, Mondeño and José Julio against a string of toros from the ranch outside Madrid belonging to the Duque de Pinohermoso. Two ears were cut by Puerta on his second bull; Mondeño, the goodlooking but moody and sort of spooky-acting kid who kept talking about becoming a monk, heard two ovations, while José Julio did zilch.

Back in my rathole at the pensión, I found myself in a rather introspective mood. Just this morning I'd been thinking almost fondly about that old four-eyed TV geek with the bow tie, Dave Garroway, and now I caught myself wishing I could flick on the tube and watch the *Friday Night Fights*. I could hear the band playing that theme that went *Da-da-da-DAH-da-da-da!*, followed by the *CLANG!* of a boxing bell, then a musical repeat and another clang, and finally Howard Cosell or whoever the announcer is, intoning, *"The Gillette Cavalcade of Sports* is on the air!"* Then the male chorus ditty punctuated by that bell at the end of every other line:

> *To LOOK sharp (clang!)*
> *Every time you shave . . .*
> *To FEEL sharp (clang!)*
> *And be on the ball . . .*

Just BE sharp, (clang!)
Use Gillette Blue Blades
For the quickest, slickest shaves of all!

What's the matter, Marlo? I asked myself. Getting homesick? Had enough o España? No way, I answered. I'm just in a funk. Need some action. Yeah. Well I had a feeling I might get some the next day. Action, I meant.

Chapter 12

Marlo Joins the Reds

On the morning of Saturday, April 30, I walked over to the tobacco factory. Saturday was a work day there, and the employees were, I supposed, hard at work inside, rolling cigars or whatever it was one did in a tobacco factory. I glanced at my watch: 10:45 a.m. The morning break was still fifteen minutes away, so I decided to go inside and see what was really happening.

I walked through one of the big, open doors on the side of the factory and into a dark and gloomy place which smelled like I'd stuck my head into a cigar humidor. Just off a sort of dingy lobby area was a huge, open room with people, mostly dames, sitting on stools at high, wooden tables, spreading tobacco leaves on the surfaces which were covered with pads of some kind. They were then cutting the leaves with strange knives of a half-moon shape, sort of rolling the blades back and forth as they cut the tobacco shipped to Spain from Cuba. Then they rolled the cut leaves into cigars. I confess I was a little disappointed; my old man had always told me that havana cigars were the best because they'd been rolled on the thighs of beautiful women. I'd been lied to, it appeared. And not only were the leaves not being rolled on thighs, most of the workers present were old bags, not gorgeous chicks. Worse, some were men. If I knew I was smoking a cigar which had been rolled on some guy's thigh, I'd probably puke. Jesus!

I walked further into the big room. Nobody seemed to pay any attention to me. A couple of nuns were walking the aisles between the work tables. What were nuns doing in a tobacco factory? Beat me. Up at the front of the hall was an old coot seated behind a table on a sort of raised dais, and he was reading from a book. Obviously, this was the workers' entertainment while they toiled at their workplaces. I paused to catch what it was the viejo was reading, and I soon realized it was a biography of Generalísimo Franco. At this point, young Francisco had just entered the military academy, so there was a long way to go, to book's end. I wondered how many times some of the older employees had heard this book read. Well, what the hell, I thought -- if this were Havana, they'd probably be listening to the biography of Fidel Castro. At least that's what I'd heard. Which made me stop and think: How much longer would Spain be buying tobacco from a Cuba that was looking more and more each day as though it were leaning toward joining the Soviet bloc? After just over a year in power, Castro was making a lot of changes, playing up to the Reds.

The Reds! Could there be some connection? I mused. Tobacco from an increasingly Red-tinged Cuba and Spanish workers reputed to be Reds? It bore keeping in mind.

Through the open windows of the factory came the tolling of the cathedral bells, and all the workers began standing up and walking toward the exit doors, ready for their break. I went out with them, keeping an eye out for Carmen. I didn't see her, but I did come across Mercedes and Bimer, who hinted that perhaps I should come back to the factory after the corrida. I might be able to help, they said, but when I pressed them for details they just laughed and skipped away like a couple of carefree, young gypsy girls. Which made sense, because that's what they were. I left, figuring I'd be seeing Carmen at this afternoon's corrida, anyway.

And I was right. She was there, as were Faraón and Doña Luna, on yet another day in which La Maestranza was lleno hasta el reloj. She seemed a little cool, however, and she was coy about where she'd been of late, telling me that I'd know all about it soon enough. I sighed. Dames! I decided to concentrate on the corrida.

The cartel for this, the penultimate corrida of the feria, boasted one Cobaleda bull for the rejóneador Don Angel Peralta and -- this was more like it! -- six Miuras for Curro Girón, Diego Puerta and Tirón Poder. But my expectations were not met, I'm sorry to say. One ear was cut by Girón on his first, but the rest of the astados stunk up the ring. Poder was the pits: a bronca after each bull, plus one more, accompanied by a hail of cushions, on his exit. Maybe he'd decided to quit trying, now that he'd opted to take Don Pedro's dinero.

After the corrida, as had become the norm, Carmen once again ran off to some mysterious assignation. This was starting to bug me. I muttered a dirty word and, instead of going to El Bodegón as usual, I continued on to the tobacco factory.

When I got near the place I could see that it was all dark. Closed for the weekend, obviously. Nobody was about, so I walked around to the other side, in the Calle Frontera. This was where deliveries arrived and departed, and tonight there was a canvas-covered truck backed up to a loading platform, its engine idling but its lights doused. I could see shadowy figures loading boxes into it from the factory.

I walked up to the edge of the building, keeping to the shadows, until I was behind a bush growing alongside the portal to which the camión was reversed. In a moment a man inside the factory called out something, and the two who'd been doing the loading shouted back and then went inside, leaving the vehicle unattended. Quickly, I scrambled up onto the tailgate and crawled into the cargo area of the truck, most of which was filled with sealed cardboard boxes with no markings, each maybe two feet square. I climbed over the cartons and found a place in a far corner, behind some of them, and I settled back to wait.

In a minute the men came back, loaded a few more boxes, then slammed shut the tailgate. They went around and got into the cab, cranked the engine and pulled away. I found my pocket knife and cut a small slit in the side of the truck's canvas cover, enough to see out just a little. We were bouncing along the Paseo de Cristóbal Colón, paralleling the Guadalquivir; the lights of Triana twinkled on the other side of the river. Right about then we should've been passing La Maestranza, on the other side. We kept on going, always with the river off to the left. Now the empty wastes of Cartuja Island could be seen in the moonlight, across the Guadalquivir.

Eventually we pulled into some kind of warehouse on the river and the motor was switched off. The two guys got out, came around back, and let down the tailgate, laughing about getting all those boxes of cigar covers out of the truck. Cigar covers? Holy moley, had I wasted my time, clandestinely coming along on what was nothing more than a straightforward delivery of bona fide factory products? Damn!

Well, I'd be discovered if I stayed where I was, so I decided to make a move. All the voices seemed to retreat some distance from the truck, so I thought if I could get out and just start unloading the boxes myself, they might mistake me for one of their own. After all, the place was pretty dark. So that's what I did. Then I heard footsteps coming my way; I mentally braced, to see if I'd pass the test.

"Who the hell are you?" a voice challenged. I turned and faced Danny Cairo, who was wielding a crowbar.

"Hiya, Danny," I said, pushing my hat brim back a little with a thumb, then pulling out a fag from my pack of Camels. I offered him one.

"Carmen's novio!" he said, as his buddy El Castrado hurriedly limped up, ready to tackle this stranger in their midst. Warily, they both took a weed from me, and I lit up for everybody. Then I explained that I was here to help, making it sound like Carmen had filled me in on everything.

"Say, how'd you catch on to me so fast?" I asked, smiling.

Cairo looked at me like I was an idiot. "There are only two of us here beside you, and neither of us is wearing a trenchcoat and hat."

"Oh, yeah," I said. The guy was pretty sharp.

"Rock!" Carmen's voice called out. I looked to my left and saw her in a doorway down at the end of the warehouse. She was wearing yet another red gypsy-girl dress with a red bloom in her hair.

"Hi, toots," I said. She came over to me, but she acted sort of strange. She didn't give me a hug or kiss or anything. She seemed all business. I spoke up, acting like I belonged there, saying I was ready to help. Carmen looked as though she were trying to make up her mind about something, then turned to Danny Cairo and El Castrado and told them I was okay. El Castrado seemed to object but Cairo reiterated the bit about me having foiled the cops earlier in the week, enabling Carmen to get away, and that seemed to settle the matter. I was then told to continue unloading the truck of the boxes of cigar covers, prompting everyone to laugh. I laughed, too, although I didn't know what the joke was.

It wasn't a hot night, but even so, after a few minutes of moving the cartons while wearing my trenchcoat and hat, I was sweating. Each box weighed maybe ten or twelve pounds -- no more. Thus the "cigar covers" couldn't be guns, grenades or dynamite, as the cartons would be heavier. So what could be inside? Money? Drugs? Red propaganda leaflets? Or actual cigar covers? Nah, I said to myself, there's no such thing, unless you're talking about cellophane wrappers, and these boxes were *too* heavy for that.

I kept working. Cairo and El Castrado were at the far end of the warehouse, and I couldn't see Carmen. I'd just about emptied the truck when one of the cardboard cartons got away from me and fell from where I stood on the rear of the truck bed, to the concrete loading dock. It split open when it hit the pavement, and dozens of slightly shiny, disc-like objects poured out. I stared at the pile of -- what? They looked like . . . like . . . rubbers!

"Holy moley!" I gasped. "Condoms! These boxes are filled with condoms!"

Carmen appeared out of nowhere and walked up to the spilled pile of dully-gleaming discs, hands on her hips, and sneered at me. "Of course they're condoms!" she barked at me. "What did you think we were dealing in, Rock? Rosaries? Catechism booklets?"

"But condoms are the most illegal things you could possibly be messing with in España Católica!" I shot back. "This stuff is hotter than a truckload of *Playboy* magazines dumped into the center aisle of an evangelical Baptist tent revival in Alabama! If you're caught with it, Franco's cops'll bury you *under* the jail! You'll never see the light of day again!" I took off my fedora and mopped my face and neck with a handkerchief. The sweat wasn't just from my exertions.

Carmen still had her hands on her hips and the sneer on her face. "You fool!"

she shouted. "Don't you realize that what you see here is just el diamante de la asta -- the tip of the bull's horn? Our organization deals in abortion, marijuana, euthanasia for the terminally ill, birth control -- things the workers can't get under the fascist Franco regime! These condoms will be distributed to the working people all over España!" By now, Cairo and his pal had returned, crowbars in hand. Danny was watching me closely, but El Castrado seemed to be hypnotized by the scattering of contraceptive devices on the warehouse floor, a sort of wistful look on his face.

"Uh . . . I see," I said, trying to act more at ease. "Hey, just one question. I figure your pals in the tobacco factory are clandestinely importing these condoms from your comrades in Cuba, along with the tobacco, then storing them there someplace, maybe in the basement, until you can move them out for distribution." Carmen nodded at this. "But I saw those nuns patrolling the joint like cops. How do you get the stuff past the good sisters?"

Carmen smirked. "We tell them they're cigar covers," she said. They never know the difference. How could they? Only yesterday, there was an accident and a box broke open when it was dropped -- just as happened here tonight -- and some condoms spilled out. Sister Simplicidad was patrolling the area and picked one up and unrolled it. She asked someone what it was, and was advised it was a new form of cigar covering, to keep the product dry in wet weather. The sister handed the condom to a worker and resumed her partol, commenting only, 'By the saints, cigars are getting bigger!' So you see, we have no problems from that quarter. The nuns, in case you are wondering, were assigned to the factory by the government, in an effort 'to foster purer thought,' as they put it."

"Ummm . . . I see," I said, mopping my neck with my pañuelo yet again.

"Well?" queried the gypsy girl. "Now that you know, are you with us or against us?" She glared at me.

I didn't want any part of this nutbrain scheme. Get connected with it by the cops even slightly, and I could kiss my taurine P.I. license goodbye. And find myself back in the slammer, as well. But if I told Carmen that, I could say sayonara to her, that was for certain. She was already acting a little weird toward me, and this would finish everything off for sure. So . . .

"Hey, count me in," I said, trying to look enthusiastic.

Carmen and the two men huddled and apparently decided to trust me. They told me to watch the stuff in the warehouse while they went back to the tobacco factory for the final load. I said okay. When the three of them turned their backs to me and began to walk away, I quickly bent over and scooped up a handful of rubbers. Naturally, Carmen would choose that moment to look over her shoulder and catch me in action. She glared at me, then turned back around and walked out of the place, not looking back again. Obscenity a brick!

I sat down on one of the boxes and lit a fag. Everything was quiet, and it stayed that way for maybe an hour. The warehouse doors were all shut and locked so when I heard the door at the end of the place being unlocked, I quietly pulled out my rod. The puerta opened slowly and the shadowy figure of a man wearing a gorra slipped in.

I crept around a tall stack of boxes until I was behind the guy. It was pretty dark, but I could see him fairly well. "Manos arriba!" I snarled. But instead of putting up his mitts, he looked like he was going for a gat inside his jacket. I fired and his gorra leaped from his head and slid across the concrete floor. He froze and put up his hands. In one of them was a silver flask.

"P-por favor!" he pleaded. "I -- I was just lookin' for Carmencita!" The voice sounded familiar, although somewhat slurred. I walked over to a wall switch and flicked on the lights. It was Poder, dressed like a worker.

"What the blue blazes are you doing here?" I demanded. "And why are you looking for Carmen? I thought you'd agreed to Don Pedro's deal."

"You!" he exclaimed, staggering back a step. "Uh, yeah, I did. Por supuesto I uh, I jus' wanted to, uh, say goodbye to her, tha's all." The guy was pretty drunk. He put the flask back in his jacket pocket.

"I'll bet," I growled. "Well, Carmen's not available any more. You got that? Now clear out, and don't try to get near her again!"

Poder hiccuped and, swaying, went over and picked up his cap, poking an index finger through the hole I'd blown into it. A stupid smile crept over his mug. "Now I get it," he said. "You got the hots for Carmen y'self!" Then he laughed. "Hey, you poor sap -- don't you realize her love affairs ain't never lasted longer'n six months, at best? Huh? An' you wouldn't do no better, neither! Th' only one she could really go for full time is me!" He reached into his jacket pocket and brought out the flask of liquor again, and took a big slug from it.

"Why, you --" I guess I went a little crazy. I holstered my .38 and went for his throat with my bare hands. Before I could reach him, he'd dropped his flask and pulled a stiletto from someplace. I grabbed his wrist and the two of us crashed into a stack of boxes, then rolled around on the floor, fighting for control of the knife. I finally wrestled it from Poder's grip and held it to the matador's adam's apple.

"Stop!" screamed a woman's voice. Carmen's. I looked up and saw her in the doorway, terror on her face. In her hand she was holding some tarot cards. I looked down at my hand gripping the blade at Poder's throat. Por Dios, what was I doing?

I released the matador and got to my feet, dropping the stiletto into a trenchcoat pocket. As I did so, I heard Danny Cairo and El Castrado talking to each other as the loading door was opened. In a few moments, they were back inside the warehouse. By this time, Poder was also standing, albeit somewhat unsteadily, trying to appear unperturbed by our little tussle. He obviously knew the other two hombres, for he mumbled something to them and they nodded to him.

"Pues!" declared Poder, puffing himself up. "I gotta go. But first, I wanna invite all my friends to th' big corrida tomorrow -- especially thems that loves me." He looked at Carmen and smiled an obscenity-eating smile. Then he hiccuped.

"Why, you --" I yelled for the second time in the past few minutes, once again going for Poder with my outstretched arms, but Cairo and El Castrado stopped me before I could reach him. With a sloppy, hand-saluting brindís, Poder, still smiling, turned and staggered away. As he opened the far door of the warehouse I could hear a band playing a pasodoble, and the thought passed through my mind: what was a banda taurina doing in this part of town, at such an hour?

Carmen walked up to me, her pretty upper lip curled into a sneer. "You certainly made a fool of yourself!" she spat at me.

That really got my Jockeys in a wad. "Oh, yeah?" I snarled at her. "I stick up for you, and you tell me I'm making a fool of myself! Why, you little flirt -- I oughta . . . I oughta . . ."

"What?" she demanded. "Kill me? I know you have a pistola. Are you going to shoot me?"

"No, baby!" I protested, horrified at the very idea. My anger was gone, replaced by desperation. "I --"

"Sí!" Carmen interrupted me. "I think you will end up killing me! But Destiny is the master!" She threw the tarot cards onto the floor. The only one that landed face up was the one of Death wearing a trenchcoat. Wait a minute! Was that really a tarot card? Never mind, I told myself.

Afraid I'd just make matters worse by arguing, I turned and stalked out of the place. Outside, the banda was now playing that *Fate Theme*.

Chapter 13

Death and Betrayal

On the last day of the feria, Sunday, May first, Sevilla was all abuzz. The word was out that Tirón Poder was going to retire immediately, and that today's corrida would be his despedida, when he would cut the coleta. I was having a carajillo and a cigarette in a sidewalk cafe in the Plaza Nueva when I heard the news. Well, I said to myself, that cinches it. He's definitely decided to go with Don Pedro's buyoff deal. That bit last night at the warehouse had just been his farewell to Carmen. Maybe this thing'd turn out okay after all -- for Don Pedro, anyhow, assuming he could really spare all that loot. But what about for me? I lifted my fedora with my right hand and with my left ran my fingers through my hair. Hombre! Things weren't easy.

The big corrida finale of the feria featured bulls of Albamadera for Curro Romero, Tirón Poder and Escamopayo. The whole town was agog, for these were the three hottest names in the taurine world of Sevilla at present. Romero had only one year of alternativa behind him, yet he was the senior matador on the cartel. The afición seemed to be split on the subject of Curro: half thought he was great, half thought he was sinvergüenza. But one thing was for sure -- he was a hell of a draw.

Poder had of course been going great guns since taking his own doctorate recently -- at least until a couple of not-so-hot performances of late. But with his stunning retirement announcement of earlier today, el público would have been fighting for entradas to La Maestranza -- had there been any available, which there weren't.

Last on the bill was the exciting young Quinn Helado, formerly of Poder's maletilla "cuadrilla" and the newest member of the club of full matadors. As the up-and-coming challenger Escamopayo, he had already impressed the windbag Faraón, as well as many others -- including, obviously, Doña Luna Jezebella de Avaricia, collector of men.

Soon the banda taurina was playing *La Giralda* and the paseillo was underway. The three matadors approached the barrera where, from left to right as the toreros faced us, I, Carmen, Faraón and the beminked Doña Luna were sitting. Escamopayo made a big show of presenting his capote de paseo to Doña Luna. On the other hand, Poder, who looked like he'd had a few drinks, did his best to appear as though he did not see either Carmen or Doña Luna at all, and was, in fact, engrossed in thoughts as to how best to rearrange his sock drawer at home. I tried to suppress a grin over this, but then my jaw dropped when Carmen winked at Curro Romero and blew him a kiss. The kid from Camas, already with a reputation of being a ladies' man, reacted immediately, smiling broadly and presenting her with his own dress capote. Inside, I was steaming.

Both Carmen and Doña Luna were trying to spread their champions' capes on the barrera. Faraón, between them, was ineffectively purporting to help both, but the capotes were so wide that it became clear they would overlap if one of the females didn't move hers down some. And neither of these babes was about to do that. First, Doña Luna tried to place the right corner of Escamopayo's capote over the lefthand end of Curro's, but Carmen quickly yanked hers out from under the other and flopped *it* on top. Furious, Doña Luna sank her long, crimson fingernails into the back of Carmen's little brown left hand.

"Puta!" Carmen shrieked, now reaching across the girth of a startled Faraón to grab a fistful of Doña Luna's golden coiffure. The latter screamed and, in turn, launched herself at her attacker's own wild mane of glossy black hair, crying out, "Basura gitana!" The two dames became engaged in a full-fledged catfight, cursing like sailors and locked in combat over the bloated form of a terrified Faraón, whose stubby arms were flailing wildly. The crowd began cheering as though watching a championship boxing match. Hair, flower petals, diamonds and mink fur flew through the air in all directions.

The battle royal ended -- in a draw -- only when the contingent of twenty gray-green-uniformed Guardia Civil, their black patent leather hats gleaming in the sunlight, descended from their block of seats on the sol side of the plaza and marched across the sand to the scene of carnage in the barrera sombra sector. There they drew up in a semicircle facing the two cursing, scratching, fighting and spitting dames and unholstered their pistols, aiming the weapons at the babes. Faraón, caught in the middle of the melee, could barely keep his bulging eyes in his head when he saw all those drawn rods pointing his way. To be completely honest about it, I felt the same way. If those guardia *did* shoot, I just hoped they were accurate. As everybody in Spain, including Carmen and Doña Luna, knew full well that the Guardia Civil didn't mess around and wouldn't hesitate to shoot to preserve public order, the chicas reluctantly let go of each other and sat back in their respective seats, fuming. The crowd cheered; what a show! They'd gotten their money's worth already!

Both women were showing facial scratches, their clothes were torn and their hairdos were pretty well destroyed, but Doña Luna came out with the short end of the stick, since Carmen's hair was already sort of wild-looking anyway, while the doña's had been carefully coiffed to begin with, and her mink coat now looked like it'd contracted the mange. Faraón had not gone unscathed, himself. His derby hat was crushed and the end of his cigar splintered, as though it had exploded. Holy moley, I thought.

The roar of the crowd subsided to a loud buzz, most unusual for the normally staid Maestranza, the guardia returned to their seats in the sun, and the corrida commenced. To the spectators' disappointment, Curro's first appearance of the afternoon was one of shameless routines. You could've driven two andaluz oxcarts side by side between him and the bull during his faena, and he killed the thing with a sneak attack into the side of the beast's neck with the sword. He received a bronca for his efforts -- or lack thereof.

Poder, up next, took a not-so-secret swig from a flask supplied by a worried-looking Garbaje, then went out into the ring and acted as though he were trying to emulate Romero, and a second bronca rocked the plaza.

And then Escamopayo came out and put everybody into a good mood, generating a show which obviously impressed Juan Belmonte, who was watching from behind the callejón burladero marked *Ganaderos*. His wolf's chin supported a big smile as he chatted with his neighbor, no doubt stuttering characteristically as he did so. Then Helado went in with the estoque hasta al puño and the crowd went wild. Two ears.

With his second toro, Curro executed a single beautiful verónica which caused his supporters to go insane with joy. Faraón even tried to stand up, so excited was he as he screamed, "Curro Romero is the first man of the world! I, Faraón, say it!" After that, Romero lapsed into his disgraceful style, but those who loved him didn't seem to mind; they'd had their show. After another terrible kill, he received a mixed reaction of jeers and cheers. Could this kid really make a career of this farce act of his? I asked myself. Nah, I answered. No way. Pretty soon people would see through the phoniness. By '61 or '62 he'd be gone, washed up, I felt sure.

Poder now prepared to face his own second astado. In his case, however, the crowd didn't make the same allowance for his first bronca as they had done for Curro, and he was greeted with pitos and catcalls. At dedication time he walked over to where we sat and, his montera outstretched toward Carmen and a serious expression on his face, he spoke to her, ignoring Doña Luna. He didn't seem to have drunk any more.

"To the good times we had together, chica," he said, "I dedicate this last bull of my career." He then turned and tossed the hat to her over his shoulder. Carmen caught it and sat with it in her lap, an expression of confusion on her face. And then, ignoring the boos and jeers, Poder went out into the ring and put on the greatest performance I have ever seen in a plaza de toros. His critics were converted to roaring, deliriously happy worshipers in record time.

Even Faraón was yelling olé and clapping his meathooks as he cried, "Tirón Poder is the second man of the world! I, Faraón, say it!" And then suddenly Poder was in the air, flung upward as if a rag doll, and the crowd was screaming in terror. Quickly, Escamopayo was in the ring, taking the toro away, and Carradino, Garbaje and others were carrying the limp body of Poder through the callejón at great speed. Curro was doing his part to help out by crouching down behind the burladero and keeping out of the way.

Carmen leaped over the barrera and ran after the entourage, and after a second's hesitation I did the same. Everything was pandemonium. They took Poder not to the infirmary but into the chapel, where they laid him on a sort of bier in front of the statue of la Virgen de la Macarena. When I busted into the darkened room and saw the carved stone image, I froze for a second and thought: pigeons. But I quickly shook off that notion.

I rushed up to Garbaje and, grabbing him by the lapels, shouted, "Why the hell didn't you take him to the enfermería?"

Little Garbaje hung his head. "Ah, señor," he sighed. "This is more dramatic. It is the way things are done in great tragedies. Have you never seen a bullfighting movie?" I looked around: the dying torero laid out like a corpse, the solemnly grieving cuadrilla, the frantic and weeping Carmen, the stunned onlookers, all in the dark and gloomy setting of the chapel. Yeah, I had to agree with Garbaje -- it was dramatic, all right. And this was certainly tragic. So I guess he had something there.

Carmen was kneeling down beside the prostrate Poder, who was white as a sheet. I whispered a question to Garbaje: shouldn't a doctor at least look at him? No, the mozo de estoques replied, such was not necessary, since it was obvious that the cornada was fatal, and the presence of medical personnel would merely diminish the drama and tragedy. Yeah, I nodded; I probably shouldn't have even questioned the point.

The mortally wounded matador was apparently delirious, for he was babbling to Carmen as though he'd never agreed to Don Pedro's deal to leave her alone. He would take her to Hollywood, he gasped, where she would become a star, greater than even Doris Day. He would obtain for her an autographed photo of Neil Sedaka singing *Stairway to Heaven*. He would -- then he grimaced in pain and ceased promising stuff. Carmen tried to smile, to make him buck up a little, but, being a dame, she just boohoohooed all over the place. Outside, the crowd roared -- they had already forgotten about their former favorite and were engrossed with new action in the ring. Carmen looked toward the chapel doorway, distressed.

Garbaje, infuriated by the fickle *muchedumbre*, ran to the door and jerked it open. Shaking his fist at the screaming *público*, the diminutive ex-matador de toros yelled, as loud as he could, his hands now cupped to his mouth, "Are you happy now, you animals? Are you happy?"

Wasting your breath, amigo, I thought, but Garbaje roared at the beast yet again: "Is everybody happy?"

And to my astonishment, the crowd roared back.

"Hell . . . yes!"

"Is anybody sad?" he then screamed.

"Hell . . . no!" howled the mob.

"Then do the locomotive, and do it . . . slow!" cried Garbaje, who began pumping his right arm back and forth like a piston and taking exaggerated, high steps, as he proceeded "steppin' it out" into the callejón, all the while chanting, "P O! D! E! R!" Then, faster, "P - O - D - E - R!" And a third time, faster yet, *"P-O-D-E-R!"* followed by, "Whattaya got?"

"Poder!" bellowed the crowd, which then cheered madly and applauded.

Glowering, I ran over to the doorway and out into the callejón, grabbing Garbaje's arm. "What the hell are you doing?" I shouted, over the clamor.

Garbaje lowered his head and sheepishly said, "I -- I'm sorry, señor. I lived in the U.S. for awhile as a joven and was a cheerleader for the South Chimichanga (Texas) High School Fighting Burritos. I'm afraid I just got carried away."

I let go of his arm and went back into the chapel, disgusted. In the gloom I could see Tirón Poder's body, stretched out in front of La Macarena. He was covered in blood and was barely breathing. Carmen was standing now, her grief replaced by anger. "I should have known you were a loser!" she shouted, pointing at the expiring torero. Then she pointed at the image of the Virgen and cried, "I'll deal with *you* later!" Next she turned toward the door to the callejón and wailed, "Curro, te quiero!" One arm was dramatically extended. It made me want to puke.

Carmen started to go back into the ring, but I grabbed her wrist and dragged her out through the patio de caballos. I wanted to talk to her, private like. The enclosed area which was the scene of such bustling activity prior to and after a corrida was quiet now. The matadors' cars were parked off to one side, headed out -- Poder's purple Roadmaster, Curro's magenta Chevy Bel Air convertible and Escamopayo's red T-bird. From inside La Maestranza the roar of the crowd indicated that Escamopayo was wowing them with his last bull.

Still gripping Camen's wrist, I shouted at her, "Do you mean it? Do you really love that creep Romero?"

She twisted and fought to free herself, but I held on. Finally she put her face close to mine and spat, "Sí! I love him! I will go away with him! I will be his woman forever!"

"But . . . but . . . *why?*" I sputtered. "The guy is a joke! Why would you possibly have any interest in the likes of him?"

She looked at me and shook her head slowly, as though she were dealing with an idiot child. Then she smiled a defiant smile and, her nostrils flaring, she proudly pronounced, "Because common sense and the truth are no longer of importance to me -- I have become . . . *¡una currista!"*

"That does it!" I yelled, pulling something from one of my trenchcoat pockets without actually thinking about what I was doing. I looked down at my left hand; it was holding the stiletto I'd taken from Poder at the warehouse the night before. From inside the plaza the band suddenly played the *Fate Theme.*

Carmen's eyes fixed on the gleaming knife. "I knew it!" she shrieked. "I knew you'd kill me! I saw it in the cards!" I still had hold of her wrist, though she was fighting to get loose.

I looked at the stiletto as though mesmerized. Finally I said something. "Curro, huh?" The crowd was roaring again inside the bullring. Then, still holding onto the gypsy girl, I lurched over to Curro's magenta Chevy ragtop and circled the car, quickly slashing all four of its tires. From within the plaza, the *Fate Theme* blared forth yet again.

Wild-eyed and grinning insanely, I looked at Carmen and cried, "How do you like *that?* Huh?" She fought some more, and at last I released her. She ran toward the plaza and collided with Garbaje, who was coming out the doorway, his face a mask of agony.

"Muerto!" he was sobbing. "Tirón is dead!" He fell to his knees in the sawdust of the patio de caballos and hung his head, his body heaving. Carmen pushed him aside and ran back into the bullring.

I looked at the stiletto in my hand, then threw it into a far corner of the patio, observed by the one-legged gatekeeper who had appeared on the scene. I walked out into the Calle Antonio Díaz without saying anything to the man, and I kept going, toward my pensión.

Old Don Pedro had certainly played his cards right, I thought as I walked in the direction of Sierpes. His buyoff deal with Poder wasn't to kick in until after the last corrida of the feria, and Poder hadn't made it. The ganadero was out nothing, except for the peanuts he'd paid me. Peanuts for him, anyway. I wouldn't be going back to see him -- there was no reason for me to do so. I'd blown the assignment. Sure, Poder was out of the picture, but now Curro was in. And I had a feeling that was worse. Much worse. Don Pedro could keep his money; I hadn't earned any more of it. I kept walking in the purple crepúsculo of the mild spring evening.

Chapter 14

A Fateful Ending

Monday, the second of May, dawned bright and sunny. I threw my stuff into my old B-4 bag, checked out of my dump and began walking the kilometer or so to the Estación de Córdoba. I'd call Don Pedro from there and give him a final report. I owed him that, I told myself.

Along the way, I stopped at a news kiosk and bought a local paper whose headline screamed, *¡Curro Executes Devine Verónica!* A subhead read, *Tirón Poder Killed in Ring, Escamopayo Cuts 4 Ears.* The byline, I noticed, was Faraón's. Further down the page, a smaller headline announced, *Red Plot Against God and Spain Foiled by Police.* I skimmed the copy, which was datelined Sevilla and detailed a coordinated police raid on the tobacco factory and a warehouse on the Guadalquivir Sunday night which had resulted in the arrest of several men, including one ex-novillero, all notorious Red subversives involved in the distribution of "banned items." Well, obviously they got Cairo and El Castrado, I thought as I read the piece. The "items" were unspecified but the paper declared them to be "the work of Satan and the International Red Conspiracy." Happily, no mention was made of Carmen or, for that matter, any other dames. I puffed my cheeks and blew air out. That had been close!

I started to fold the paper and put it in my coat pocket, but then I saw a small article in the bottom corner of the front page with the heading, *Sculptor's So⟨ Reconsiders Retirement, Wants To Do Statue of Curro.* ¡Carajo! I thought. Don' people ever learn?

I continued on to the station and was standing in line at the taquilla when tw⟨ mugs dressed as I was walked up to me, accompanied by Captain Zitcara, wh⟨ was in uniform and who said, "That's him." A shiver went up my spine. If I wa being hauled in as part of the plot against God and Spain, I was dead. The shorte⟨ of the two plainclothesmen spoke to me, flipping open a wallet with an I.D. car⟨ in a plastic window. There was a picture of a bull's head on the card, and I coul⟨ read the words *Policia Taurina.* I groaned. But at the same time, I was relieved the taurine cops don't look for Reds.

"Señor Felipe Marlo?" he asked. "Alias Señor Rock Dean?"

"Yeah," I sighed. I sat my B-4 bag on the dirty, tiled floor of the station hall.

"Do you know what the penalty is for slashing the tires of an automobil⟨ belonging to a matador de toros, señor?" he asked me. I shook my head, no⟨ Damn! I felt like obscenitying in the milk of my own mother!

"Two months in the taurine jail, señor," he advised me.

I bent down and picked up my bag. "Let's go," I said. Zitcara was smirking⟨ Someplace, I knew, Lieutenant Inmoral was leering.

We walked out of the station and turned left, headed toward where I suppose⟨ the Taurine Police HQ was located. As we walked, I reached in a trenchcoat pocke⟨ and pulled out the flower Carmen had laughingly tossed to me what now seeme⟨ like a lifetime ago; it was crushed and withered, but it still smelled like Carmen.

From somewhere down the street, a band played the *Fate Theme.*

The End

Printed in the United States
18058LVS00005B/67-384